ONE-MAN STRIKE FORCE

Firecloud stormed into action, the whirlwind
suddenness and fury of his attack taking them
all by surprise.

He charged into the line of black-clad Front
guards at a full run, bouncing them off the walls
like pool balls on a break. He dashed the man
nearest him against the wall with a headbutt to
the chest. As the man was sinking, he snatched
the guard's knife and swung it backward in a
horizontal arc, slashing a second guard open
across his midsection. Another charged from
his left and Firecloud thrust the bloody six-inch
dagger into his stomach, then hauled it up
between his ribs, twisting the blade.

But all at once a powerful forearm locked
around his throat and arched him backward.
Firecloud struggled for air . . .

SwampMaster

SWAMP MASTER

JAKE SPENCER

DIAMOND BOOKS, NEW YORK

SWAMPMASTER

A Diamond Book / published by arrangement with
the author

PRINTING HISTORY
Diamond edition / February 1992

ISBN: 1-55773-661-8

Diamond Books are published by The Berkley Publishing Group,
200 Madison Avenue, New York, New York 10016.
The name "DIAMOND" and its logo are trademarks
belonging to Charter Communications, Inc.

PRINTED IN THE UNITED STATES OF AMERICA

10 9 8 7 6 5 4 3 2 1

Special thanks are due to: Ann S. Gushue of the Eastern National Park & Monument Association Bookstore in the Castillo de San Marcos, the public relations folks at CNN, Elmer Kosinski for the research materials, Jerome Preisler, and my parents for giving birth to me.

This book is for Suzanne, who keeps me in line, and for Jones, who keeps me smiling while she bends me out of shape.

Prolog

Long ago, the people across the ocean were having a Fire Dance. Panther was a great speaker and leader, so they let him lead. Twice he ran up to the flame and made signs. Everyone thought he was wonderful. The third time he picked up a brand from the fire and ran toward the woods. He ran so fast that the people could not catch him and soon the forest was burning. But the shaman made medicine for rain and put out the blaze.

Panther came back. Some said, "Don't let him lead again." He had friends, however, who convinced the people to let him lead, though this time they made him pledge to keep his hands clasped behind his back so that he would not be able to reach for another firebrand.

But he outwitted them, and went up close to the fire and stuck out his head. His hair ignited and he ran off. Again the people could not catch him, and the forest burned right over until the village shaman was able to make another rain. As the first drops of water fell, Panther found a hollow rock out in the woods, and he hid in it, and kept the rain from putting out his fire. It rained and rained, but he was safe.

Now and then he came out and set fire to the grass, and each time the people made rain and put it out. Eventually they couldn't find any more burning and assumed Panther was finished up. But he still had some fire left in his hair, and he crept out of the hollow and got into the ocean, keeping his head above the water to prevent the flame from being doused as he swam.

He came across to our land, and soon the sky here was thick with smoke. Some claim our grasses had been smoldering well before he arrived and that he just hastened along what was already fated. Others deny this. In any event, our medicine was not potent enough to check the flames. The fire burned for many months. By the time it died away almost everything had been destroyed, and the One Tribe had splintered into many clans. To this day the clans fight over what remains of the land they once shared in peace.

Now you know how life got to be the way it is.

Chapter One ═══════════════

A pair of sharp, hidden eyes watched the soldiers on the beach.

They were laughing over an obscenity one of them had spat at their captive. Seemingly oblivious—or perhaps merely indifferent—to the vulgar insult, the woman gazed with a kind of numb, mesmerized fascination at the wavelets scrolling gently over her bare toes. Her failure to react annoyed the soldier holding her rope leash, and he gave his end of the rope a sudden, hard yank, tightening the slipknot around her neck. She bellied to the surf, came up on her knees wet and gasping, flopped back down as the rope was snapped a second time.

"Better watch out for crabs, squaw-slut!" the man clenching the rope taunted. "You don't wanna pick up any more than are already crawling on your filthy skin!"

His companions erupted into more loud, jeering guffaws.

Nearby, their stalker gritted his teeth with barely suppressed fury.

After a few moments the three troopers lost interest in the woman and sat heavily down on the sand, dumping their backpacks, resting their automatic weapons across their laps. One of them uncapped his canteen, took a deep pull from it, then passed it over to the others, who guzzled thirstily in turn.

The long trek through the swamp had exhausted them. Sweat ringed the silver eagle insignias on the crowns of their field caps. Their dun-colored, lightweight tropical

tunics and uniform pants were spattered with mud, as were
their combat shoes and leggings. Two of them had rolled
their sleeves up almost to the armbands bearing the haughty
National Front emblem: a dark blue swastika in an orbit of
twelve white stars—each star representing one of the
original secessionist states—set against a bold red field.

Several yards inland, where a wall of mangroves but-
tressed a low ridge against the sea's advance, the stalker
watched from his treetop vantage.

His keen eyes hardened as they focused on one of the
armbands. Amid the sun-splashed beauty of the Cape Sable
shore the swastika emblem was like a razor blade implanted
in a large exotic fruit. It had its own secret, malign power.

John Firecloud switched his gaze to the woman.

She was young, perhaps twenty-five or twenty-six, and
unhealthily thin . . . almost emaciated. He suspected that
her features might have been very pretty before hard times
had stamped them with suffering and weariness. Her long
black hair was matted and dirty. Her dress, a traditional
Seminole one-piece garment, was torn and ragged, its
formerly colorful patchwork dulled with old, worked-in
grime. A more recent crust of mud had partially rinsed off
when she'd been dropped into the water.

The soldiers had walked the woman through miles of
dense forest without sharing any of their provisions with
her. Firecloud had been tracking the group for hours, and
they'd appeared to have already hiked a substantial distance
when he first spotted them near the southwestern bank of
Whitewater Bay, which marked the lower boundary of his
tribal ground. Firecloud himself was from the last permanent Seminole camp in Florida, but there were small,
fly-by-night settlements and isolated single-family *chickees*
scattered throughout the Everglades. The Front's slave-
gathering raids were becoming increasingly widespread and
intrusive; he supposed the woman could have been captured
anywhere between here and Homestead, far to the east.

A breeze huffed through the mangrove canopy, and the

covering rustle of leaves allowed Firecloud to shift position without risk of being heard. He'd been nestled, motionless, in the fork of two branches for a while, and his muscles were cramping.

He flexed his shoulders and neck to loosen the kinks.

Cooling fingers of wind whisked the hair off his back in a thick swirl, flapped the ceremonial breechcloth draping the thighs of his faded dungarees, slipped under the bandanna around his forehead. He would have welcomed the gusts unreservedly after the sticky, humid air of the interior . . . but the way they whipsawed between southwest and southeast troubled him.

That, and the clouds.

Out over the Gulf of Mexico the sun was dipping toward a billowy cumulus formation. Though benign when moving about the sky in loose, unlayered drifts, the clouds had begun to stack—an ominous sign that a severe storm was coming.

Firecloud had originally intended to strike against the soldiers after dark. If they'd camped in the woods overnight, as their initial course had seemed to indicate they might, he could have picked them off among the tangled wilderness that was his natural element. But then they had suddenly cut toward the open beach—heading, he'd assumed, for a prearranged rendezvous with either a larger ground force or some kind of vehicle transport.

At that point he had come close to jettisoning the idea of a night attack. Now it seemed entirely out of the question. The upper portions of the clouds hadn't yet flattened into anvil-shaped thunderheads, indicating that some time remained before they would open their guts, but he couldn't accurately predict how *much* time. Storms struck at the Cape with awful destructive force, and he wanted to be gone, heading back to his village, before this one hit.

Still scanning the horizon, Firecloud began to mentally grope for a plan.

And then he saw something against the fleecy backdrop of the clouds.

Something which raised his hackles, and made his mouth go dry, and shook him with a terrible sense of urgency that pushed his concerns about the coming storm to the back of his mind.

It appeared to him as an airborne dot, no larger than a pebble, in the not-too-distant south—the direction of Vaca Key and the Front's recently established military airbase. It surged toward the mainland, growing rapidly in Firecloud's sight.

He blinked once, twice, and it was the size of a plum; he blinked again, and it was larger than a man's fist. Another two eyeblinks, and it had taken on definition. It looked like a strange, giant wasplike insect.

Now he could hear it, buzzing at first, the buzz becoming a whine, the whine pitching to a crescendo and then separating into two distinct sounds: the drone of powerful turboshaft engines, and above that, the regular *whup-whup-whup* of whirling rotors.

Firecloud recognized it beyond a doubt as a Sikorsky AH-60B Strikehawk. He was all too familiar with that particular aircraft—both its design and the telltale sound of its approach. Excepting the tactical nukes, it had been responsible for more carnage during and after the invasion than anything in the Front's armament.

The Strikehawk had been born in '97, a hybrid of the H-60 troop carrier and ultra-sophisticated air assault technology, some of which was pirated from the Soviet Hind. Tricked out with a vast, state-of-the-art array of weapons and computerized instrumentation, it was a fearsome death machine.

Pylons on the gunship's external stores support system (ESSS) stub wings carried a mixed bag of sixteen missiles, including air-to-air Sidewinders and TOW and Hellfire air-to-surface missiles equally capable of vaporizing buildings and tanks—as Firecloud had often witnessed with his own eyes. Each weapon wing could be optioned for a second, inner pylon supporting a nineteen-tube rocket launcher pod.

The 20-millimeter cannon which thrust from its chin turret like an enormous, menacing proboscis fed off a 750-round magazine and could belch its deadly fire at a rate of up to three thousand rounds per minute.

There were 7.62-millimeter swivel-mounted machine guns behind port and starboard gunner's windows.

In addition to its formidable warload and a two-man flight crew, the Strikehawk had the ability to carry nine fully combat ready troops.

John Firecloud's heart knocked against his ribs.

The chopper was closer, flying in low perhaps two miles offshore, a distance its blades would easily chew up in a minute or less. Its rotors *whupped* loudly. Their noise frightened a gaggle of pelicans that separated from the water just beyond the breakers.

Firecloud took a couple of deep breaths to slow his galloping heartbeat.

Part of him wanted to abandon the woman, to slip down off the tree and fade into the brush. To be gone. He didn't even know her. And it was insane to think he could do anything to help her. *Suicidal.* Wasn't it?

He looked downbeach.

The troopers had risen in anticipation of their pickup. The soldier that held the rope leasing was handing it off to the man beside him. His pockmarked face bore a nervous expression. The third soldier stood waving his arms high above his head at the arriving helicopter.

The woman continued to stare apathetically at the waves.

"Gotta go empty my tank, Vic. All the fancy hardware in those birds, you'd think some genius would'a thought to put in a toilet," the man with the acne-pitted face said to his comrade. He patted himself in the general region of his bladder. "Be careful of the honey, in case she gets any dumb ideas. I'm gonna go hose the trees."

"Whyn't you let loose right here instead of bothering to walk up the ridge? If fish piss in the water, so can we," the other soldier said as he wound the rope around his wrist.

"Nah. You never know, might be brass snooping from the copter. Surprise inspection or some shit like that. Wouldn't want some jealous lieutenant on my back just because he sees I'm a bigger man than him. You catch my meaning."

Vic grinned lopsidedly. "Yeah, right, give me a break."

The first man turned and started toward the tree line, the bottoms of his heavy combat shoes mashing broken bits of seashell into the white silicate. Behind him the sixty-foot shadow of the chopper cruised over the water's surface, mere yards from shore.

Firecloud tensely nibbled on his bottom lip as the soldier walked in his direction.

He could still quit the scene. Be gone. Be safe.

But his mind kept echoing the soldiers' mocking laughter. Their laughter as they had tripped the woman into the surf.

They would make her their slave, rape her again and again, and when they had used her up they would either kill her or let her die of sickness and starvation. Her body would be tossed into a mass grave outside one of their concentration camps and they would pour lime over it to dissolve her rotting flesh.

Firecloud pressed a finger to the protective medicine pouch of *aha lvbvkca* and cedar leaves hung from his neck, and uttered a silent prayer to gods he scarcely believed in anymore.

He ran the fingers of his other hand down the smooth, curved fiberglass and graphite limb of the compound bow slung over his shoulder. Eight steel-tipped broadhead arrows nosed out of the snap-on quiver.

Their lethal sting was something in which he had *absolute* faith.

His decision made, Firecloud climbed off his perch and went scrambling down the tree trunk. This time he didn't need the fluttery murmur of the leaves to conceal the sound of his movement. The descending copter made racket enough.

His feet quietly touched ground moments before the acne-scarred man reached the trees.

The trooper stood whistling before a tall red mangrove whose twining prop roots snaked aggressively toward the sandbelt. He had not been in a good mood, but a sense of imminent relief had improved it—that and simply being off the beach. He hadn't really thought anyone would be scoping him if he took a leak down there; at least not anyone who mattered. The thing was, he hadn't wanted to watch the copter land. Because watching it land made him think about having to board it in just a few minutes. And when he so much as thought about boarding it, his stomach rolled as if it were already struggling with gravity.

If he'd told Vic that, Vic might have gotten the impression that he was some kind of wimp. Which was far from the case, as the Indian woman could attest. He had showed her just what kind of man he was when they'd broken into the clapboard shack she had been living in. Yeah, he'd gotten her underneath him and showed her, and it had been fine.

A justifiable hatred—not a fear, oh no, if anyone ever suggested it was some kind of irrational fear, he would beat that person to a pulp—of flying did not make him a coward. Man, he believed, had not been meant to fly. Birds flew. Goddamned bugs flew, which was why they had been given wings. Human beings did not have wings. Because they were not meant to fly. Simple logic.

He loosened his Sam Browne belt, unzipped, and began extricating himself from his pants.

He never finished.

Without warning, a hand shot out from behind and clamped over his mouth, its thumb and forefinger pinching shut his nostrils. Simultaneously another hand came around and gripped his throat. He was pulled backward, off balance. He tried to breathe, tried to scream, could do neither. His air was cut off, he was choking. His feet flailed, heels skidding on the mushy ground. He brought his own hands up and pried frantically at the arms wrapped around him. His nails bit into them, but they wouldn't unlock. Their muscles bulged. The powerful fingers gripping his throat tightened. His Adam's apple was being crushed. His windpipe was swelling shut. Blood rose into his mouth, filled it, rose into his nose. The pressure in his head was enormous. He was drowning, drowning in his own blood. A haze fell over his vision. Red at first, then shot with black. Then the haze became a solid *wall* of black.

Just before the end he made a desperate attempt to beg for his life but could only manage a tiny, sputtering sound.

Then he went limp.

John Firecloud let the body spill out of his arms.

Blood spouted from its nostrils and gaping mouth as it crumpled into a mesh of prop roots.

Firecloud looked at the soldier and noticed the spreading wet stain on the crotch of his half-fallen pants. Death had robbed him of whatever dignity he'd possessed . . . just as he'd robbed it from the woman.

Still doesn't make them even, Firecloud thought.

He turned and watched through the trees as the Strikehawk banked for a landing. It hovered about ten feet above the ground for several moments, the wash of its rotors whipping up a funnel of sand, then settled gently onto its landing gear.

The men on the beach approached the chopper cautiously while its slowing blades beat lazy circles in the air, their captive trailing along behind.

Firecloud nocked an arrow into his bow and waited. The helicopter had come down with its starboard side to him, which meant he would be out of the pilot's and co-pilot's direct line of sight. A lucky break. Now if he could only have another . . .

Upper and lower doors opened on the Strikehawk's fuselage like a square, robotic mouth.

His breath catching, Firecloud anxiously peered inside.

And got his second break.

The cabin was vacant; even the big 7.62 sidegun was unmanned. One of the men in the cockpit must have opened the doors remotely.

Firecloud exhaled with a grateful sigh. He had counted on the Strikehawk having a reduced crew since cabin space was needed to accommodate the ground patrol and their captive. But even a third of its maximum troop complement would have been sufficient to make him a vastly outnumbered goner. That there was no one aboard besides the flight crew was a discovery which exceeded his best hopes. Possibly the absence of any effective threat to their occupation had resulted in a slackening of the Front's military procedures.

The odds were still four to one against Firecloud, but he felt that he at least had a fighting chance.

He readied the bow for firing, testing its draw.

Watching. Waiting.

Inertia had finally brought the Strikehawk's blades to a halt. The aircrew had popped their windscreen canopy, and the co-pilot was outside the front of the craft having a cigarette. The man named Vic and the other foot soldier had led the Seminole woman aboard, after which Vic had emerged from the copter alone, walked slowly over to the co-pilot, and grubbed a smoke off him.

The two of them talked and puffed while in the cockpit the pilot undid his safety harness and relaxed with his helmet visor up, stretching his arms, occasionally joining in on the conversation.

Several minutes later the co-pilot stubbed his cigarette

into the sand and gazed over at the trees. He said something to Vic, who turned in the same direction.

"Ray, you done yet?" he shouted, taking a last drag off his cigarette and flicking away the butt.

His only response was silence.

Firecloud added a little more tension to the bowstring.

Vic looked at the co-pilot and wagged his head, a prosy grin on his face. "Guy's bladder must hold more water than Lake Michigan," he remarked. He cupped his hands over his mouth and looked back at the trees. "Yo, Ray! You playing with yourself in there or what? We gotta take off before the bad weather hits!"

There was another parcel of silence broken only by the rhythmic slap of the waves and the cries of the gulls that had flocked inland before the advancing stormfront.

Vic's grin dwindled. "Bet he went and took a catnap, damned if he ain't sawing wood," he grumbled, shaking his head with greater annoyance. "I'll go and fetch him."

Firecloud heard more than a trace of the South in the tone and cadence of his voice. He wondered briefly if the man was a native of Florida; there were many collaborators, a percentage of whom had become full-blown National Front recruits.

Vic started quickly up the loose-packed sand toward the ridge less than thirty yards away.

Firecloud let him walk for ten yards, then took aim and fired.

An instant after the arrow whooshed from the bow he saw Vic stagger backward and look down at the shaft suddenly jutting from his chest, his face clenched with agony and utter bafflement.

He looked back at the trees with that same pain-wracked, stunned expression, opened his mouth as if to shout, and wheezed out a foam of blood and saliva.

His hands gripped the arrow and tried to pull it free, but only succeeded in further mauling the lung in which its tri-bladed head was imbedded. A scarlet flower bloomed in the center of his service blouse.

He gagged, pale pink blood bubbling over his lower lip and chin, and swayed forward.

Firecloud was off and running across the strand before Vic's face smacked the ground.

For a moment neither the pilot nor co-pilot could grasp what was happening. They stood watching with frozen, wide-eyed incomprehension as the man with the bow dashed toward them.

Then the co-pilot snapped back to awareness, looked desperately around for cover, and broke for the chopper's open passenger door.

Firecloud let him go. It was vital that he deal with the pilot next. If the man in the cockpit pulled down the armored canopy, then he would be sealed off from attack.

As if reading Firecloud's thoughts, the pilot reached for the raised windscreen panel above his head.

He was a slice of an instant too late. Firecloud had halted less than fifteen feet from the chopper and loaded his bow. His firing hand a blur, he loosed the arrow, slipped another from the quiver on the bow's handgrip, and fired it in rapid succession.

Had the pilot's helmet visor been down, he might have lived a bit longer. But it wasn't, and he didn't.

The tip of the first arrow ripped into his exposed right cheek and plowed an exit wound through the left. Gaudy fletching protruded from a face that immediately stretched around the shaft like a distorted funhouse mirror-image.

The second arrow drove home just as the pilot reflexively turned, gaping, toward his assailant. It socked into his right eye and burrowed deep into his head, throwing him spread-eagle backward across the cockpit.

His legs jerked twice then ceased to move.

Firecloud narrowly scrutinized the corpse for a moment, his lips compressed into a grim, tight line. He'd halved the odds against him. The Strikehawk was brain-dead.

A fighting chance, yes.

He raked his glance over his shoulder toward the cabin entrance.

And saw the surviving ground trooper jump from the boarding step and come tearing at him in a low, humpbacked charge, hands wrapped around an M-16. The co-pilot was in the sidegunner's station, calling to the soldier at the top of his voice.

"Come back, you idiot, I can't get a shot off with you in the way!" he shouted from the copter. "Goddamn it, I said you're *blocking my fire!*"

The soldier disregarded him. His eyes met Firecloud's with a steely, vengeful glare as, still running, he triggered a burst from the rifle.

Firecloud chucked his bow and dodged sideways just before a hail of lead riddled the ground on which he'd stood, churning up dry geysers of sand. The soldier swung his head around to see where he'd landed, pivoted toward him, triggered another volley. Firecloud managed to avoid the fire with a lightning quick tuck-and-roll.

"Gonna get you for Vic and Ray, bastard!" the soldier screamed, pivoting again to keep up with Firecloud's zigzagging scramble. His berserk grimace revealed a mouthful of crooked, decayed teeth. "I'm gonna blow your guts right out your ass!"

The gun muzzle chattered, pulverizing a mound of ocean debris. Shell fragments and chunks of seaweed and driftwood sprayed chaotically into the air.

Firecloud ducked, bellyrolled, weaved. He was tiring, losing his wind. Every muscle groaned from exertion. He had to put an end to the barrage—*fast*.

Powering to a low crouch, he launched himself at the man with the gun, barely skirting a murderous stream of bullets. Caught off guard by his sudden move, the soldier tried desperately to recover from his surprise and draw a bead.

Like the Strikehawk's pilot, his reflexes were a hair too slow, and that slowness cost him his life.

Moving with a speed and fluidity that was almost balletic, Firecloud came in under the M-16's barrel and then sprang to his full height, hooking the barrel between his left forearm and bicep. At the same time he slammed the heel of his right hand against the soldier's head at a point just above the nose and between his eyebrows, shattering his glabella.

The man died instantly as jags of bone ripped through his brain. He collapsed, his finger spasming on the gun trigger and squeezing a round harmlessly into the air.

Firecloud tore the M-16 from the soldier's convulsive grasp as he fell.

The rifle felt uncomfortable in his hands.

He did not like guns. Guns made killing easy—and so depreciated life.

Did not like them, but knew how to use them.

He spun around, poised to fire the M-16 at the helicopter.

The chopper's sidegun was pointing back at him. The co-pilot held it steady with his right hand. His left hand was twisted in the Seminole woman's hair.

He pulled hard on a fistful of hair and she shrieked, bending backward into him, her spine arched against his shoulder.

Firecloud fixed him in a hard, cold stare.

"Go ahead, Indian, do me," the co-pilot snarled. "But you'll be doing the bitch, too. That's if I don't put you down first."

Firecloud was silent.

"I'm not sure what's happening here, but if this is over the woman, you can have her," the man in the helicopter said. "Flying the chopper's my business. She isn't. All you've gotta do is toss the gun and I'll let her go."

Sure you will, Firecloud thought, still saying nothing. He was positive that the instant he relinquished his weapon he would be as dead as the soldiers sprawled about the beach . . . and the woman would be left at the co-pilot's mercy.

Neither his dark eyes nor his rifle wavered. He took a slow step forward.

Thunder rumbled over the Gulf.

"Stay where you are, man!" The co-pilot wrenched the woman's head back again, and she cried out sharply, her cheeks blotching with hectic color. "I can hurt her if I want to," he yelled. Listened to the thunder. "I can hurt her bad!"

Firecloud kept his gun leveled. Letting each second live. Noticing every movement, as the shaman, Charlie Tiger, had once taught him.

Each movement means something, the old man had said. *Observe. Then participate.*

He took another step.

"Hold it!" the co-pilot screamed. "Is she gonna have to catch more punishment? *Is she?!*" He pulled her hair a third time. Tears burst from her eyes, and she squirmed in his grasp, causing his weight to shift.

His hand slipped back from the trigger.

Just a little.

Just enough.

"No. No more," Firecloud muttered under his breath, firing the M-16.

It went off with a blinding roar, recoil slamming its stock against Firecloud's shoulder, empty casings leaping into the air around him. Thrown suddenly clear of the girl, the co-pilot dervished toward the far wall of the cabin, his head vanishing in a grisly eruption as a half-dozen slugs plowed into it at once.

A shapeless, bloody pulp from the shoulders up, the co-pilot's body rebounded off the wall and toppled to the copter's steel floor with a dull clang.

Firecloud stood for a moment before going over to the woman in the copter. He needed to pull himself together. He felt queasy and light-headed. Completely spent.

It wasn't just exhaustion. That was only a small part of it.

Most of it was the killing. He had seen too much. Done too much. Killing in a world that was itself in its death throes. It all seemed so ultimately pointless.

He took in a great swoop of air, waited another few seconds, and started forward.

The woman was leaning against the frame of the cabin door, staring out at the beach, her face shiny from tears. The apathy and submission that had marked her expression before had been overlayed with a kind of dazed shock.

She did not acknowledge Firecloud as he entered the cabin.

The craft's interior smelled to Firecloud of metal and rubber and air conditioning and oil—but predominantly of blood. There was a great deal of blood around. And clumps of flesh. And hair.

He avoided looking at the body of the co-pilot and kept his gaze on the woman.

The dead man's blood was all over her, too.

"We, hayone," he said to her softly, using the traditional Seminole words of greeting. He noticed that her rope leash hadn't been removed. It looped around her neck and ran limply between her shoulder blades to her feet.

She kept looking outside as if he weren't there.

Firecloud wondered if she might be unacquainted with the ancient tongue.

"You're going to be all right," he said in English. "I'm Seminole. From the Whitewater Bay camp, not far from here. I can take you there and—"

"And what?" she hissed, rounding on him with an unexpected suddenness that actually made him flinch.

"And what?!" she repeated, *demanded*. The muscles of her face, previously static, were twitching like snakes.

He looked at her for a long moment, surprised and mystified. "You—" He hesitated awkwardly. "—You can stay with us. If you want."

"You think *that's* what I'd want? To go back to the *swamp*?" she cried, her voice rising to a shrieky pitch.

Firecloud stared at her as if at some improbable mirage. He felt lost, unanchored.

"What I wanted, you son of a bitch, was to go with *them*," the woman snapped, waving her fists as she spoke. "To live some place where the food and water isn't radioactive and the damned White Trash muties aren't running wild. Where there's some kind of *civilization*." Tears started spilling down her gaunt cheeks again, and her voice became low and husky. "They'd have gotten me out of these rags. Given me fine things. Taken care of me."

Firecloud felt a profound sadness settle in on him like mist.

"You were tied like a dog," he said. "They abused you."

She threw her head back and laughed bitterly. "A game. The rough stuff's just a game with men like that. I could have put up with it. What would it have mattered? How much does *anything* matter these days? They wouldn't have hurt me. They liked the things I did to them."

She looked at him and broke into her humorless laugh. When the laughter subsided, her anger seemed to drain away with it, and the glaze slid over her eyes again. The flat, bleak expression returned to her features.

"I'm getting out of here," she said.

And simply left.

The wind was high, and dark angry clouds were massing over the beach. The woman's hair swirled wildly around her head. She walked away, the rope leash dragging behind her like an absurd tail, furrowing the sand.

There was a stab of lightning, a vicious crack of thunder. Sand rattled against the hull of the chopper. Gritty particles tried to invade Firecloud's eyes, and he was forced to squint.

He watched the woman until she disappeared far down the curve of the shore and he was alone with the men he had killed and their deathbird.

Pointless, he thought, unable to know that same mechanical bird of death in the very near future would fly on a mission to save his life and the lives of many, many others.

Now he only knew that he had to be well gone from the beach before it took the main brunt of the storm. It was not hurricane season, and for that he was thankful; nonetheless, the charcoal-gray clouds and harridan winds promised turbulent, dangerous weather.

Stepping outside the chopper, Firecloud hunched his shoulders, leaned into the blowing sand, and hurried toward the relative safety of the forest.

Chapter Two ═══════════════════

Late afternoon sunlight filtered weakly through the over-growth as John Firecloud plunged deeper into the swamp. He was thinking about the old man, and that was dangerous— with an enemy very likely near, Firecloud knew he must remain ready, alert, focused on the moment. But despite that knowledge, the thought continued to beat in his mind with its own painful, insistent rhythm.

The old man was dying.

He was dying, and there was nothing to do but accept the fact. The life that had been trickling out of him for years like air from a pinhole leak was now escaping in an unstoppable rush. When Firecloud had seen him earlier that day, the flesh on the old man's face had appeared almost transparent, like waxed paper wrapped around a socketed, cadaverous skull. He hadn't even been able to muster the strength to speak. And the sound of his breathing—that bubbly, laboring wheeze—had evoked in Firecloud a child-hood association that, in context, was far from pleasant.

It had reminded him of a straw sucking the last bit of drink from a glass that was nearly drained.

Firecloud moved through the thicket, its heat a pressing physical burden. Sweat drenched the bandanna he wore around his forehead and the brown hair that fell thickly to his shoulders. All around him mangrove bushes stood like weird spiders on withered, yellow roots. The ground was becoming soft, but he proceeded noiselessly, avoiding the sticky patches of marl and plant rot waiting to suck at his feet, alert for hidden root tangles that might trip him up.

As a boy he had been taught to walk in perfect silence. He could still remember the old man telling him how white people walked with their toes pointing out to either side, clomping and thrashing like bull manatees in heat. He had demonstrated the clunkish stride for Firecloud, who laughed hysterically at his burlesque. And then the old man's tone had become more serious, and he'd showed his student the Seminole way. Walking with your toes pointed in the direction you are headed. Cutting a narrow path and registering one foot in front of the other. Touching the ground with the ball of your foot and rolling slowly toward the arch, while scanning for rocks, fallen leaves, anything that might make a sound and betray your presence.

Again the old man had demonstrated.

Firecloud hadn't laughed.

That had been years ago. So many years.

Now the thought recurred like the cyclic, ominous thunder that had rolled in off the ocean preceding last week's storm. The old man was dying.

Firecloud hadn't wanted to leave his side. Not when the pitifully thin filament of his life was liable to burn out in the space between seconds. But two young boys of the tribe had claimed to have seen someone poling a skiff through one of the watercourses that crisscrossed the reservation's outskirts, compelling Firecloud to investigate.

He paused. Directly in his path huge green fronds leaned as if in benediction, fronting a cathedral stand of cabbage palmettos and mangroves. Through the foliage at his left he had glimpsed water.

Firecloud turned and, crouching slightly, peered through the ferns and vines that screened the pool. The skiff was a narrow, seven-foot oblong resting in the gloom at the water's near bank. A rope moored it to the denuded remains of a fallen gumbo limbo sapling. It was unoccupied, the long wooden pole that was used to steer it through the murk laid across the bow.

John Firecloud's keen eyes continued to probe. The prostrate tree to which the boat had been tied was half in, half out of the water. It groped at the air with branches that resembled skeletal fingers. A crayfish scuttled into the water from one of the branches, vanishing in a swirl of bottom mud.

The sawgrass near the unsubmerged portion of the tree was flattened in places. The slight depressions ran off to the left along the pool's margin. Each roughly approximated the contours of a human foot.

Firecloud cut his gaze in the direction of the footprints. A burlap sack lay crumpled on the ground perhaps fifteen feet from the dead gumbo limbo sapling. Old, coppery blood-stains splotched its fabric.

The lid of a nearby cooler was propped half-open by an overload of Budweiser cans and crushed ice.

Firecloud's hand relaxed around his speedbow, and he smiled thinly. He straightened, made an opening in the curtain of growth with a swipe of his free hand, and stepped through.

The broad chunk of a man standing over to the left held a Remington 870 slide-action rifle. A machete hung from his leather belt scabbard. He wore a camouflaged bush hat, khaki shirt, and dungarees, the legs of which were tucked hip-deep into a pair of rubber waders. The triangle of fuzz sprouting from beneath his open collar was the same carrot-red as his walrus mustache and the hair bordering his hat. His cheeks were ruddy and glossed with perspiration.

The man quickly swung his gun up toward the parting foliage . . . and just as quickly lowered its muzzle, a toothy grin of recognition lighting his face.

"Now this is what I call a fine coincidence," he said, as Firecloud approached. He spoke in the low rumble that was his best version of a whisper. "Fine coincidence," he repeated, his meaty hand gobbling up Firecloud's and pumping it heartily.

"Bill Coonan. I should have guessed it might be you," Firecloud said. His own smile remained subdued. "A couple of boys from the village saw you while they were out on the roam. It put a scare into them."

"Hell, I ain't that ugly. Ain't wearin' a National Front armband, neither."

"The children have more enemies these days than just the Front soldiers. Collaborators. White Trash. Slave traders."

"I s'pose." Bill suddenly looked eager to change the subject. He raised a hand and made a swatting gesture near his face. "Can't say I'd mind if the skeeters was as afraid of me as yer brats. Damn bugs'll suck a man dry. I seen a few were bigger'n hornets, no exaggeratin'. Muties, I reckon."

"Maybe. Or maybe they're just well fed. Fresh blood's easy enough to come by. There's been plenty spilled since the invasion."

"See you're in a dandy mood today," Bill said, cocking an eyebrow. "Hell, we both oughtta quit bitchin' and just be glad the storm didn't blow us all to kingdom come."

Firecloud shrugged and stared contemplatively down at the still, opaque water. It seemed to draw in all available light like a black hole.

After several moments his eyes shifted to a mound of earth on the opposite bank of the pool. There was a shallow groove in its side, and furrows and scratches on the crest that a grown man's hand might have easily fit into—although it was apparent from the clawed, tapering shape of the imprints that no human had made them.

He looked at Bill. "A twelve-footer."

"Or better. Wouldn't waste my time huntin' a gator smaller'n that, leastways not in this heat. Been waitin' for the sucker to come for air, but I think it's about time to give him a holler. Now you'll see blood spilled, by God."

"The meat from an alligator that large makes for bad eating. Too tough."

Firecloud's remark was superficially casual, but Bill caught the underlying accusation. "That's right. It's his gnarly hide I want. Front officers want to keep their painted ladies—not to mention their wives—hot and happy, so they deck 'em out in gatorskin shoes and handbags. If we can't get rid a' the goose-steppin' assholes, we might as well make a buck off 'em." His green eyes narrowed. "I never fault any man for the way he earns a livin', Johnny. To each his own, that's my policy."

Firecloud said nothing. He was thinking of the woman on the beach as he'd seen her walk away, the leash still dangling from her neck.

"I'd best get to business," Bill said, turning away.

He squatted at the rim of the pool, set his rifle on the ground, and cupped a hand over his mouth. His thick neck muscles bunched, his Adam's apple rode up his throat, and sound boomed out: *"Ooonk! Ooonk—ooooonk—ooo-ooo-ooooonk!"*

He waited, scrutinizing the water, then took a deep breath and repeated the sound several times.

Bubbles popped at the water's surface.

"Oooonk! Ooooooooonk!"

More bubbles broke through the water, then two dark, parallel lobes, and a moment later the hooded yellow eyes of the alligator were up and beading Firecloud and Bill in a cold reptilian stare.

Bill grabbed his Remington. In a flash he was on his feet and aiming the gun at a point between the creature's eyes.

The explosive report of the rifle made Firecloud blink. There was a dull echo as the shells smacked into the surface of the pool. Water sprayed, then surged upward in a high, foamy column.

And suddenly the gator burst clear of the churning water, monstrous jaws snapping, long horny tail lashing crazily. It hung in the air for a frozen instant, twisting and jerking like a puppet suspended from invisible strings, and then splashed back in. It flip-flopped just beneath the surface, exposing its pale, mottled underbelly, righted itself, turned over again. Blood ribboned through the water.

Then the frenzied motion ceased, and the alligator was floating near the pool's rim. Its body rose and fell with the undulations of the calming water, one widespread foreclaw thrusting upward like a grotesque aquatic stalk. Pulped brain matter brewed from the jagged crater that had replaced the crest of its skull.

Leaving his gun behind, Bill sloshed forward until he was almost hip-deep in the pool, and wrapping his big hands around the gator's closed snout, hauled it onto the bank.

He released the shattered head, and its weight hit the moist ground with a loud *splat*. The gator's tail and limbs jittered reflexively, making smaller, squishing noises in the mud.

Bill gazed at the quivering reptile and shook his head. "Too stupid to know yer dead, poor bastard. Well, I'll get ya settled."

Bill knelt, took one of the gator's forelegs into his right hand, and a hind leg into his left. He lifted the creature, turned it so that he was looking down at its pale, exposed belly, and then cracked its still-quivering body sharply over his knee.

The animal's backbone snapped. Its body writhed in a final shuddering convulsion, as if suffused with voltage, then was finally still.

Bill rose, letting the carcass slide limply to the mud, and examined his bloodslimed hands. His face screwed up, and he grunted with distaste, like a drill sergeant who finds grime in the latrine during barracks inspection.

"Messy work!" he exclaimed a trifle breathlessly, wiping the gore onto his shirt. "Thirsty work, too. Gonna have me a cold one 'fore I get to skinnin' the beast."

He went to the cooler. "How 'bout it, Johnny? Join me?"

Firecloud, who had been watching him with stony detachment, merely shook his head.

"Suit y'self, then."

Bill got out a beer, popped the fliptop of his can, and took a drink. He swished the liquid around in his mouth before letting it go down.

"Don't know what's eatin' ya, buddy, but it ain't too late t'change yer mind about havin' some'a this brew," he said, sighing contentedly and dragging the back of his hand across his lips. "Brought along more'n two six-packs—"

"The old man is dying."

Bill looked at him, ballooned his cheeks, allowed the air to slowly whistle out.

Firecloud's expression remained impassive. He had hoped that speaking the endlessly looping thought aloud would vent off some of its thunderous internal pressure. But the words had sealed themselves against emotion.

A limpkin cried into the silence. A frog dove into the pool, raising a tiny splash in the murky water. The alligator's blood pattered quietly from its ruined head to the ground. Mosquitoes droned around the widening red puddle.

Dusk was near, and the thicket was cooling.

"World's done a whole lot a' turnin' since our hellraisin' days at the orphanage," Bill said at last, his voice uncharacteristically gentle.

Firecloud gave him a somber nod.

"How long's he got?"

"Could be any time now."

Bill finished his beer, crunched the empty can, and tossed it into his boat.

"Don't need a weatherman to know which way the wind blows," he muttered under his breath.

He strode over to Firecloud, and when they were only inches apart placed a firm hand on his shoulder. His clothes carried the odor of perspiration and the swamp and rubbed-in blood. Around the bristling red growth on his face, his cheeks were mud-streaked and a little drawn, but his blue eyes were unwaveringly bright peering out from the shadow of his hat brim.

"Johnny, I know how you feel about the old man," Bill said. His voice remained soft but had gained a certain intensity. "I care 'bout him, too, in spite a' what he thinks. He took me in all them years ago, same's he did you, never mind I wasn't Seminole. So don't think that what I'm gonna say makes me heartless."

Firecloud nodded again, faintly.

"Old man's a dreamer. An' it's my refusin' to buy into his dreams that's kept us at odds all these years. But their price is too high. Always has been. 'Cause dreams ain't worth a damn in what's left of this rotten, nuke-blasted country. An' livin' out the old man's won't do nothin' but put ya in the grave alongside him."

He paused a beat and studied Firecloud's features for some clue to his thoughts. But they revealed nothing.

"I know what's in the wind for you, know all the Indian fables and mystic crap. I also know what's real. There ain't no warriors, Johnny. Ain't no heroes. Man's either a survivor or a casualty, those are the only choices. I made mine a while back. Your turn's comin' soon, an' I hope to God you don't blow it."

Bill fell silent then, and for a while the two men stared at each other in the dimness.

Finally Bill looked down, took his hand off Firecloud's shoulder, and sighed. He stretched, pressing his fists into the small of his back. His spine crackled.

"Well, I've put in my spare change," he said. "Things'll work themselves out one way or another, I reckon."

Firecloud's expression had not altered. "Will you be coming to see the old man?" he asked flatly.

"Right now I ain't plannin' any further ahead than separatin' that gator from his hide before the skeeters beat me to it," Bill replied, a bit too quickly. He adjusted and readjusted his hat. "It's you that oughtta be gittin', Johnny. Not me."

With that, Bill returned to where he had left his kill, fighting off the cloud of buzzing insects that had gathered around it. Drawing his machete, he made an incision near the hornback ridge at the base of the gator's head and moved the knife along the length of the carcass, slitting it open. Then he turned the gator belly up, made some more precise cuts, and began methodically peeling away the hide.

Firecloud stood watching in silence. As he'd stood minutes ago, while Bill had addressed him first with concern, then overlapping frustration, and finally—when declining to visit the old man—a kind of fumbling uncertainty.

We're like two dogs picking at the same bone, he thought, knowing it would have been futile to try and convince Bill that survival sometimes hinged on dreams and that one sometimes had to fight for them to live with dignity . . . or even to go on living, period.

Bill Coonan had had the clear option of either accepting or rejecting Seminole traditions from the day the old man had brought him onto the reservation. And he'd tossed them away like unwanted baggage.

It was different for Firecloud; the tribal legacy ran through his veins.

He could not make himself forget that the name Seminole was rooted in the Spanish word *cimarron,* which meant "untamed." Nor could he forget that of the three thousand Seminole that had resided in Florida prior to the Cuban invasion, a third had been exterminated and hundreds more interned in forced labor camps.

The seventeenth-century conquistadores had considered the Seminole to be a bold, fearsome people.

What must the Front soldiers think of us? Firecloud wondered.

What must they *think*?

Still in silence, he turned and slipped into the brush, retracing the path he had taken from the village, without once looking back. And as he walked on, he became possessed of the unsettling and wholly irrational notion that the ground behind him was pulling away a thousand or ten thousand miles for each forward step that he took; that the gulf separating Bill and himself was now as wide as a canyon, now a mountain range, a sea, an entire continent— and would soon be as vast and unbridgeable as the black emptiness between stars.

The queer feeling stayed with Firecloud until long after he'd reached home.

Chapter Three ═══════════════

Something had awakened him.

Some sound . . .

Firecloud jerked bolt upright, his awareness congealing. The second or two of fuzzy disorientation he experienced after opening his eyes was unusual. His mind was trained to remain keyed for signs of possible danger even in sleep. But last night his rest had been infested with nightmares and frequently broken.

Firecloud shook his head, blinked once, twice, and then was free of the cobwebs. He stared into the darkness of his lodge.

There had been a sound.

He heard it again. A low creak. Outside.

Someone was climbing the ladder that rose up to the lodge's narrow veranda.

Naked, he sprang from his pallet and crossed to the window with catlike speed. A breeze sifted in through the cheesecloth insect screen that was tacked to its glassless frame. Firecloud cautiously looked out, keeping his body flat against the adjacent wall. The hut fronted eastward, and he registered that dawn was near, the sun a thin line of lava-orange smoldering across the distant horizon.

His eyes angled to the left and down, toward the entrance ladder.

The floor of the lodge was seven feet off the ground, supported by wooden posts imbedded deep in the marl. The woman scaling the ladder had gotten halfway to the top, and though her face was vague in the semidarkness, he was able to recognize her by her shape and the way she moved.

Had his unexpected visitor been a certain or even potential enemy, he'd have reached for one of the dozen razor-honed throwing stars mounted on the wall within easy reach of where he stood.

Instead he turned to reach for some clothes.

Firecloud was already slipping into his jeans when she knocked. Tugging them around up his waist, he hurried to the door and opened it. Though he could feel his body gearing down from the taut combat-readiness of seconds past, Firecloud did not completely relax. His nerves continued to hum with a duller kind of apprehension.

Ella Parker was one of three women who had for the past week been taking turns keeping a death vigil at the old man's bedside. When Firecloud had returned from his encounter with Bill in the swamp yesterday, she'd given him the bad, if not entirely unexpected, news that the old man had lapsed into a coma.

What reason would Ella have for calling on him at this hour other than to inform him of the worst?

He opened the door, steeling himself.

And saw no grief on her broad, unlovely face, but rather an open and excited smile.

He looked at her, perplexed, and feeling oddly untethered, wary of being dashed against his own upcropping hope.

"What is it?" he asked, anxiously.

"He's come to!"

The plump, fiftyish woman huffed breathlessly from the exertion of running across the camp and her hurried climb up to his door. Her hand went to her large bosom as she took in a great swoop of air. *"He's out of the coma—"* She gulped more oxygen. *"—And wants to see you!"*

Firecloud caught himself just as he was about to ask if she was certain. It was the sort of question that utter surprise often prompted, and it was also completely idiotic. Of course she was sure.

He stepped past her onto the deck and clambered down the ladder, shirtless and barefoot. The sawgrass-carpeted ground was spongy and damp, the breeze cool, gusting off the salt marsh on the reservation's western fringe. Goose bumps erupted on his flesh as he crossed the plaza.

At his left were several plank huts like his own, arranged in a slightly irregular semicircle; to his right the sturdy driftwood longhouse which functioned as a mass shelter during hurricanes. He passed these dwellings and then the *tipaci*, his tribe's communal eating place. Central to the thatch-roofed, open-sided arbor was a cooking pit in which a flame had once burned constantly. But the Front bombs had irradiated most available crops and livestock, and no one cooked anymore. The star-shaped pit was now dark and filled with scavenged canned and bottled foods—grim evidence of the nuclear strike's lasting consequences.

An even more chilling reminder lay just ahead of Firecloud.

He did not want to look. At least he thought he didn't.

But, in fact, some mutinous part of him *did*, and it was that which prevailed.

In a small pen just beyond the *tipaci* a goat sniffed at the ground where yesterday its calf had fallen from the womb two-headed and limbless. The stillborn atrocity had been quickly buried amid ritual chants for divine favor. It had risen from the grave in Firecloud's hammering nightmares.

In his dream the malformed creature had wriggled from the hole, shedding loose divots of earth, bleating as it pushed upward, its heads flapping loosely at the end of their shared neck. One of the heads had been pulped and was dripping blood. The other had fixed him in a black-eyed stare. The mutation had squirmed toward Firecloud, stretched caterpillarlike on its belly, its umbilicus dragging behind. There had been a glistening trail of afterbirth.

Firecloud had stood paralyzed with horror and loathing as

it came and came and came at him, while a loud, cheerful voice sang to the background accompaniment of whirling carnival music, *"He had a mismatched body with two left heels, long dick hangin' out like a four-yard reel . . ."*

Then, in the dream, Bill Coonan had appeared. The woman from the beach shuffled dazedly behind him on her leash. They'd been hiding somewhere, perhaps behind one of the lodges. And Firecloud had realized it was Bill who had been singing the vulgar ditty, and was still singing it as he charged at the crippled goat calf, hauling the woman behind him so that she was forced into a run, his heels kicking up mud, his machete raised above his head and then coming down in a clean whistling arc to slice the creature in half a moment before it would have flopped onto the toe of Firecloud's buckskin boot.

Now Firecloud surfaced from his memory of the dream like a swimmer gasping for air. He tore his eyes from the goat pen and sprinted across the remaining ten yards to Charlie Tiger's lodge.

Fast up the ladder, then.

The door was ajar. Ella must have neglected to shut it in her haste.

Firecloud pushed it the rest of the way open and entered.

The old man's deerskin pallet was empty.

Firecloud's brow creased, and he combed his fingers through his long hair. Less than twelve hours ago the old man's physical condition had deteriorated so badly that his nurses had held a mirror under his nose to see if it would fog.

Where could he . . . ?

Firecloud took another step in. His eyes peered into the riot of shadows that an oil lamp farther back flung about the four walls.

A large cedar chest in the middle of the room was draped with animal hides and geometrically patterned swatches of fabric. On the floor over to the left, the flickering lamplight revealed a jumble of ceremonial gourds, rattles, hand drums, and small clay dolls. There were boxes filled with terrapin shells, and others containing red, yellow, and green *sapiya*, magic stones carried by their owners to bring power in love, the hunt, and battle. An open pulverized-bark scroll overspread a tabletop.

The lamp was perched on another table near the wall opposite Firecloud. There were two large high-backed wicker armchairs behind the table.

Charlie Tiger sat back on one of them, rolling a cigarette. His thin silver hair was tied back in a ponytail that had slipped forward over one shoulder. He had on a loose patchwork robe, the sash of which was drawn tight around his withered frame, and slippers.

The old man's eyes gleamed warmly as they looked up from the makings on his lap and gazed at Firecloud. The parchmentlike skin of his face, pulled taut over jutting cheekbones, was latticed with innumerable deep grooves— amid which the small, dry smile he offered Firecloud was almost lost.

"Shaman. *Father*—" Firecloud swallowed again. He felt relief, joy, and bewilderment all at once.

"For months Ella and the other women have forbidden me my licorice twists—too much sugar's bad, they say— and my morning smoke," Charlie Tiger said quietly. "There were even times when they hid my tobacco pouch, and I allowed them to think that I didn't know where." The smile lines at the corners of his mouth lengthened and curved upward. "Well, much as I wish otherwise, I haven't been able to get my hands on any licorice for a while. No stores. At least none close enough for a sick old man to reach on his own. But the tobacco comes from right out in my garden and there's plenty around. Today I'm going to have a cigarette. Let them try and stop me this morning, or so much as complain, and they'll quickly learn what a difficult patient I can be."

Firecloud was still staring at him with that same joyous, puzzled absorption. His head felt light. He fumbled for words. "I came to visit yesterday. Toward evening. And you were . . . I spoke and touched your hand, and you didn't—"

Charlie Tiger raised his hand to silence him. "I had gone *inside*. Do you understand? To draw what energy I could . . . and there was less than I had anticipated. But enough so that I can speak with you now." He paused, motioned with his chin. "Come, John Firecloud. Sit beside me."

Firecloud did as he was asked. As he sat, he noticed that the play of the flame over the interwoven shoots of his chairback formed a net of shadows on the ceiling above the old man. Beneath that black netlike pattern Charlie Tiger looked like some small, helpless creature on the verge of being snared.

Charlie Tiger watched Firecloud settle into his chair. His eyes were very bright and kind in their deep pits. Returning the old man's gaze, Firecloud was overwhelmed with a surge of love for him, and he resisted an impulse to reach out and touch his cheek.

"I woke today amid memories of my youth," Charlie Tiger said, presently. He was busy with the makings on his lap again, sprinkling tobacco onto a cigarette paper. "It's natural, I suppose, to reminisce about summer when winter has you in its coldest, hardest grip. Even the most torturously hot spells seem . . . less severe . . . in retrospect."

The old man paused for a stretched second, spreading the tobacco evenly along the paper's crease with a jaundiced fingernail.

"As a boy I was all skin and bones. A weakling, I must admit. Have I ever told you this?"

Firecloud shook his head, and then realized that Charlie Tiger wasn't looking at him.

"No," he said aloud.

"I didn't think so." He licked the edge of the cigarette paper and began rolling it about the tobacco. "Nor have I ever told you about the burning of my village. When I was eleven."

Firecloud's mouth drained of moisture. Not only hadn't the old man told him, he hadn't *known*.

A feeling he did not completely understand touched his heart. Part of it was fascination, and part was . . . he had no word for it. It was like standing at the brink of some preordained leap and realizing that the drop is greater than you'd believed possible.

"Do you know anything about the dredgemen?" The old man's lips tightened when he said the last word, as if it carried a rancid taste.

Firecloud nodded slowly. "They were the ones that cut the canals here in the Everglades. In the 1920's, I think."

"They are the ones that plowed up Seminole graves and called them *aboriginal mounds*. The ones that stole the bones of our dead and the jewelry in which they were buried, and called them *souvenirs*. To build their canals and levees and roads, they ripped into land that had belonged to our people, land that we had dwelt on and cultivated for a dozen generations . . . and they called that *reclaiming the Everglades for civilization*." He sighed. "They called themselves Cracker Boys. A very jolly name."

Charlie Tiger pinched the end of the cigarette and then put it in his mouth. He struck a wooden match against the edge of the table in front of him, held its flaring tip to his cigarette, inhaled, and released smoke through his nose.

The smoke hung sweetly in the air, and the old man peered into it as if there were some cryptic message to be read in its whorls.

"The American Steel dredge machine—that was the kind they used—was a loud, belching iron monster. It had a hull that was sixty feet long and half as wide. There was a towering A-frame at the front end from which cables supported the swinging boom. The jaws of the dipper had teeth of steel and could chew up more than a square yard of earth at a time. The beast was powered by a locomotive

engine, and when they were digging . . . *feeding* on our
land . . . you could hear them for miles on end. The roar
when the boilers were fired was ear-shattering. *Whoom!*
That was it. That was the noise. It would startle the birds
into flight. And once the steam was up, the pistons and
gears would clatter and thump and howl, and always in the
background was the rumble of the engine . . ."

Charlie Tiger trailed off, his eyes seeming to gaze
through an imaginary tunnel into a distant quarter of the
past, and Firecloud suddenly knew that this was the
first—and last—time in the old man's life that he would
speak of what he saw at the far end of that corridor.

"Our village . . . the village I was born in, was located
on a tract of land which the developers wanted to run a
highway through. They offered our elders money to resettle.
I don't know how much, it doesn't matter. They wouldn't
leave. Then the dredgemen, the Cracker Boys, came and
threatened to remove us by force. They looked like giants to
me, these white men, and they had guns with them,
and . . . and I remember that they *stank*. They stank of
whiskey and meanness.

"They left without starting any real trouble, that first
time, promising to come back unless we pulled up stakes. I
suppose the village counselors petitioned the Bureau of
Indian Affairs. The land belonged to us by government
treaty. But the developers had money—" Charlie Tiger
grinned crookedly. "—And the people at the Bureau belonged to them."

He took a drag of the cigarette and went on.

"One day, some weeks after the Crackers paid us their
first visit, I woke to a great commotion outside my lodge.
This was August, and the heat was stifling though it was
very early morning. Anyway, I soon discovered that my
parents, along with the other adults, were out in the plaza.
As I said, there was a lot of hubbub, and some of the voices
were harsh and angry, but most were just afraid.

"I found out much later that they had been given a final

ultimatum to either abandon the village that same day . . . or have it torn down around their heads. They were out there, the adults, trying to decide on what to do. Knowing our people as I do now, I'd guess that if there were fifty of them taking part in the discussion, there were as many clashing opinions. But finally they came to an agreement—as is also our way.

"I remember my parents coming into the lodge and leaning over my bed. The look on my mother's face in particular is very clear, because she put it so close to mine that our noses almost touched, and because it was so sad. Her eyes were overbright, and I believed then that if the tears began to fall they would never cease.

"My mother told me to dress quickly, because all the children of the tribe would be gathering in the plaza. We were going to be brought to the bank of Whitewater Bay, less than a mile distant, where we were supposed to stay until one of the women came for us. We would have to wait a few hours, she said. But I could hear the uncertainty in her voice—and something else. Something which every Native American recognizes in his kinfolk, something which was driven into our souls by the white man. Something hard and sharp which let me know I was not to ask for any explanation.

"There were thirty of us children taken to the bay. The hours passed, each more slowly than the last, it seemed, and no one came to fetch us. All through the day I remember thinking, *The dredges are silent*. The thought stuck like a thorn. I knew the men that operated them were hostile, and I had grasped the fact their conflict with the adults had not been resolved. Yet the dredges were silent. I wondered where the dredgemen had gone, you see. Where they'd gone and what business they were up to."

The old man's cigarette was spent and tobacco grains spilled from the stub as he deposited it onto the table. He did not, as was typical, pour the remaining grains into his tobacco sack. It was a break with habit to which Firecloud at the time attached little significance—though he would afterward.

Charlie Tiger looked directly at Firecloud then, and his glittering eyes remained locked in that position until he was finished.

"The sunlight waned," he said, his voice hardly more than a rasp, "and the sky became spread with stars, and we grew hungry, and cold, and more afraid. I was neither the youngest nor the eldest. Nor, I'm absolutely certain, was I the bravest. I don't know why I broke away from the group and began walking. The urge just took me, and I did. The night was dark, and the other children were preoccupied, and none of them noticed I had gone. I walked for what must have been thirty minutes.

"And then I saw the flames. The glare made my eyes water. I could see trees burning, their tops like orange crowns, and beyond them a solid wall of fire, and above that wall the smoke blotting out the stars. I knew at once that it was the village. I knew, also, that no one would ever come for me or any of the others waiting by the river. I knew what the dredgemen had been up to. And I cried bitterly.

"I returned to the bank and told all of them there what I'd witnessed. Some refused to believe me; they wanted to go inland, to see for themselves. So we did, and they got their proof, and it was horrible. There were tears of grief and terror and rage. The night seemed like the last night of the universe . . . but of course it wasn't.

"And even as I wept I was aware that in a few hours the sun would rise in the east, as always. The earth would still be making its rounds in space. And we would be alive.

"What we needed to do, then—the only thing we could do—was try and stay alive.

"When morning came I took charge of the group. Why me, and not someone else? I can't tell you. Anymore than I'm able to explain why I had wandered off into the darkness the night before. But there was a kind of *knitting* around me. I felt it along with the rest. And I accepted it. I accepted responsibility for the group. And it was *heavy*.

"First I led us in the search for food. Later I led a party of boys to the smoking ruin of our village, and we salvaged many of the scrolls and objects you see lying around this hut. Then I led us to a place we could make camp. And finally I led us here, *and we survived*."

He leaned closer to Firecloud, his face sallow and haggard, etched with weariness . . . and so terribly ancient. "Mind you, son, that life is hard, and heaven often seems indifferent, and our only power as single individuals is to oppose the forces that press upon us. I credit myself with having some intelligence, and curiosity, and above all else *will*. As a young man these three qualities propelled me down the paths of knowledge, and I became a shaman. I am proud of my accomplishments. But I also know my limitations. The world has been remade, and our people carry their lives on their fingernails. New, dark forces have gathered against them, and their reaction has been to pull their heads down in the swamp like children huddled under a blanket. Waiting for their oppressors to reach in and throttle them."

Firecloud looked at him. His guts felt like stone. The precipice was high, the temptation to back away strong.

"There are two kinds of courage," the old man went on. "That of the man who fights for himself, and that of a man who fights a cause *greater* than himself. This second level of bravery renders the first trivial." He gazed piercingly at Firecloud. "The people do not need a medicine man for a leader but a *warrior*."

"Father, I—"

He wanted to shout: *Shut up! I've always known this day would come and you'd do this to me and I don't want to hear it!*

But his throat locked on the words.

And when Charlie Tiger reached out suddenly and took his hand, Firecloud did not pull away.

The shaman's rawboned hand was icy cold.

"The task falls on you," he said. "Do you accept?"

And in the moment of depthless silence that followed, something went out of him. Some almost palpable essence. It seemed to exit through his pores and rustle in space between the two men.

Firecloud's mind circled back to the image he'd had yesterday of the old man's life rushing out of him like wind through a massive rent, and his heart was clutched by an awful certainty that the last remaining measure of that life had departed.

But though Charlie Tiger had sagged in his chair, had visibly shrunk, his eyes and craggy features still held a steady, regardful expression.

Firecloud met his gaze and nodded.

"Yes," he said shakily.

The old man's grip on his hand tightened, and they sat together without speaking.

After a while a bird crowed outside, and both of them glanced briefly at the window.

The sun had climbed to the bellies of the lowest clouds.

"I'm tired, John, and my tongue hurts from the wagging it's done. We can talk more later on. In a few moments I'll want Ella—I'm sure she must be outside chewing her knuckles—to come and tuck me in. But first there's one more bit of history I have a wish to relate." He paused and then spoke with slow, careful intensity. "The root of our tribal name has another connotation besides 'untamed.'"

Firecloud's eyes widened incredulously. "How did you know I'd been thinking of that?" he gasped.

"Shhhhh . . ." Charlie held up a preemptive hand and continued in his deliberate tone. "It also goes to mean 'runaway,' you see, because during the 1840's many of our clans participated in the Underground Railroad, helping fugitive slaves escape to areas of safety in the free states."

He gave Firecloud's hand a sharp squeeze.

"You'll remember that."

It was not a question.

Firecloud nodded again.

"Good." The old man let his head sink onto the back of his chair and closed his eyes. "Now I'll have my nap, if you'd be so kind as to go rein in Ella."

"Father, how did you—?"

But Charlie was already snoring, and Firecloud's question went forever unfinished and unanswered.

He turned, went out the door, and stood on the veranda.

The sky overhead was painted a dozen shades of pink and gold and violet; a million tons of dust raised by tactical nuclear bombs had turned the atmosphere into a gaseous prism.

As the old man had predicted, Ella Parker was waiting in the plaza, wringing her hands, looking anxiously in his direction.

He waved to her, descended the ladder, and walked slowly back to his lodge in the gorgeous, terrible post-nuclear dawn.

Chapter Four ═══════════════════════

The symbolism was beautiful, Wiley Pike mused. Just beautiful.

He took another bite of the meal that he'd ordered up from the swank Italian joint in the lobby, chewing slowly, savoring the taste. Best food he'd ever eaten. The main course had a name he could hardly pronounce, and until the kid from room service had wheeled it through the door, Pike hadn't had the foggiest idea what kind of dish it would be. Could as easily have been fish as fowl, dairy as meat. He hadn't known, had simply gone for the most expensive item on the menu.

It proved to be delicious. Morsels of choice veal sautéed in wine sauce, served with these exotic mushrooms that were big and fat as Pike's fist. He'd never seen anything like them. Fantastic. The appetizer, come to think, had been nothing to snub your nose at, either. In its case he had known what he was getting beforehand, the ingredients were listed in English on the menu—go figure the why's and why-not's. Seafood salad with lobster and shrimp and scallop and something that was either squid or octopus. Just to put a nice topper on things, Pike had asked for a bottle of white wine, his choice of which was based on the same criteria he'd applied to ordering the meal: Most expensive in stock, if you please. They'd delivered a vintage Sauvignon. He guessed the tab on the dinner was maybe two hundred Free State Union bucks—money nobody would ever collect.

But what had he been thinking of a minute ago . . . ?

Oh, yeah. Right. Nuking Free Atlanta. Bio-nuking, more exactly.

The symbolism of it. So perfect. So absolutely rich.

Of course you had to have a sense of history to appreciate the parallels. The connections. Take, for instance, the way the basic physics and working principles behind the creation of an atomic blast corresponded with how the old United States had gone up in flames.

In the simplest kind of bomb you had a number of blasting caps, or lenses, arranged around a sphere of fissionable material such as plutonium or uranium. The lenses had to ignite in flawless sequence for the nuclear reaction to occur. This reminded Pike of when the various survivalist groups of the twentieth century had united around a core of common belief to touch off the Second American Revolution. Until very close to the turn of the century, they had feuded self-defeatingly. But despite having wasted too much time squabbling among themselves, their founders remained his sainted heroes.

Pike could name most if not all of those trailblazing organizations. They'd had such *inspirational* names. There was the Ku Klux Klan, grandfather of them all. And the American Nazi Party. The Universal Order. The Social Nationalist Aryan People's Party. The Sword of the Covenant. SS Action Group. The Posse Comitatus. And over a half dozen others.

By the late 1990's the early visionaries had stopped their senseless bickering. And what had bridged their differences? What had gotten them to jump off their own special-interest soapboxes? What had made them join forces in bringing down the Zionist pig, so-called democratic government that had sapped the vigor and reproductive capability of the White Race by fluoridating their water supplies? That had mongrelized white bloodlines with civil rights legislation?

Identity, was what.

Identity. The spiritual and philosophical center around

which they had joined hands. The heart of their faith and strength. The raw fuel of insurrection.

If the survivalist groups had been the Revolution's explosive triggers, then Identity was its plutonium. It was—

The telephone blatted, interrupting Pike's reflections. He got up from behind the small oval dining table near the French doors which opened on the terrace, crossed the room to the nightstand, and answered the phone.

Though Pike was right-handed, he lifted the receiver with his opposite hand and held it against the nuggety lump of scar tissue that was his left ear. The bad ear was deaf to all but the nearest and loudest sounds, and he took advantage of every chance that he got to use it. He wasn't sure why. Maybe he was afraid he'd totally lose hearing in it one day and constantly needed to reassure himself that it was still functional.

As he'd expected, his caller was the guy that owned the shoeshine place downstairs. Pike's shoes were ready, and he wanted to know if Pike would like them delivered to his room. Yes, Pike said, I'd appreciate that. And thanks for the fast service.

Click.

Pike smiled. This was living in style. Who'd ever have thought that he, a hardscrabble-poor farm kid from Burlington, Wisconsin, with no formal education to speak of, would be staying in a first-class room at the Omni Hotel in Atlanta and have a brigade of peons serving him hand and foot? Not his father, for sure. Definitely not that sorry prick.

But everything had its time and its season. He'd found that out during the Revolution.

Pike returned to the table, speared a veal tip with his fork, washed it down with some wine. Then he sat back in his chair watching the sunset through the open balcony doors, plunging back into his thoughts.

Wiley Pike had been introduced to the Identity Movement while doing a five-year prison stretch for arson back around '93 or '94. His cellmate in the federal pen, Homer Buntline, was a believer and had given him a wealth of literature issued by the various Identity ministries. His three favorite tracts had been *The Holy Book of Adolf Hitler, Know Your Enemies!,* and a pamphlet entitled *The Negro: Serpent, Beast and Devil.* Written in simple language that even Pike—whose last acquaintance with school had been when he was eleven and in the fourth grade—had no trouble reading, these works had put forth the Movement's fundamental tenet, namely that the Jews were descendants of Satan who had as their goal the extermination of all God-fearing white Christians. The devilspawn had in those pre-Revolutionary days maintained control of America's political establishment, and were leading the nation down the doomsday path.

During his prison stay, Pike found illumination. The realizations had struck him like a string of flashbulbs going off behind his eyes. *Pop! Pop! Pop!*

And he had been far from alone.

Under Identity's guidance, the right-wing organizations found a common ground. Whatever their individual causes, they could, every one of them, subscribe to the preachings of Identity ministers. Every major national crisis throughout history had sprung from the same infernal well.

Two misguided World Wars with the great brother nation of Germany? High taxes, interest rates, and debts which resulted in widespread business bankruptcies and farm foreclosures? The drug and AIDS epidemics? Impotence-causing fluoridation? The Jews along with their pawns, the subhuman Blacks, Asians, Latins, and American Indians, were the instigators.

They were responsible.

They had pledged their souls to the antichrist, and the blood of patriotic Americans was their sacrament.

By 1997 the numerous survivalist groups had merged like metals in a forge around their Identity beliefs. In the passion and excitement of this coming together, their shared desire to overthrow the United States government became pressurized.

Reaching critical mass.

There it was again, Pike thought. The symbolism. The *poetry.*

Known as the National Front, the new coalition flourished amid prolonged economic downturn and widespread middle-class discontent.

It cultivated supporters in the highest ranks of the military. Gained crucial access. Became well armed.

There were riots. Assassinations. Commando raids.

The violence compounded itself.

The National Front's power base grew.

In 1999 twenty Western and Midwestern Front-controlled states seceded from, and declared war against, the fractured remnant of the Union.

And America *burned.*

Someone knocked on Pike's door, startling him. He'd been lost in thought. That was happening to him often these days. Maybe too much. Had to watch it. Stay sharp. He'd been given a great responsibility. A once-in-a-lifetime honor.

He rose, smoothed the legs of his slacks, patted his hair in place. Who could be knocking? He glanced at the closet, made sure it was closed, the briefcase with its precious contents safe inside. He wondered if he ought to get his gun out of the dresser, tuck it under his shirtflap just in case. Then he remembered the shoes. He'd told the guy on the phone to send them up.

It was only his shoes.

The flunky kid at the door was about thirteen and dark-complected. Inferior genes. He handed Pike his loafers in a paper bag. Pike eyed him mistrustfully, took them out, inspected them. They looked good. Spit-polished.

Pike grinned. The country had turned over on its head, the whole fucking deck of cards had been scattered, mushroom clouds had bloomed over sections of both coasts—but here in Free Atlanta you could still get excellent service at the Omni. Still get your shoes shined while you waited in your room. He supposed that sticking to the old routines was what kept a lot of people from going crazy.

He put the loafers back in the bag, nodded his acceptance at the kid, and shut the door in his face without thanking or tipping him. Maybe that was a mistake. He was supposed to blend in for the next few days. But what the hell. What the hell. You couldn't go being friendly to a mutt. Handing him money. Not even when you told yourself he'd get what he deserved within a week anyway. It was a matter of principle.

You had to draw the line somewhere.

Pike set the bag with his shoes in it on the closet floor beside the briefcase. His eyes lingered on the briefcase. He reached out, touched it. Delicately. Tenderly. Felt a thrill as his fingertips made contact—and an urge to open it. To look at the canisters.

"And to him was given the key to the bottomless pit," he thought suddenly, recalling a passage from Scripture.

He wanted to see the canisters.

Pike went to the sliding doors and pulled the drapes across them. Then he went to the window and closed the curtains. Almost certainly no one would be spying on him, but he had to take every precaution.

He returned to the closet. Squatted before the briefcase and laid it flat on its side. Dialed the correct numbers into the combination lock. Thumbed open the catches.

His breath trembled with anticipation.

"And he opened the bottomless pit; and there arose a smoke out of the pit, as the smoke of a great furnace; and the sun and the air were darkened by reason of the smoke of the pit."

The three canisters arranged in a row inside the briefcase were a bright, shiny silver. Each was the approximate size and shape of a coffee thermos. Each encased a five-kilogram sphere of plutonium which, when detonated, would yield an explosive force equal to that of thirty thousand tons of TNT.

The nuclear charges alone were enough to incinerate Free Atlanta.

But each bomb also packed a special surprise. A gift, you could say, for those lucky folks that might survive the blasts.

"And there came out of the smoke locusts upon the earth . . ."

Pike ran his fingers over one of the canisters. Its surface was smooth. Cold. But, oh, the power within. The searing, purifying energy waiting for release. And the little something extra.

The booby prize.

The vial, pregnant with plague.

Pike grinned broadly, thinking of the operative that had met him yesterday at the Peachtree Center MARTA station. Of the frightened, almost sick, expression on his face. The man—who Pike knew only as Mason—had been there to deliver the briefcase, which had then contained a packet of forged ID as well as the bombs. He'd been so relieved to turn it over, one might have thought it were blistering his fingers. And the odd way he'd looked at Pike as the transfer was made, then afterward had gone bolting off down the railway platform . . .

It was like he was as scared of me as of it, Pike thought. *Like I was some kind of Dark Angel.*

And wasn't that what he'd become? The Messenger of God's Wrath? King of the Bottomless Pit?

Wiley Pike expelled a gale of laughter.

In one week the leaders of three major territories which had emerged out of America's ruins and remained independent of the Front—the Texan Territories, the Free State Union, and the Japanese-controlled Eastern United States—would convene in Free Atlanta for a trade and mutual defense summit.

In eight days Pike's bombs would unleash holy fire and plague, annhilating the city and everyone in it.

The Dark Angel, he thought.

The Plague Bringer.

King of the Bottomless Pit.

He laughed harder, more hysterically. Laughed until his eyes were tearing and he was clutching his sides and rocking back on his heels.

The laughter went undiminished for a very long time.

Ed Mason woke up acutely aware of two things, and two things only: He was in a strange bed, and he was thirsty as a bitch.

He'd awakened like that before. Plenty of times. The price to pay for having one too many. He didn't remember having gone out drinking, not yet, but not remembering immediately was par for the course. He was sure it would all come to him in a minute. Right along with a flare of meteoric pain across his temples and nauseous heaves that would send him pelting for the bathroom . . . wherever the hell the bathroom was. And the cramps.

Ed shut his eyes a bare instant after opening them. Shut them tight. Making the most of the calm before the inevitable storm of aches and shakes.

Hangover number 5,783 incoming, he thought resignedly.

Ed groped for his memory, but it wriggled away into the murk. He supposed he'd been on a humdinger of a toot. Which was excusable, considering the pressure he was under. The constant pressure. Every now and then a man in his situation needed to ventilate.

Ed Mason's situation being that he was a citizen of Free Atlanta engaged in selling critical intelligence to the Front.

His job as a foreman at the Hartsfield International Air Cargo Center put him at the hub of shipping activity in the Free State Union. He had carte blanche at the cargo terminals. On any given day he could plug into a wealth of sensitive information simply by examining bills of lading and freight forwarding orders. He knew the movements of food, medical and technical equipment, war materiel, and other essential goods.

Ed wasn't a very political man. If he had to cast his sympathies one way or the other, he supposed he'd throw in with the National Front. But he was primarily concerned with doing as well as he could for himself in a crumbling world, and his Front contact in Florida paid generously for the data Ed provided.

Spying wasn't Ed's exclusive sideline; every so often he and a few of his pals would get together on a cargo theft. Plunder was bountiful. Dozens of existing air freight companies leased warehouse space at Hartsfield's facilities. In addition, there were rooms stacked ceiling-high with crates that had been gathering dust since before the outbreak of Revolution II.

Ed and his crew concentrated on merchandise they could unload for the quickest profit. Cigarettes. Booze. Razor blades. Occasionally handguns and ammo. When it was booze, Ed would hold onto a few cases, and he and the boys would score some chicks, have a good time.

He wondered fuzzily if that was what had happened to him. He couldn't remember, but it was possible. There might be a woman in a shower not ten feet from him, soaping her curves while he lay here like some kind of cripple . . .

Better find out.

His eyes still shut against the light splashing in from a nearby window, Ed tried to sit up using his arms as props.

His arms didn't budge. Neither did any other part of him.

He tried again, his eyes snapping open like camera shutters. Next in line behind his confusion, fear waited to sink its teeth into his heart.

A half-second later, Ed Mason felt the cold bite.

There was some kind of frame around the bed. Around

him. Metal uprights supporting horizontal overhead bars. Ropes, weights, and pulleys were rigged to the frame.

Ed's arms and legs hung suspended from straps at the end of the ropes.

Traction! Merciful Christ on his heavenly throne, he was hanging like a slab of beef. In *traction*!

Ed reared violently, and immense pain tore through his body in an unbelievable, almost unbearable series of power dives, climbs, and loop-de-loops. His jerky, thrashing movements slackened the ropes attached to him, and the slack was taken up by the counterbalancing weights. The weights clattered as they slid up and down the traction frame. A machine at the side of his bed beeped frenziedly. An IV stand teetered.

He tried to scream, and the walls of his throat scraped his vocal cords like sandpaper. The sound that finally escaped his parched lips was an almost inaudible rasp.

And suddenly he knew what had happened to put him here; it all came back, his memory fast-forwarding images against a white screen of agony . . .

He had met with Lieutenant Slade, his regular contact, across the border outside Jacksonville. Slade had a task for him, not the usual harvesting of information. This was special and took priority over everything else. The Front needed a courier. Someone trustworthy. Ed was offered five thousand dollars, his choice of currency, to convey a briefcase to a man in Atlanta.

"This will be your final assignment in that city," Slade had said to him, a peculiar, guarded look coming over his ice-blue eyes. "You are to leave there within seven days of delivering the briefcase. Absolutely no later. In gratitude for the loyalty you have shown over the years, I will personally oversee your resettlement here in Occupied Florida."

Ed hesitated. Five thou, he'd never been offered a deal that sweet before. It was tempting—but it also made him wary. Why so much cash? And what was this shit about having to get out of Atlanta? He *liked* where he lived. And his friends. And the scams he had going at the airport. Besides, he didn't want to become involved in anything too dangerous. Too far out of his league.

He inquired about the contents of the briefcase, and the lieutenant was reluctant to tell him. Ed became adamant. He had to know what he was getting into. Slade finally relented, but the guardedness never left his eyes, and Ed believed he was being given an edited version of the truth.

Even trimmed down it was chilling.

"The briefcase contains explosives," Slade said. "It will be completely safe to handle them until they are primed. Their detonation at strategic locations throughout Atlanta is planned to coincide with a meeting of top-level dignitaries from enemy Territories. We expect that life in the city will be—" He paused, seemed to choose his next words carefully. "—Seriously disrupted for quite a while afterward."

Ed felt a trickle of sweat between his shoulder blades. "You're saying that whether or not I take the job . . ." He wet his lips with his tongue. "Whether or not I accept, I'd better be lamming out of Atlanta."

"In extra light shoes, my friend," Lieutenant Slade had said, winking.

Following that exchange very little had remained for Ed to consider. It was better to leave town with five thousand dollars spending money and Slade's offer to help him relocate than without either.

A day later Ed turned over the briefcase—which must have weighed almost fifty pounds—to the man he'd been told to address as Mr. P. They rendezvoused on the subway station beneath Peachtree Center, exchanged some code words, and completed the transfer.

By then Ed was a nervous wreck. Primed or not, the bombs he'd been carrying packed enough whammy to do tremendous damage—much more, he suspected, than Slade had cared to let on. Adding to his jitteriness was the fact that Mr. P had the look of a hardened nut case. Ed hadn't been disturbed by the ear that looked like a roasted walnut. Slade had described it in advance as an identifying mark, so the disfigurement hadn't surprised him. It was not the ear. It was his smile. The faint smile that never touched his eyes. Ed was positive that Jack the Ripper had worn an identical smile. And John Wayne Gacy. And that fruit in New York City just before the war—Uncle Uzi.

It was the grin of a wolf watching a young lamb from the shadows.

Ed had handed Mr. P the briefcase and gone bolting off down the platform, infinitely glad the delivery was behind him.

He was climbing up to the street on the escalator when he decided that he had better also put Atlanta in the background. Pronto. Never mind that Slade had told him he had almost a week to make preparations. Slade hadn't seen Mr. P's crazy smile.

Ed ducked into a bar on the way to the indoor parking lot where he'd left his car. The drink he ordered failed to calm his frazzled nerves, so he had another shot, and then a few more. It took five whiskeys to do the trick. When he had finally stopped trembling, Ed got his car and drove to his apartment in East Point. He was home and packing inside of twenty minutes. For a man who'd lived in the same place for a good many years, Ed had few belongings, and even fewer that he cared about enough to take with him. He had no hobbies. He almost always ate at the airport's employee cafeteria and didn't own a full set of dishes. His furniture would have been refused by the Salvation Army had that organization still existed. The high-resolution TV he'd kept as gravy from a long-ago airport heist formerly had been a valued possession, but it was worthless to him now that the only station in broadcasting range was the Freedom News Network, which he hated.

Yet, despite his lack of attachment to material objects, Ed had found himself becoming increasingly maudlin as he began cramming his summer clothes—he wouldn't need the warm ones where he was bound—and some assorted odds and ends into a single valise. He didn't have many roots, but those there were clung to familiar soil. He would miss his crew. And the heists. And the partying down afterward.

While giving the apartment a final once-over, Ed found an unopened bottle of whiskey in a living room cabinet. Another forget-me-not from an airport theft. He cracked the seal and had a nip, hoping to bolster his sagging spirits. The drink did indeed make him feel better. He had another swig. A third. Some more.

Fifteen minutes and a third of the bottle later, Ed staggered out to his car. He tossed his suitcase in the trunk, tipped a salute to Atlanta, and sped onto the highway.

His plan was to take I–85 to its intersection with I–75 at Spaghetti Junction, then bullet south past Macon into Occupied Florida. Once there, Ed would get in touch with Slade and have the lieutenant make good on his promise to find him a new residence.

Lying in his traction frame, Ed remembered that it was Spaghetti Junction that had done him in. Its multileveled knot of ramps and bridges, entries and exits, and hundred-fifty-foot-high flying ramps simply did not mix well with the alcohol in his bloodstream. Ed became confused, and somehow missed the I–75 turnoff. He got more confused, and somehow his foot missed the gas pedal, going down on the brake instead.

Another vehicle had been nudging his tail.

It rear-ended him.

Ed could remember the pain smashing into his neck and back. Could remember being whipped toward the steering wheel. He could remember the faraway sound of breaking glass, tinkling softly. And after that, nothing. Until now.

Watching a nurse appear in the doorway of his hospital room and step briskly toward his bed, Ed thought suddenly of the suitcase and the bombs inside it, the bombs he'd been told would go off in about a week. He thought of the bombs, and then a question swept into his mind on a crashing wave of panic: When *was* now?

He bucked against the weighted ropes of the metal contraption they'd put him in, his respiration quickening, his mouth pulling into a rictus of agony and horror.

"Mr. Mason, it's all right, you're in a hospital."

The young nurse's attractive features showed intense concentration as she tried to get a handle on the situation. She had just a second ago registered that her patient had come to. Now she was afraid he'd gone into convulsions. She hit the emergency call button and then put her hand lightly on his full body cast, trying to soothe him while reading on the monitors.

The screens showed that his vital signs were okay.

A groan escaped his working lips.

"Please, you have to settle down," she said. "You were in an accident, and you've been unconscious, but everything's going to be fine."

"How long?" he croaked. The tube running from his nasal passages down into his throat made speaking painful.

She smiled. "You were brought in yesterday, if that's what you're asking."

Ed's terror was reduced by a fraction. He still had six days. Thank God.

"When can I get . . . out?" he said hoarsely, wringing the words out with monumental effort.

"A doctor will be here in a second, and he can answer—"

"A few days," he rasped. "C-c-can I be outta here . . . in a . . . few days?"

A frown crossed the nurse's forehead. She was fairly new to the job and was trying to recall what she'd learned in training about dealing with a patient that was both hysterical and unaware of how badly he'd been hurt.

"You must understand that you've suffered some severe injuries, among them a concussion and broken bones," she said, keeping to herself the fact that some of those shattered bones were in his neck, back, and pelvis. She wished the doctor would hurry. "It's too early to predict how long your convalescence will take, but rest assured you're in the best of—"

"Gah . . . gotta get ou-out," he spluttered. "Few days."

She looked at him with compassion. "I'm sorry, Mr. Mason, but realistically I think we're going to be together for a bit longer than that. Perhaps in a few weeks you can—"

Eddie moaned. Weeks, she was telling him. *Weeks!*

The woman's lips were still moving, but Ed Mason no longer heard her. He was listening instead to a mental echo of his own voice—his and that of Lieutenant Slade.

"You're saying . . . whether or not I take the job . . . I'd better be lamming out of Atlanta."

"In extra light shoes, my friend."

He was stuck. Trapped. While time ran down like a lit fuse.

There was only one way out.

His eyes white terrified circles, Ed looked past the nurse and directly into the face of the doctor coming through the door.

"I . . . gotta t-t-talk to the . . . Union D-D-Defense Force," he blurted weakly. "And talk to them . . . *fast.*"

Front Commander Joseph Forster Groll was admiring the scale miniature carnival on his desk when Fran knocked at the door. He ignored her. She could wait. Here in Occupied Florida he had a great many responsibilities and few diversions. Let Fran wait. Probably just going to announce that annoying ramrod Slade anyway.

He proudly studied the carnival on his desk. His latest customization was an excellent, realistic bit of work. Sometimes he himself was impressed by the quality of his craftsmanship. The boy's tiny plastic head did indeed appear to be crushed under the foot of the performing elephant.

The child is not to blame for what happened, Groll thought. His imagination often sketched in personalities and backgrounds for the newly remolded characters. It was interesting to try and understand what had led to their circumstances. Were there ascribable reasons, or had it been chance? Could their torment have been avoided? *It is true that he was ill-behaved, but the parents were responsible. They were touching each other and neglected their child. If they had been supervising him, he could surely have been prevented from leaping into the ring and antagonizing the beast. He—*

More rapping at the door. Groll shook his head in disgust, wondering how well his secretary would be able to knock with arms that ended in stumps.

"What do you want?" he snapped.

The door opened a crack, and Fran's head thrust into the room. "Lieutenant Slade is here, Commander. Should I send him in?"

"Let him wait five minutes. Now get out of h—" He saw her gaze skitter from his pinched, sallow face to the edge of his desk, then back to his face again. "Yes?" he said, his manner becoming warily defensive. "Is there something more?"

She tucked her lower lip between her teeth.

"Is there something more?" Groll repeated tightly.

Her cheeks flushed. "Your condition, sir. I think . . . today's heat . . . has aggravated it."

He wiped a hand across his chin and it came away wet. Then he looked down and saw that a small puddle had formed on his desk below the blotter.

He blinked, once.

Above him the ceiling fan spun. It was a prewar relic that barely stirred the air enough to disturb the flying insects.

After a long moment Commander Groll's attention returned to Fran. Thin eyebrows twitched above his frameless round glasses. A small crease appeared at each corner of his mouth. Otherwise, his features were rigid.

"I . . . I thought with the lieutenant coming in, you would want to know," Fran said.

"Yes. I can see that you always keep my best interests in mind." He envisioned her severed hands nailed to the wall, her wrists spurting. "Now please leave me. I must prepare."

Finally alone, Groll reached into a drawer and extracted one of several dozen neatly folded white handkerchiefs. He opened the handkerchief, dabbed his chin, wiped the wet spot on the desk. Wiped hard, as if scouring resistant grease off a fry pan. Fran was patronizing and crudely deceitful, but perhaps there was truth in her observation about his Salivary Overproduction Syndrome. What she called his "condition." The hideous climate did seem to be affecting it adversely.

When the steel surface of the desk was rubbed free of moisture, he held the handkerchief primly between two fingers and studied it. Its middle was saturated. The white square of cotton was like a flag of surrender.

His mouth contorted with distaste, Groll let the handkerchief drop into the trash can.

As he rose to wash, Groll was once again looking at his one-ring carnival big top. His eye fell on the Human Caterpillar in the trapeze launch. What was the hapless fellow doing up there? Receiving punishment for some unspeakable act? Would he ever manage his way down?

It was deepest mystery.

Groll's washstand was in a corner behind and to the left of his desk. He went to it, removed his glasses, carefully folded the stems, and set them down. He rolled his shirt sleeves over his elbows and washed his hands with a hard-bristled scrub brush, paying meticulous attention to his nails and cuticles.

The framed portrait of Heinrich Himmler on the wall above him seemed to regard his actions with stern approval.

Satisfied that his hands were thoroughly clean, he lifted a washcloth from the pile beside the basin, dipped and wrung it, then spread it over his face. The cloth felt much cooler than the air in the office. The air was stifling. Almost everything about Florida stifled him. The humid heat. The constant bombardment of skin-frying UV's through a nuke-blown, ozone-depleted atmosphere. The fallout and contamination. The inadequate, frequently nonexistent plumbing and electricity. The diseased, anarchic blast survivors in Miami, Tampa, and other urban centers. The brutish White Trash. The Indians.

If not for the traveling carnivals Groll would have found life intolerable. The traveling carnies, and of course the glittering promise of Disney World, which would soon be transformed in keeping with his own aesthetic.

Groll inspected himself in the mirror as he toweled dry. He saw his features adopt the same stringently approving expression as the framed face of Himmler, saw his head nod.

His ablutions had taken four minutes exactly.

He was back at his desk when Slade was admitted into the office sixty seconds later.

Lieutenant Varnum Slade was physically everything Groll wished he could be, and so Groll deeply resented him even while prizing his ruthless intelligence. He stood over six feet tall, had the thick upper torso of a weight lifter, and was much lighter of foot than most men his size. The erect confidence with which he moved fell just short of cocksure swagger and was therefore rather a blunt statement of strength. Restless savagery lunged behind his cold, hard eyes like an aquarium shark behind plate glass.

He crossed the room and came to attention, clicking his heels and offering Groll the Front raised-arm salute.

"Let's make this fast, Lieutenant. We have a number of matters to discuss, and I'm very busy today." Groll gestured impatiently to a chair on the opposite side of his desk. Perhaps Slade was the embodiment of the Aryan ideal, but the general enjoyed reminding him that he was also a subordinate.

Slade sat across from Groll and regarded him in silence. His full lips did not move. His ice pick gaze stirred the old, hated sound of children's mocking laughter in the back of Groll's skull.

Groll took a fresh handkerchief from his desk drawer and patted a dribble of saliva off the left side of his mouth.

"So," he said. "Brief me."

"The search for the AH-60B Strikehawk lost between Vaca Key and Cape Sable has been terminated. It is assumed that the helicopter dunked into the sea after encountering a violent weather disturbance. As the disappearance occurred nearly two weeks ago, currents would have swept any wreckage out—"

"This is farcical! Do not waste my time with nonsense about a missing helicopter!" Groll exclaimed angrily, leaning forward until he almost rose off his seat. "Atlanta, Slade. Tell me about Atlanta."

Slade seemed unruffled by the general's outburst. "All goes well. I received a cable from Pike this morning. He has obtained the bombs and will spend the next twenty-four hours reconnoitering the predesignated blast sites."

"And the courier?"

"We will take him out shortly."

"I'm puzzled, Lieutenant," Groll said, suspicion darkening his features. "By now he should either be in Florida or dead. And what do you mean by *take him out*?"

"My sources in Atlanta report that he was critically injured in an automobile accident which occurred while he was leaving the city," Slade explained in a quiet voice. "He is hospitalized and believed to be comatose. I have put—"

"*Believed* to be comatose? *And what if he isn't, you stupid lump of muscle?!*" Groll screamed. He pounded the desk repeatedly with his fist, and the vibrating blows caused several members of his carnival troupe to tip over. "*How dare you be so calm when the entire operation may be in jeopardy!*"

Slade remained placid. "As I was about to say, Commander, there are agents in place who will ensure that the courier is eliminated before he has a chance to talk. He is,

at any rate, just a small cog and knows nothing that can
endanger the mission."

"And what of Lansman, the scientist? What of him? I
suppose you are going to tell me he was *also* in some kind
of accident!"

"The captive biophysicist is being transported here under
heavy guard. I expect him to arrive no later than tomorrow
morning."

Groll sat for a moment, glowering at Slade. A thick rope
of spit began coiling down his jaw, and he quickly swiped
it away with his handkerchief, reminding himself that he
must try and stay calm.

There are three principal salivary glands communicating
with the human mouth. The parotid secretes a clear, watery
fluid; the sublingual produces mucus; while the submaxil-
lary may supply both. Groll's salivary glands had been
chronically hyperactive since childhood. Anger stimulated
the sublingual more than the other two, affecting the
composition of his saliva, making it thick and ropy. He was
especially humiliated by this type of secretion.

Stay calm, an inner voice warned again.

His eyes straying to the carnival, Groll reached for a
spectator that had toppled from the stands when he punched
the desk. He took up a fallen clown with the same hand, and
then sat examining both figures.

The matter of the courier faded in his thoughts as he was
struck by sudden, giddy inspiration.

"Have arrangements been made for this weekend's performance?" he asked, his free hand going into the breastpocket of his uniform shirt.

"I booked the carnival myself. The Praetorius Circus and
Curiosity Show—one of your favorites, I believe."

"Yes. Praetorius's collection of freaks is . . . exqui-
site." The general spoke with something like awe. "He has
Siamese Twins. One-and-a-Halfs and Pickled Punks.
Dwarves and Pinheads and a Seal Boy."

Groll produced a cigarette lighter from his shirt pocket.

He fired it and held it to the backs of the two figures. The red plastic they were made of began to soften and give off dark blobs of smoke. The smoke had a strong, tacky odor.

Slade sat impassively, watching Groll's hands. Sickly white and busy, they reminded him of small, bald subterranean creatures that lived an existence of total darkness.

He was pleased that Groll had subsided. The lunatic was his commanding officer—at least for the present—and it was important to keep a working harmony with him.

Slade wanted no setbacks in his climb to power.

Now Groll was smiling avidly, spit glistening on his chin. The figures in his hand were cooking. A large blister swelled from the back of the clown and popped. Droplets of liquified plastic spatted the desk blotter.

Suddenly Groll flipped the lighter shut, set it down, and shifted the clown to the hand in which he'd been holding the lighter. Still gripping the spectator in his other hand, he pressed the pair of figures together, back-to-back.

Cooling rapidly, they fused.

"Now Groll's Carnival has Siamese Twins," he muttered, turning the joined figures over in his palm. "One is very frail, the other a simpleton. Their relationship is characterized by dislike and mistrust, but they have certain interdependencies which make separation impossible. Survival hinges on inescapable bondage." He opened an animal cage resting on a miniature flat. "A grim drama," he said under his breath, and gently placed the figures in the cage near the lion.

Groll looked across at Slade, and his face assumed an odd, mildly surprised expression, as if he'd only then realized that he wasn't alone in the office.

"Ah, Lieutenant," he said in a genial tone. "Have you ever tried to imagine the result of an operation in which normal human legs are transplanted onto the stunted body of a dwarf?"

"I am afraid not, sir. My mind tends toward the pragmatic."

"Yes, yes, I suppose it does," Groll said thoughtfully.

There was an extended pause.

Slade sat through it with a feeling akin to déjà vu. He and Groll had had similar discussions before. They always followed a set dialectical pattern.

Finally Groll asked, "The transplant . . . could such an experimental surgery be arranged?"

"We have many surgeons with the skill to perform it. And there would be no problem finding a pair of inmates in the detention camps who would make excellent subjects."

Groll's small eyes brightened. He slurped a tiny head of foam off his bottom lip. "When Lansman arrives we could perhaps induce him to participate. His knowledge might be useful."

"Something to consider, Commander."

"You will see that the operation is scheduled."

"Gladly, Commander."

"And attend to that minor snag in Atlanta."

Slade nodded.

"Excellent!" Groll clapped his hands happily. "Now I think it's time we both carried on with our business."

Slade nodded again, waited an appropriate number of seconds before rising. Groll's moods pendulumed easily. He did not want to seem overanxious and provoke another tantrum.

"Have a good day, my general," he said at length, and stood up.

Groll did not respond.

He sat engrossed by his carnival.

Slade turned on his bootheels, stepped briskly toward the door, and exited.

Chapter Five ═══════════════

Water splashed softly against the bow of the canoe as it slid into midday dimness, the man in the slender dugout steering it expertly, his squawpole rising and falling with a steady, unhurried rhythm. Downstream, the creek spooled through the vaulting cypress dome like a black satin ribbon, stitched here and there with golden sunlight.

The air was without a quiver of a breeze, the slough almost currentless, but the foliage along the bank rustled with animal stirrings. A small yellow warbler drank raindrops stored in the cupped leaf of an epiphyte. A swamp rabbit sprang into covering shrubs. Otters bobbed. Geckos climbed on adhesive feet, and box turtles dragged with labored slowness. A frog thrashed helplessly on the venomous skewer of a scorpion's tail.

The ubiquitous mosquitoes milled and buzzed.

The canoe swung around a mat of twigs and decayed vegetation, and soon afterward the leafy ceiling opened up and the crowded stand of pond cypress was left behind. As the shade tattered, the man working the squawpole was enveloped by soupy heat and the fragrance of tree-climbing orchids.

To his right the bank began to elevate; peat, clay, and muck gradually acceding to jagged spurs of Miami oolite. This porous limestone forms the bedrock of southern Florida and is a major component of the Atlantic Coastal Ridge, running southward along the East Coast from Ft. Lauderdale to Florida City, then curving west for many miles into the Everglades wilderness. Near its western extreme the ridge breaks down to forested outcrops which dot the saw grass with oasislike patches of deeper green and are high enough above sea level to remain relatively undamaged by the fires, floods, and man-made catastrophes that often sweep the prairie.

One such tropical hammock was the destination of the man in the canoe. He had started out early that morning. He reached it after tediously poling through the backwater for six hours.

He had made the trip two times in as many days.

Pushing against the bottom, he guided the canoe toward shore. Then he waded out and dragged it clear of the water.

He climbed the embankment with the canoe in tow. His boots were waterlogged and muddy. His jeans were soaked to the knees. The muscles of his arms and shoulders were sore from nonstop poling. Sweat plastered his T-shirt to his chest and back.

The slope was not especially steep, but its footing was pebbly and loose, and he had to sidestep clumps of grasping vines.

He minded neither the aches, the sticky dampness, nor the awkward, tiresome haul. He was glad to be where he was. Somehow the pain in his heart was less acute here.

Reaching the upper rim, he hid the canoe in a snarl of scrubby buttonwoods, spreading some palmetto fans atop it for added camouflage.

From where he stood John Firecloud could see the cypress casket which held the body of Charlie Tiger. It had been conveyed to the hammock by canoe yesterday, twenty-four hours after the old man had died in his sleep . . .

. . . Twenty-four hours after he had told Firecloud the story of the dredgemen, and invested him with a tribal status he'd never wanted, and given him a mission he didn't think he could fulfill.

The last time Firecloud saw him alive, his father and mentor had been dozing contentedly in his favorite chair.

Firecloud had gone to call Ella Parker.

Charlie Tiger had passed on before Ella reached his cabin.

Now an old, dark-blue mourning cloth enclosed in a square the place where he used to sit. Now Firecloud was going to his coffin.

It rested on a bier of logs some ten or twelve yards from the edge of the hammock in a shaded grove of tall, straight oaks.

The Seminole customarily lay their dead with the feet to the east. It is said that the spirit must travel in the opposite direction to reach the netherworld, and for three days a fire is kindled several yards west of the casket to illuminate its journey. Firecloud had dug a small flame pit, filled it with pitch—a fuel he knew would burn even in rain—then surrounded it with a windbreak of large rocks. He checked on the fire, saw that it still crackled, then went to stand by the casket.

John Firecloud put little stock in traditional beliefs. He was not a religious man. But Charlie Tiger was. Had been. Honoring him, Firecloud bent his head and voiced a prayer for the deceased:

> *"Come back.*
> *Before you get to the king tree, come back.*
> *Before you get to the line of fence, come back.*
> *Before you reach the crossroad, come back . . ."*

As he chanted, the old man did come back—in his memory. There was no order to the recollections. They were like randomly tossed snippets of film reel.

He saw Charlie Tiger with Bill Coonan and himself on the night the nuclear mushrooms had ruptured the constellations. Firecloud was fifteen, Bill seventeen. They were huddled together on the floor of the shaman's cabin, Charlie Tiger between the boys, and outside a great hell-born dragon roared, and its breath baked the air, and its feet

pummeled the earth. They held each other's hands without
shame in the raging throat of the holocaust, and in one of
the thermal flashes Firecloud saw the old man's cheeks wet
with tears. Their eyes brushed. Firecloud looked away
without saying anything and tightened his grip on the bony
fingers. Giving what he could, aware of his own courage for
the first time. Feeling it expand like an inner muscle.
Feeling its solidity and wanting to explore its capacity.

> *"Before you get to the door, come back.*
> *Before you get to the middle of the ladder, come*
>   *back . . ."*

Firecloud was looking at Charlie Tiger through the eyes of
a boy not yet thirteen; it was November, 1997, and the place
was the social worker's office at the orphanage. As Firecloud
entered the room, Charlie Tiger sat very straight in an armless
wooden chair, a black, floppy felt hat on his lap. His brows
were arched and thick as caterpillars, and the silver-gray hair
cresting his high forehead was woven into several long braids.
He looked a handsome thousand years old.

"You're too pale for a Seminole," Charlie said. The
candid warmth of his gaze was unexpected. Firecloud, who
had never had anyone to cry out for when the nightmares
woke him, held it in suspicion. Charlie Tiger grinned. "You
look like the powdered doughnut I ate for breakfast this
morning," he added.

Firecloud resisted a smile—this bright-eyed Methuselah
seemed kind, but in the shelter one quickly learned that trust
could be a trapdoor.

"I'd like you to come live with me on the reservation,"
the old man said. "Get some sun on your face."

Firecloud challenged him. "I have a friend, Bill Coonan.
He's white. If I go, he goes, too."

"Well," Charlie Tiger laughed, spreading his hands. "If
you've chosen a brother, who am I to argue?"

That day Firecloud ceased to be parentless.

"Before you get to the fire, come back . . ."

More jumbled memories. Charlie Tiger taking him on a trip into the woods to gather plants and roots and berries, sharing his formulas for herbal remedies. Tutoring him in the martial arts. Watching with interest and pride as he and Bill championed their matchball team to a victory against players from an opposing village. Looking hurt and angry during one of his many quarrels with Bill as the distance between them grew. Puttering among the corn rows in his garden. Setting animal snares.

Firecloud saw Charlie Tiger's body encased in funeral wrappings and covered with bay leaves meant to ward off evil spirits, the men fashioning the casket, Ella and the other women weeping profusely as they made a selection of his favorite belongings to be placed inside it.

There was something they had failed to include which he would surely have wanted.

"Charlie Tiger, come back, come back."

As Firecloud completed his recitation, he was picturing his father in the hour before his death, absently discarding the remainder of his cigarette. It had seemed an odd thing for the old man to do. He had always saved the grains from exhausted stubs, and his frugality had increased after the bombs fell.

He had known his life would end that morning. That was apparent now. He had known, and he had wanted to speak his final words to Firecloud, and smoke some of his homegrown tobacco.

And he had wished aloud and wholeheartedly for licorice twists.

Firecloud unzipped his leather waistpouch and took out the cellophane package he had brought. He'd scavenged through gas stops all along Highway 41 to obtain it, keeping a constant lookout for Front motor patrols and roving bands of White Trash. Looters had completely picked over the majority of the stations. He had covered over thirty miles of road and been in a dozen ransacked minimarts before finally getting lucky.

He reached down and put the pack of red licorice twists on the coffin lid.

"That's a good boy, yes 'tis."

Firecloud almost jumped at the sound of the female voice behind him.

He spun around.

The woman stood in the ring of shade thrown by the oaks. She was tall and black and had the taut shape of a healthy forty-year-old. But Firecloud's sharp gaze quickly picked out signs of substantially greater age: the wiry and mostly gray hair showing under her straw planter's hat, the lines on her forehead running from the corners of her mouth to her jaw. Something in the way she looked at him, too. A wistful yet vaguely amused glint which often came into the eyes of those looking at youth from its far side.

She wore green military fatigue slacks, hiking boots, a square-necked, horizontally striped blouse gathered at the waist, and two dark-blue beaded necklaces. The blouse and strings of beads were clearly of Seminole origin.

"Guess I must've startled you. Sorry about that," she said evenly, then smiled and nodded her chin at the casket. "I'd been here paying my respects since this morning, and just a short while ago decided to take a stroll around. This sure is a beautiful, tranquil spot for Charlie Tiger to rest." Her smile broadened. "My name's Ardelia, by the way. Ardelia Martin. The friends I've got seem to prefer calling me Dee."

He stood there for a bewildered moment, unable to think of anything to say.

"Charlie'd appreciate you bringing him his candy—and the right candy at that. Been hard to come by since Revolution II." The woman strode forward until she was only a couple of feet away from him. "He was always hankering for red licorice . . . used to call it his sweet tooth medicine. 'Course I mean the original red twists, not those cherry-flavored ones that're about the same color. He bought a pack of them by mistake once and almost took a fit. Went back and gave the storekeeper an earful, like the poor man had done something wrong just by *stocking* it." She paused thoughtfully, nodding toward the casket. "I don't believe most people would have bothered. To get Charlie exactly what he liked, I mean. They'd reason that close was good enough, that a man in his condition wouldn't much know the difference."

Firecloud had managed to wipe the expression of utter puzzlement off his face, but there was nothing he could do to erase the feeling itself.

How had the woman known his adoptive father? What was she doing here?

He looked at her questioningly. "*Most people*, if they were not Seminole, would think the idea of bringing a dead man his favorite candy—or for that matter *any* sort of food—was laughable. A quaint Indian custom."

"You remind me of Charlie, son. So much it *hurts*. Waiting to see if I'll tell you the things you want to know without having t'be asked." She gave him a good-natured smile. "Y'know, more than twenty years back this Baptist minister came around with some kind of *ologist* or other from the Smithsonian in Washington. Offered Charlie Tiger a nice piece of change to talk about your people's religion. Charlie pocketed the money, figuring he'd speak the truth when it suited him, pawn off some hokum when the questions got too close to the heart of what was sacred. Public relations, he called it.

"Anyway, the reverend was asking him about funeral services, wanting to know why a dish of the food a dead man was fond of eating was sometimes put on his coffin. 'When is the deceased going to eat this food?' he said, with this attitude like he'd scored a big debatin' point on behalf of the Lord. Well, Charlie just looked at him in that calm way he had and answered real quiet, 'He'll eat it the same time the white people's dead rise up and smell the flowers you put on your graves.' " She laughed suddenly. "That about says it for Charlie, hey?"

Firecloud was again caught speechless. The thing was, her little anecdote *did* say it for Charlie—better than any of the sincere but tired remarks from the tribal elders at the funeral ceremony, better than their best parables, better than anything he'd heard from anybody. Her words captured the essence of the man Charlie Tiger had been, and they were, for that reason, important.

And, yes, they were *funny*.

He was surprised to feel laughter building in his chest, and very nearly astounded when it burst from his lips and he heard himself laughing along with Ardelia Martin, this mysterious yet irresistible woman, this complete and total stranger, who had presumably known his father for years and certainly known him well enough to sum him up in just a few sentences.

"Well, didn't that feel good, son," she said after a while, rubbing her eyes. "Kind of like a massage for the place inside us where the grief gets stoppered."

Firecloud nodded. "Ardelia . . . Dee . . . I haven't told you my name—"

"I know who you are, John Firecloud. I meant it when I said I came here to say good-bye to your pa . . . but I was also looking forward to meetin' you."

His eyes went wide with open curiosity and wonder.

"I also suppose there's plenty you want to know about me," Ardelia went on without pausing, "and I intend to answer your questions, all of 'em. But not here, and not now. Now's for remembering Charlie. You come to my home. I'll fix something to eat, and we'll talk. And since nobody in the Master Race ever gets in thick with a gal who has skin darker'n his morning coffee—" She held out her hand, turned it palm up, then palm down. "—You don't have to worry about me being in on any National Front shenanigans."

She made a wry face. "Have we got a date?"

He looked at Ardelia Martin for a long moment, feeling as if the ground beneath him were a mechanical platform that she could on a whim crank up at dizzy angles.

Which only made him more fascinated by her.

Finally, he nodded and said: "You haven't told me where you live. Or when I should come."

"Anytime tomorrow'd be fine," she said, delighted. "I rise before the birds. And as to the directions, I got them written down here." She brought a folded sheet of paper out of a pants pocket and gave it to him. "Ain't but a three- or four-hour walk from your village."

And of course she would know where that is, Firecloud thought.

He tucked the paper into his waistpouch.

"Now then," Ardelia said, "everything's settled. Almost, I mean."

Firecloud waited.

"This ain't quite playing fair, but *I've* got one quick question, and only one, and I'd be obliged if you could answer it before I leave."

He nodded to indicate that she should go on.

Her eyes locked with his. "Did Charlie ever talk with you about the Underground Railroad?"

The earth seemed to shift under him again, but this time it felt like a lurch toward the future he'd promised his father he would seek—and perhaps for that very reason, he managed to keep his balance.

Looking at her expectant face, he said, "The last thing you choose to mention is nearly the last thing he spoke about before his passing. He was very general on the subject. I didn't . . . I don't . . . see how it relates to me. But I want to, Dee. I want to know."

She nodded with a small grunt of understanding. "And the fact that he saw fit to raise the matter means you're *ready* to know. But I couldn't get you involved until I made sure. Because the course ahead, should you choose to take it, is most secret—and dangerous." She paused, appearing to gather her thoughts. "Son, I'll explain this a lot deeper tomorrow, but for now what I got to say is that the Midnight Special's rolling again, deliverin' good, desperate folks to liberty like it did over 150 years back, when my great-grandma was a young woman that escaped the Georgia slave compounds and took refuge here in Florida among the Seminole—*your* ancestors. Oh yeah, the Railroad is back in service, and its whistle blows for anyone tryin' to find safety from the National Front's oppression, and there are hidden tracks laid all across this hunk of busted-up real estate we once called America, bound for Free Atlanta. And what the Railroad needs are men and women who can be brave, who'll risk their lives bringing fugitives on board, and stoking the engine furnaces, and making certain the lines stay open until the Front's dark empire can be brought down." She sighed. "What it needs, John Firecloud—"

"I think I know, Dee. I think I understand."

They were both silent for a moment, listening to the bird chatter and the faintly crackling flame at the head of the casket.

Firecloud watched a large tree snail slide across a limb, the rainbow-hued cone of its shell spectacular in the sunlight.

"Well, leave it to me to go on tootin' after I said I was going to keep my mouth shut," Ardelia said. "I'd best be along. You have the way of getting to where I live, and I hope to see you there."

"I'll come. Tomorrow. Before noon, probably."

"Then be ready for a big lunch," she said, once more sounding immensely pleased.

She smiled and held out her hand, and he took it gently and briefly, and then she turned and began walking across the hammock.

"Dee?" he called after her.

She looked over her shoulder.

"I don't know how you came, but I have a canoe. If you'd like, I can take you home."

"Now that's a gent," she said, and shook her head, laughing a little. "And I appreciate the offer. But my stomach prefers travelin' on land, and these old legs of mine could use some stretching. Besides, I know my way around more shortcuts than even you Indians."

She waved and left.

Firecloud went to stand beside the coffin of his father.

A bird screeched from a nearby treetop.

It was a lonely sound.

Chapter Six ══════════════════════

At 9:00 A.M. on the day she was expecting John Firecloud over for lunch, Ardelia Martin sat in a splash of lemon-yellow sunlight at the table near her small kitchen's east-facing window, preparing the meal they would eat.

She had left her Everglades City bungalow an hour before dawn that morning, gone down to the marina, and cast her fishing line off a pier where the sheepshead usually converged.

By the time the sun rose to silhouette the disintegrating pleasure boats anchored in the slips, she'd had three bites—all hefty two-and-a-half-footers. Were only Firecloud coming, such a catch would have been more than enough to allow her to head home. But she'd also invited Saralyn, and Saralyn was never without tag-alongs. *Hungry* tag-alongs.

Dee remained at the dock until she'd hooked another couple of the stout, bucktoothed fish.

Now she was doing the messy work—a sheepshead in one hand, a scaling knife in the other, a bucket on the floor. She was in a relaxed but contemplative mood.

As she had said to him yesterday, the boy—no, that was unfair and disrespectful; you didn't go and drag someone like John Firecloud into the miserable, bloody business he was about to become caught up in, you didn't even think of doing such a thing, and then dare call him a boy—the *man* was so very much like Charlie that it pierced her heart.

How she had loved Charlie Tiger. Had loved him even

after she'd refused to continue sharing his bed . . . had it really been three decades ago? *Thirty years?*

He had been kind more often than not, and wise, and if he had his crotchety moods, Ardelia was able to abide them. It had been easy enough to bring Charlie around just by teasing him or saying one of the half-dozen silly things that were guaranteed to push his laugh button.

Ardelia had known from the beginning that their life together would always take a backseat to Charlie's responsibilities as tribal shaman—in fact, his dedication to that calling was largely what she had found attractive about him. She did not have a selfish or a jealous nature and had never sought any claim on the time he spent being a counselor and healer of his people.

But the time he spent with other women, that was hers. Or should have been. She had sacrificed for him and would have continued doing so for the right reasons. To have tolerated his unfaithfulness, however, would have made Ardelia a fool in her own eyes.

So they parted, and eventually Ardelia married a man named Robert Martin, who ran a company that rented farm equipment, and he was good to her and honest. Perhaps her love for him lacked the heat she had felt for Charlie, but there was enough of it to satisfy them both. The single regret she'd had about their long union was that it failed to produce any children.

Ardelia saw Charlie Tiger only in passing for many years.

Then Robert was killed in the bombing of Miami. As fate had decreed, he'd driven there on business the same awful day the warheads fell. Somehow Charlie got news of his death, and in the turmoil that followed the nuclear conflagration, made his way up to Everglades City to offer Ardelia his sympathies and whatever support he could.

In short order, their friendship was renewed, though both acknowledged that their moment as lovers had come and gone.

John Firecloud had never been told about her. That was

Charlie's wish, at first. He'd been too proud to expose old scars to the boy, especially those that were self-inflicted. Later on he changed his mind, maybe because he believed John had matured enough to understand that a man could have his flaws and still be worthy of admiration—though maybe Charlie more than anyone else had needed to grow into that understanding.

At any rate, by then Ardelia was the one who wanted to keep a low profile. She had become a prime organizer in the underground system for helping targeted enemies of the Front escape Occupied Florida and felt that the fewer acquaintances she had, the better.

She and Charlie had often discussed the possibility of fostering an armed opposition to the National Front tyrants. They had agreed that the key to a successful resistance was having the right man to lead it.

Six months past, shortly after breaking the news of his terminal illness to Ardelia, Charlie had suggested that John Firecloud might possess the intelligence, courage, fighting skills, and charisma to become that leader—but he had wanted to be certain before mentioning anything to his son.

Without knowing it, John Firecloud was observed and groomed to head an outlaw band that would strike blows against the empire.

He seemed ready, and Charlie'd obviously felt that he was, but she'd wanted to break things to him slower. He needed time to digest it all, to see his own strengths as clearly as she could, and his father had. To learn how to be comfortable with and use those strengths. He was still so green.

But this business with Atlanta, and getting that Professor Lansman out of the Castillo . . . She hadn't expected it to crop up. How could she have? Ready or not, Firecloud would have to dive headfirst into the rockiest of waters. Assuming, of course, that he was interested in playing along with her in the first place.

She thought he would be. But maybe, again, she was projecting too much of Charlie Tiger into him.

Ardelia gathered the fish scrapings into a mound with a wet cloth, then swept them off the edge of the table into the waste bucket. She sighed. Oh yes, she saw Charlie in Firecloud. In his reserved yet proud bearing. In his economy of words and movement. And the way he had seemed to take the whole of her in with his gaze, filing a hundred little details into his memory.

Had she not known otherwise, she would have assumed he was Charlie's son by birth.

After the sheepshead fillets were arranged in a large, covered dish, Ardelia went to the counter beside the sink and began slicing up the tomatoes, cukes, onions, and greens for her tossed salad. The vegetables were all freshly picked. She would sooner have put crayons in her stomach than canned vegetables, being as how their taste was about the same, though the former came in a wider variety of pretty colors. Nor would she have relished the idea of eating produce cultivated outdoors in soil that was loaded with enough strontium 90 to make earthworms curl up dead and radiation meters do the hop.

The alternative she'd found had been to convert the glassed-in Olympic-size swimming pool of an abandoned Holiday Inn down the road into a greenhouse. She had filled the pool with a truckload of uncontaminated Louisiana topsoil that Saralyn and a couple of her friends had brought across the border, and planted the enclosed garden with seeds she'd foraged from the shambles of a local supermarket.

The water Ardelia used to raise her crop came from the same source as the water she drank and washed with: an artesian spring near her property that drew from the aquifer and, unlike rainwater, was almost free of contamination.

She was realistic enough to know that it was impossible to completely escape the fallout, that to one degree or another it permeated her physical environment, that every breath of air she took filled her lungs with at least a trace of radioactive dust. But she did what she could to keep herself healthy and prayed for the best.

Ardelia glanced at her wristwatch, an old reliable ladies' Timex that had kept on ticking even immediately after the thermonuclear blasts, when the EMP was most concentrated.

It was ten-fifteen. Almost time to start the barbecue. The fish would do nicely on the grill, sprinkled with red pepper, onion, paprika, and garlic to add some Cajun zing. Ardelia had picked a few ears of corn, which she would also put over the coals.

She was reaching for the sack of charcoal briquets in the nook beside the sink when she heard footsteps on the front porch. More than a single pair. And they were loud.

She froze.

Lyn did not walk so heavily. Nor Firecloud, she was sure.

Then who . . . ?

She lived alone in the area. Her closest neighbors, a thirtyish couple and their teenaged son, were ten miles to the north. They drove down to see her once or twice a month. Maybe it was them. Maybe, but she didn't think so. She would have heard their jeep.

She stood listening.

There were voices. Harsh. Deep. Male. And shrill giggles. A woman, too? A child? If either, then she wasn't dealing with a Front patrol.

Which left another frightening possibility.

She heard the doorknob turn.

She had to think. It would do no good to panic.

Think.

Ardelia was absolutely sure now that her visitors were no one she expected. Saralyn would not try the door. She would know it was locked and use her key to enter. And John Firecloud would have announced himself. Whoever was on the porch must be assumed to be hostile. *Think, think.* What if she tried to escape through the back door?

No, it wouldn't work. They might have the house surrounded.

A glance out the window revealed that the backyard was empty, but they could be in the brush beyond, flat to the ground and waiting.

Okay, she was forced to stay put. *Which means what, Dee?*

The bungalow would offer her little concealment. All the rooms were on the lower story except for the guest bedroom in the belvedere, and that could be quickly searched. No, it would do no good to look for cover.

She could not hide. She could not flee.

All she could do was fight.

Something smashed against the door, rattling its hinges. The bottom of a foot, or a large fist.

"Hey! You in there!" a voice shouted. "Gitit open! Gitit, or we bust in!"

"Boombada boom! We bust the door down!" a second voice hollered.

Then a higher, shrieky voice, belonging to the giggler, probably: "Shock ya! *Yaaah yaaah yeeeeaaahhhhh!*"

Grunts of laughter.

More drumming crashes at the door.

Ardelia heard the dry rasp of her own breath. Beads of cold sweat had formed on her nose and forehead. She felt the hair on her scalp bristle at the nubs.

The demented raving substantiated her worst fear: She was under attack by White Trash.

The door thudded and shook. Its boltlock racketed in its socket. A chunk of plaster fell from above the frame.

Ardelia stood there in the kitchen for several breathless, endless seconds. She had to fetch her rifle, and the rifle was in a closet near the front door. She had to get to it before the door buckled.

She forced her legs to carry her forward and reached the entry hall and saw the door dancing in its frame and saw them through the porch windows just as the windows exploded in a glittering avalanche of shards and the mutant leaped over the sill, clawing aside the gauzy curtains, clawing for her, grabbing her wrist and pulling her to him before she could reach the closet, his scabbed, red-eyed face thrusting into hers as the door crashed open and the rest of them came pouring in.

"Gotcha!" the one that was holding on to her growled.

And as his fist struck her across the temple, and she began freefalling into unconsciousness, her last terrified thought was that they had her, they had h—

Chapter Seven ═══════════════

Everglades City looked like a city on a Monopoly board that had been trampled by a disturbed child.

The extravagant carnage was not the direct result of bomb detonations or colliding armies. Because it had been primarily a fishing and recreational town in the days before Revolution II, Front strategists gave it a negligible amount of attention when they composed their battle plans and marked their maps. It was located far from the major arenas of war. There were some token, show-of-force raids, true, and it had endured sporadic visitations from White Trash, but for the most part the damage had been perpetrated by its own citizens. Ordinary men, women, and even children who, infected by apocalyptic hysteria, went out looting and rampaging. Whose manner of coming to terms with chaos had been to swallow it whole.

As John Firecloud hiked along Route 29 through what was once Everglades City's commercial ribbon, the empty streets seemed to hum with a residue of the violence that had occurred there, or perhaps of the unreasoning madness behind the violence—a kind of psychic fallout no less detectable than that of the nuclear blasts. It saturated Firecloud, made him feel as if his hindbrain were being stroked with a length of barbed wire.

He wondered what the conditions in Miami or Tampa must be like.

He wished he were already at Ardelia Martin's home.

Though National Front tow crews had cleared the road of

abandoned vehicles to make it passable for military convoys, the streets flanking the highway were an obstacle course of auto wrecks. Firecloud again envisioned a spoiled, moody child kicking out at a gameboard, scattering the pieces every which way.

Here was a Honda rammed head-on through the plate glass window of Captain Andy's Marine Supplies. There, the stripped down husk of a Camaro. A burned-out passenger van lay overturned amid dunes of tinted glass, the charred bones of a human hand projecting from a shattered rear window. The pavement immediately around the hand was rust-colored. Firecloud had heard that porous concrete often retained bloodstains for decades.

He walked up Main Street, passing a shop with a dead neon sign which indicated it had been the Tropics Pharmacy, glancing into a T. J. Maxx where eight or nine gulls roosted in a stationary row on a naked, guano-caked metal clothing rack.

Their black, unblinking eyes caught the morning sun like tiny chips of mica.

At the end of the block was the local branch of the Southern Florida S & L; across the road from it was a storefront in which Ocean Air Real Estate had formerly been officed.

Both were noted in Ardelia's written directions.

Firecloud pitched his gaze up at the signpost near the corner entrance to the savings and loan. He had reached the intersection of Main and Cloverdale.

He took a right. About a mile ahead on Cloverdale, his vista dissolved into a saltwater haze jabbed by a few sailboat masts and the frame of an inoperative offshore light tower. There were clusters of sagging residences on either side of the street with small, weed-choked yards bordered by desiccated hedges or low wooden railings.

Where had the people gone? Firecloud wondered. *What had happened to them?*

The silence and desolation pressed on his nerves.

Everglades City felt haunted.

He passed open windows in which rotted curtains flapped, passed driveways blocked with rusted bicycles and mowers. His attention was briefly captured by the skeleton of a dog that had died leashed to the base of a jungle gym. The leash was stretched to its limit, and the dirt was gouged where the dog must have pawed in desperation, attempting to break free.

Starvation had finished it probably.

He broke his eyes away and walked on at a brisker pace.

He counted off another five blocks, and at the corner of the sixth paused again to check the street signs. Here Shorewinds Drive crossed Cloverdale. He swung right on Shorewinds.

Development was sparse in this part of town. Firecloud could see only five or six structures spaced over a quarter-mile section of road. Between them were vacant lots, bulldozed long ago, in which FOR SALE notices struggled to keep their heads raised above a swelling ocean of weeds and brambles. Other, virgin, tracts grew thick with lofty royal palms.

According to her directions, Ardelia lived in the third dwelling up ahead.

As he came to it, Firecloud stopped suddenly in his tracks. Instinct jacked him to heightened alertness.

The door had been battered down, and the porch was strewn with glass fragments and spears of wood from two broken-out front windows.

He had no doubt this was the right place. He was confident of his skills. He could orient himself by sun and stars, by subtle alterations in wind direction and terrain. He would not have simply made a wrong turn or miscounted the number of houses he had gone past.

The airplane bungalow with its recessed second story perfectly fit the description Ardelia had given him of her home. It was, furthermore, the only property he'd seen since entering the city that showed evidence of recent habitation.

The lawn was trimmed, the corral-style fence freshly weatherproofed, the crowns of the citrus trees dark green and fruit-studded from regular watering.

His brow furrowed.

It was true that postwar shortages had forced many into haphazard migrations. The single law of possession: If you could take something and hold onto it, it was yours. Some people lived like hermit crabs, readily changing homes when they found another that was unoccupied and suited them better.

Maybe that was Ardelia. Maybe the house he was looking at was a worn-out shell about to be discarded.

Maybe, but doubtful. He had a sense of the woman. She would value what she owned. She would stick.

And why would she keep her yard immaculate yet sleep without a door, leave smashed windows uncovered, fail to remove the glass littering her porch?

Firecloud's solar plexus suddenly tensed.

Something bad had happened to her.

He would find out what.

He sought cover. His gaze roving, his body inert. Unnecessary motions had to be avoided. They instantly drew the eye.

He was standing on a small strip of grass just outside the fence. Yards from any brush. What about the trees behind him, on the opposite side of the road? No good. Crossing the road would leave him open. The fence would have to do; a log post to the right was his nearest available concealment.

He crouched and shuffled behind it. He needed to observe. To assess his situation.

He felt vulnerable and isolated. He knew that by kneeling he was creating a high silhouette, making a target of himself. Lying prone would more effectively hide his position. But if intruders were in the house, then they had most likely staked a lookout and were already aware of his presence. He wanted both feet on the ground if they attacked.

Observe. Don't let anything slip by.

He peered around the railing post.

The house presented a blank face and numerous vantages for snipers. The deep porch with its wide eaves cast the windows and doorway into obscuring shadows, and each of the two porch columns was broad enough to shield a man from view.

The roof was all gables and overhangs, offering clear lines of fire at him. There were missing roof tiles that might be prepared loopholes. Well back from them, out of sight, gun muzzles could be angled at his head.

He dropped his eyes back to the porch. It was elevated on stone pedestals. The low risers leading up to it from the walk were covered with muddy footprints and scattered clumps of earth. The prints were uneven, better defined near the toes; whoever made them had been running or at least moving with some urgency. Their dull edges indicated that they were not very fresh. From their varying sizes and patterns of overlap, Firecloud estimated that between three and five individuals had been on the stairs. One set was very small. Smaller even than those typically made by a woman of compact proportions. *A child?* If so, he was not dealing here with Front infantry.

Plunderers, then. Maybe White Trash.

His gaze pulled back, covering the grounds in a trained, systematic fashion. His eyes ranged from right to left across an area several feet away and parallel to his front, then reversed direction, marking a larger, farther sector.

Derelict lots adjoined the yard on both sides.

He thought he saw a rustling in the weedy field to the left, focused his attention slightly away from the spot. Movement was more easily discerned by the peripheral vision.

Yes. Something—or *someone*—was there.

Hunched low in the weeds.

Creeping toward him.

Firecloud's surveillance took under eight seconds, and left him with little to consider. He had walked into an ambush. His enemies knew where he was. He did not know exactly how many of them there were, or how they were deployed, but he did know the general position of one of them.

Better to try and score a hit than let them have the first move.

His compound bow hung across his back on its strap. He reached for its grip, crisply jerked it around, and was about to whip an arrow from the attached quiver when the mutant in the weeds sprang erect, shrieking like a drunken banshee.

He was slab-armed, sway-bellied immense. His cheeks were crusted with fungal masses. A spongelike sac of tissue grew down from his forehead, occluding his left eye. His mouth was wide open as he yelled, baring teeth which had been filed to jagged points.

He wore a green Kevlar vest with no shirt underneath, shorts, combat boots, and a hip-holstered pistol.

In his hand was a leather sling. He was winding up for an overhand hurl, the loaded pocket of the sling a blur at his right.

Firecloud acted on triple reflex: almost nocking in and firing the arrow, catching himself on some intuitive alert that the screaming man was a diversion, twisting sharply around and onto his right shoulder.

As he hit the ground, another sling-wielding mutant sprang from hiding in the stand of trees across the road, and a large object flew through the air where Firecloud's head had been. It struck the fence post with a loud, shattering *crack!*

He smelled gasoline and out of the corner of his eye saw the liquid spewing from the remains of the mason jar which had hurtled past, saw the lighted Fourth of July sparkler which had been taped to the bottle roll into a puddle of fuel and set it ablaze, saw a rapid chain reaction as other spills were ignited by spraying orange-yellow firedrops.

Flame licked at the gas-and-oil-splashed log post, and it went up like a torch.

Firecloud felt a rush of crisping heat.

He clambered away from the fence, still on his right side, pushing off with his arm and foot. Fiery spatters singed his hair, stung his arms, made tiny brown scorch marks in his T-shirt.

The second mutant ran into the middle of the blacktop and halted with his feet apart in a hurling stance. He was smaller than the man in the lot and had on a camo-netted flak helmet that was garnished with foliage, a ragged sport coat over a filth-scummed tuxedo shirt, and denim cutoffs. His skin was a bruisy purple-red color, his eyes were pink, and his nose was a rotted sprout above his lips.

He reached into a large burlap tote bag on which the slogan I'VE BEEN SHELLING ON SANIBEL! was printed above an illustration of a striped conch. His hand reemerged with a Molotov cocktail.

"Look here, boy!" he screamed. *"Look! Look here!"*

His right hand gripped the ends of the sling cords and a Bic lighter; his left, the jar. With amazing speed, he put the lighter to the tip of the sprinkler, raised both arms so they were almost vertical, pushed the jar into the socket, and began twirling the sling clockwise overhead.

As it accreted momentum and began to whir in the air, his upper arm and the rest of his body remained static. Only his wrist and the weapon itself were in motion.

"Shimmy shimmy boneyard!" he babbled.

Firecloud scrambled onto one knee and brought his bow around. A projectile shirred past his ear from behind, then another: lead fishing sinkers that would split his skull like a melon if they connected.

The first White Trash was trying to take him out before he could load.

He quickly got the shaft in place and aimed at the

mutant's chest, but an instant before firing tilted the bow several degrees upward, targeting the gasoline-filled jar instead. He did not want it rolling his way when he dropped the mutant.

A third missile came pelting from the lot behind Firecloud, then a fourth. Both missed.

The fifth was not a fishing weight but a roughly egg-shaped pellet of molded clay which had been embedded with razor blades.

It caught him hard an inch above the elbow of his drawing arm. Honed stainless steel edges notched into his flesh. Pain coursed along his nerve tracks to his fingers, but he managed to keep them firm and steady around the shaft.

The White Trash in front of him shifted his weight slightly backward as he geared for his release stroke. He was howling at the top of his lungs with murderous glee: *"Die, Uncle Tommyhawk, die!"*

Adrenaline pumping through his bloodstream, Firecloud shot the arrow.

By the age of thirteen he had been an expert archer who could hit a standing cornstalk at three hundred yards. The mutant was a fraction of that distance away.

The shaft flew smoothly, and its broad head smashed the Molotov cocktail while it was still nestled in the sling. Pieces of the jar hit the ground with a plangent tinkle.

Gasoline drenched the mutant from head to toe.

He looked down at himself in yawping astonishment as the gas ignited with a dazzling flash, a Rip Van Winkle beard of flame seeming to grow rapidly out of his chin and fall over his chest and legs.

He staggered in a circle, flailed blindly toward the trees across the road, got as far as the soft shoulder and crumpled into a rain ditch, the beard of flame now having spun itself into a cocoon which enveloped him completely.

Firecloud's quick action had eliminated one opponent, but gave him no respite. He didn't even dare pause to remove the projectile stuck painfully in his arm. Though there had been a lull in the deadly shower of missiles from behind, it was certain to resume at any moment.

He had to deal with the other slinger.

Still on his haunches, he turned from the ear-ringing shrieks and the acrid stench of broiling flesh—

—And scarcely had the time to glimpse yet a third White Trash tearing across the lawn from Ardelia's bungalow before the doll-sized mutant plowed into him.

Waist-tackled, he was slammed onto his back with a grunting expulsion of breath.

Straddling him with arms and legs, its long-nailed, sticky-cold fingers clawing viciously, the diminutive mutant wriggled up Firecloud's body to his chest.

Firecloud registered with sick horror that his attacker was a child—the same child whose footprints had been left on the porch.

"Yuh roasted mah paw!" the mutant wailed, its voice pitching high, its head lolling from a scrawny neck, flaccid, gummy lips working. Its jack-o'-lantern face was wet with tears. "Yuh done roasted Paw!"

He grieves, Firecloud thought suddenly. *Grieves because I killed his father.*

And he would kill this monstrous offspring as well, if he had to—though not without pitying him.

Firecloud bucked, trying to disengage him, but he clung, his ragged, grubby nails raking Firecloud's neck and face, his fingers unimaginably strong.

They tumbled through the fence opening and into the yard, grappling, rolled twice again, and Firecloud was on top of the White Trash, the idiot-creature writhing underneath him, his fanglike teeth gnashing, now sinking into Firecloud's arm, now tearing at his ear, his chin. His cankered, out-turned lips smeared with blood, his cheeks bulging and florid.

"Roasted Paw!" he shrieked. *"PAW! PAW! YEAAAAAR-RRRRRH!"*

He held onto Firecloud with one hand, and with the other

began clubbing the projectile lodged in Firecloud's arm, smashing his fist down on it repeatedly, raising a fresh spout of blood with each blow. Firecloud winced and felt a surge of dizziness as biting, chopping pain raced up to his shoulder.

They had barreled up against a tree trunk, the White Trash's back to it, and Firecloud shoved him, drove him against the trunk with all the force he could muster. Branches rattled overhead. Oranges fell around them. Peels of skin from the mutant's hairless scalp scraped off on the rough bark.

Incredibly, the White Trash held on, thrashing his head from side to side like a pinned animal, rabidly panting and hissing, spittle bubbling from his mouth.

Firecloud banged him against the trunk again, again, again. Finally one of his hands relaxed its grip, and Firecloud pried an arm free and delivered an openhanded blow to the left side of his face, then brought his hand back for a wallop to the mutant's right cheek.

Something gave beneath the distorted flesh.

Firecloud clapped his palm over his throat and squeezed, not a flicker of hesitation; his life was at stake, Ardelia Martin's, too, if she hadn't already been murdered.

At last the mutant's other hand fell loosely away, and with an injured squeal, he slumped against the tree trunk, his misshapen head drooping back, legs widely splayed.

Firecloud breathed great lungsful of air. Sweat ran off his face. His arm was pouring blood like an open tap, and he felt woozy, nauseous. He had to get the pellet out, staunch the flow.

He never got the chance.

Suddenly the battered White Trash shaped a gun with his thumb and forefinger, and chuckled.

Firecloud knew immediately that he was in trouble—but the bleeding had taken a dreadful toll. He simply could not make his body react before the huge shadow of the White Trash in the Kevlar vest fell over him.

He felt the cold metal snout of a gun against his temple.

Heard the click of its hammer being cocked.

Then from inches behind him, a coarse voice: "Don' move, injun. Don't even bat an eye . . . 'less you want a sloppy kiss from this heuh Colt forty-foah." There was a pause. "Bettuh gather yousself togethuh, Grundy-boy."

Sliding his back up the length of the tree trunk, the young mutant tittered, snorted, spat a wad of bloody phlegm into Firecloud's face.

"You gon' fix him, Arlo?" he said in his high, mewling voice. "Fix him foah whut he done to Paw?"

The one holding the pistol to Firecloud's head laughed. "Don't you fret, lil' cuz. Gonna settle his hash real good."

The shadow of the gun swung up.

Firecloud tired to avoid the downward strike but was too weak, too slow.

Too late.

The barrel of the gun crunched into the back of his head, and the world exploded into whiteness and then went black.

Chapter Eight ═══════════════════

Wiley Pike was whistling jauntily as he strode along the Japanese garden walk that meandered to the entrance of the Carter Presidential Center, two miles east of downtown Atlanta.

The tune on his lips was "Camptown Races."

It was a picture-perfect morning, sunny and cloudless and in the middle seventies, and here in the garden the breeze was sweet with the perfume of many flowerbeds. The colors of the petals as they were touched by the sun looked impossibly vibrant.

Pike had dressed for the exquisite weather in a light-weight navy-blue sport jacket, a pale-blue oxford shirt and eggshell-colored slacks. The shirt sleeves and pants legs had ironed-in creases that could cut glass. The new soles he'd had the shoemaker at the hotel put on his white loafers crunched briskly down on the pebbled garden path. The bionuclear bomb in the lunch box he carried was inert. He had wrapped the canister in a thick cushion of blister-packing so as not to jostle its sensitive detonating mechanisms.

The bomb, of course, was not yet primed, but you had to follow basic precautions and handle it as though it were. Just as you always assumed a gun was loaded. Even if you had removed the clip and emptied the firing chamber yourself, you assumed a gun was loaded.

For a moment, as he turned a bend in the path, he glimpsed the circular buildings of the Center several hundred yards up ahead. Then the trees and shrubs again obstructed his view. Most were exotic varieties Pike had never before seen, but he'd noticed identifying brass plaques in the weeds—it was astounding that they had escaped the vandals—and he paused often to read them.

There were Japanese maples. Dwarf junipers. Cherry trees with smooth reddish-brown barks. Corkscrew willows with strangely curved, twisting branches. Ficus. Hibiscus in luxuriant red and yellow bloom. Lily-of-the-Niles. Azalea bushes. Peonies. Rhododendrons.

So many plants! And all growing in spite of the fact that they had gone untended for years, in spite of the weeds that ran riot among them, in spite of swarming insects and intermittent drought. All of them withstanding neglect and adversity, as Pike had himself withstood the torments inflicted by his father and later by even more perversely sadistic guards and inmates in prison . . .

But he wasn't going to dwell on the bad times. The dark memories would be barred; he would not permit them to infest his thoughts. Not now.

Not today.

Today would be glorious.

Today was the day he would leave his mark on history—in more ways than one.

As his anticipation built he began to unconsciously sing aloud rather than whistle, *"Camptown races sing this song, doo-dahh, doo, dahh, Camptown Racetrack nine miles long, oh doo-dahh daaaay . . ."*

The walkway had looped around some tiered, flat rocks which had once formed the slope of an artificial waterfall. What clever landscaping! Pike regretted that the pumps which had driven the cascade had failed, that he had never seen the splashing, whitely burbling flow. Now starlings and a pair of robins perched, twittering, upon the dry rocks.

Beyond was a small pond, also man-made, with an apron of flagstones. It was several feet deep and fed, Pike assumed, by underground seepage and rain. The water was green with algae and rippled occasionally in the generous breeze. A squirrel leaned down off the apron and drank. Water skaters glided across the surface of the pond on slender, arching legs.

Pike had almost reached the entrance to the Center. An excitement that was almost childlike in its intensity thrilled in his stomach and buzzed in his head and made his fingertips blush.

One of the building's double swing doors was gone, and Pike went straight in. The transition as he left the fresh open brightness outside was extreme, and he paused a couple of feet past the entrance and fell silent. His eyes adjusted quickly, but the rest of his senses had momentarily gone numb with shock. If the grounds surrounding the Center had withstood the depredations of time and civil upheaval, then the degenerating interior of this structure revealed the very opposite.

The stink was the worst of it. He wrinkled his nose. Once, before Rev II, Pike had been in New York for a few days and ridden the subway somewhere. It had been mid-August, and down in the train station the steamy air was rife with cesspool odors: Each inhalation had been like taking a swallow of warm broth made from a bum's socks and underpants.

The smell was equally atrocious here in the Carter Center.

Goddamn it, Wiley, stop being a chickenshit! an inner voice admonished suddenly. The voice sounded very much like that of his dead father. *You're King of the Bottomless Pit, aren't you?! The Dark Angel! Remember the Glory! Get on with your Mission! Plant the Bomb!*

Pike nodded, clapped a hand over his nose and mouth, and walked on down the hall, his footsteps rebounding flatly. His pupils had dilated, and enough light trickled in through the grimy windows for him to get around without difficulty.

The exhibit halls opening off the corridor were in ruins.

Obscene graffiti covered the walls. On the floors were
flattened cartons which served as beds for derelicts. Bloated
flies with iridescent green tails flitted around the trash that
was scattered everywhere. In one room video terminals and
computer keyboards lay on the floor in a wallow of
electronic guts. The showcases along the walls of another
had been totally ransacked.

Pike glanced at some of the plastic labels which described
the vanished display items, gifts to Jimmy Carter from
friends and heads of state. Some had evidently been quite
valuable: Baccarat crystal bowls, antique silver trays and
candelabras, statuettes of gilded ivory, rare paintings. And
so on.

There had also been worthless memorabilia and a great
number of knickknacks sent in by admirers. Pike had
trouble fathoming why the former president had exhibited
peanut carvings made by some miserable, no-account
Pennsylvania steelworker or a portrait of the Carter family
that had been a first-grader's arts-and-crafts project.

Maybe he'd been a compulsive junk collector.

Maybe he'd been insane.

Certainly he had been undeserving of his grand stature.

No wonder the United States had gone down the tubes.

A biblical passage occurred to Pike: "*And the rest of the
men which were not killed by these plagues yet repented not
of the works of their hands, that they should not worship
devils, and idols of gold, and silver and brass, and stone,
and of wood: which neither can see, nor hear, nor walk.*"

He went from room to silent room, seeking the right one,
the one he had read about in the yellowed, dog-eared travel
guide.

He found it in less than fifteen minutes.

The Oval Office, or anyway, a full-scale reproduction
designed as a tourist attraction. Pike would rather have
performed his Holy Deed in the *actual* executive office of
the White House, but that was of course not feasible, and
this setting would do. Do just fine.

The room had been stripped and vandalized. There were large gaps in the wainscotting, and scribbled and spray-painted vulgarities crossed the grain of the wall panels that had not been torn down. Of the furnishings, only a bare flagpole and the presidential desk remained. The desk sat heavily atop a rotting swatch of carpet liner. Its wood was chipped and shabby. All but one of the drawers were gone.

The air in the office was musty but oddly free of the odor of human waste. Did even Huns have their taboos? Pike wondered.

Maybe so.

But he didn't.

He felt mighty, untouchable, fucking near *exalted*.

Thy wrath is come, he thought, and put his lunch bucket down on the scarred desktop and snapped open its lid catches.

Even in its blister-packing, the gleaming bomb was a sight to steal away his breath. After a moment Pike removed it from the lunch bucket, placed the lunch bucket on the floor, and carefully unwrapped the bio-nuke. Then he spread the sheet of blistered plastic open on the desk, smoothed its corners flat, and laid the bomb on top of it.

Pike regarded the silvery, phallic canister and grinned. If he chose, he could leave the bomb where is was, without any concern that it might be found and defused. The remote triggering device in his pocket had two switches: one to initiate the timed detonating sequence, another to activate the motion-sensitive, tamper-proof, fail-safe mechanism which would cause the bomb to explode if anyone so much as sneezed near it.

Pike could thumb the fail-safe stud and walk away, secure that Free Atlanta would soon go up in a ball of fire. A fireball with a special treat at its core for those who weren't instantly sucked into eternity: a dispersal pod packed with a tailor-made, incredibly virulent, heat-radiation-and-drug-resistant form of the Black Death.

The genetically altered *Pasteurella pestis* bacterium had

been hatched in a National Front lab by a team of captive biophysicists, Gordon Lansman and Frank Covings, both formerly key members of the Free State Union's most celebrated scientific think tank. Pike had himself master-minded Lansman's kidnapping and transport to Front terri-tory eight months ago.

That's just fine, Sonny, Pike's late and unlamented father spoke up in his mind. *Except maybe you ought to be thinking about what happens if somebody blunders into this place and messes with the bomb before the summit. Sure, Atlanta still gets toasted, but the Mission counts as a failure unless all them big shot politicos are in town to burn with it. And here's another question to test your little brain with: What if the bio-nuke goes off before you've hauled your own ass out of the oven?*

Pike began humming "Camptown Races" again to drown out the inner voice. Yes, there was some danger in leaving the bomb here. But dear dead dad had never understood that risk was the hard currency of greatness. The other bombs would be stashed in seldom-accessed corners of strategic locations, easy, logical choices. The Freedom News Net-work complex had been targeted because it was the com-munications hub of the Free State Union, the Omni because that was where the Tri-territorial Summit would actually convene. Furthermore, the bio-nukes had overlapping radii of destruction. Any one of them could by itself vaporize most of Atlanta, and render what was left uninhabitable. Each, therefore, functioned as a backup for the others.

Easy, easy, oh so easy.

Pike saw no challenge in walking a tightrope with a safety net below. No poetry. No *Glory*. He had selected the third detonation point in order to realize a longtime fantasy. If this matter of personal fulfillment marginally increased the chances of a premature blast, then so be it.

Besides, he did not intend to let the bomb sit in the open if that was at all avoidable. Probably he could find a decent ferret hole.

He looked around the room in the semidarkness.

The hiding place presented itself to him quickly enough to reassure Pike that the Lord both approved of, and was guiding, his actions.

What he had noticed was a rectangular section of wainscotting that bulged curiously at eye level on the wall facing him. To a less astute observer it would have simply appeared that the paneling was coming loose. Pike went and gave it a closer examination, running his fingers around edges of the raised section. The seams he felt in the wall were wide and would have been easily visible with better lighting. They convinced him that he'd found the door of a concealed maintenance cubby.

He pressed down on the upper part of the rectangle. Nothing happened. He pressed down on the left side near the seam.

The right side of the little door sprang open.

He reached a hand into the shadowed cubby and groped around. Inside were some bound coils of wire, a box of wall fuses, two spray bottles of Windex, a roll of duct tape, and an ancient pack of Marlboros with its cellophane wrapper intact. *Excellent,* he thought. In the post–Rev II world, cigarettes were a valued commodity. As good for barter as smoking. That they were still inside indicated that he was the first to have found the cubby since the war. He removed the objects, then groped around some more, measuring its dimensions by feel. It was approximately three by four by six feet. Big enough for a dozen bombs like the one he'd brought.

Yes!

He turned, got the bio-nuke, and carefully stood it at the rear of the enclosure. Before he closed the door he kissed his fingertips, then touched them lovingly against the canister. The familiar, delicious tingles shot up his arm to the pleasure center of his brain, then were relayed to his loins.

He hardened.

Pike shut the door and returned to the presidential desk. He reached into an inside pocket of his sport jacket, took out a pack of facial tissues, then folded the jacket neatly and draped it over a corner of the desk. He went around to the other side of the desk and climbed up it. He undid his pants, let them crumple around his ankles, and pulled down his briefs. His flesh was still rigid and palpitant.

He would take care of that, in addition to doing the other thing.

There were enough tissues for him to be able to wipe both ends.

He squatted, and emptied himself in the Oval Office. As he'd always dreamed of doing.

Ten minutes later he left the Carter Center the same way he had gone in, giving the birds and trees and shrubs and blameless blue sky his cheeriest rendition of "Camptown Races" as he stepped into the fresh garden air, feeling dapper in his good clothes, feeling consummately fulfilled.

Feeling Glorious, yessirree!

Chapter Nine ═══════════════════

John Firecloud fought to regain consciousness, the struggle drawn in hallucinatory images.

For a while his mind groped through layers of solid blackness. Then the blackness became a sooty fog upon which muddled impressions of the objective world impinged. He felt undifferentiated pain. He had the sense of being shaken. Lifted, carried, then dropped. *Roughly.*

Time lapsed.

There was wind. The wind blew strong, but did not dispel the mist. The wind was its conspirator. It existed only to make the mist roil more thickly and inescapably, to thrash him, and confuse him with idiotic grunts and roars, and suck the breath from his lungs.

Then, seemingly from overhead, a sound he knew. The blat of helicopter blades. He peered upward, was unable to see the chopper. Was sure it was near, though. Coming nearer. The steady, repetitive thud of spinning rotors gained volume, and he kept looking for the aircraft, but it remained unseen, hovering above the highest fringe of mist. Above the wind.

Suddenly a rope ladder rolled down through the grayness, and he heard a voice call his name. The voice was faint and oddly mutable. *It's the wind,* he thought. *The wind changes it. Wind wants to take it away.*

At first the voice sounded like Charlie Tiger's. Then Ardelia Martin's. Finally it sounded like his own . . . but that was ridiculous. Wasn't it? No more ridiculous than

believing it could be his deceased father calling and calling
him.

Urging him to reach up and grab the ladder.

But he felt so weak.

For your life, John! the voice cried. *For your life!*

So weak, he tried to say, and couldn't. His mouth would
not work. Something stopped it from shaping the words.
The ladder dangled and flapped in the gibbering wind.

Catch it! For your life!

Firecloud reached for the bottom rung with numb,
clumsy fingers, missed, tried again more desperately,
grasped and missed again, tried still another time, somehow
managed to snatch hold.

He clung to the ladder in the hostile fog and wind,
groping for the next rung and the next, dragging himself up,
his body seeming to weigh a ton, his head malleting.

The wind shrieked and buffeted, and like a thing alive
tore at the ladder, spun it, snapped its rungs and wound
them around Firecloud's arms until he was entwined from
wrist to shoulder, his arms straight out at his sides. The
rescue had become a cruel trap. He was caught like a fly on
the tongue of some monstrous amphibian, the ladder reeling
him up and up—

He came back to reality gagging.

And saw the pair of White Trash—a man and a woman—
leaning over him, and smelled the poison wind of their
breath, and at first wondered if he had slipped from one
surreal nightmare into another.

Then he remembered his hike into Everglades City, and
the ambush, and began wondering why he was still alive.

He blinked the gauzy spots from his eyes and quickly
took inventory of himself.

He was faceup on a wood floor, cruciform, unable to
move. Something was crammed between his teeth. A hank
of cloth? Yes. No. Not just cloth. Too hard. Something
else, wrapped *inside* the material and wedging down his
tongue. His mouth was taped shut over it. He concentrated

on breathing through his nose. Deep, regular breaths to suppress the gag reflex. Okay. All right. His throat unclenched. *Why couldn't he move?* A pole of some sort across his shoulder blades. It ran the length of both outstretched arms, and they were bound to it with a nylon rope that had been looped many times around his back, shoulders, and neck. Additional straps of rope fastened it to his wrist and elbows.

A tender, pulsating lump had risen on his head where the gun had struck. His face was a collage of stinging bites and scratches. Pain gnawed through his wounded arm like rat's teeth; the gash itself had an open, tacky feel, but he thought the bleeding may have slowed or stopped. Bruises on his arms, legs, and ribs achingly declared that he'd gotten worked over while out cold.

He stamped down on the fear and sense of helplessness. He had to finish taking stock. To think and analyze.

He'd been brought indoors. Into the bungalow, he suspected. His captors wouldn't have taken him far.

He did not recognize either of the White Trash above him from the ambush.

The man was a young, bald, scarecrow-thin albino, wearing iridescent pink shorts, an orange short-sleeved polo shirt with an alligator emblem on the right breast, and red hightop sneakers. He had double fissures on his upper lip—a harelip. Blotches of pus orbited the almost translucent blue pupils of his bloodshot eyes. His skin was sloughy and ulcerated where it had been cooked by UV's, and there was a weeping tumor on his neck. Scrawled across his face in what appeared to be woman's lipstick or marker ink were three inverted capital letters, two E's on his right cheek, an L on his left: EEL.

The mutant noticed Firecloud's eyes upon him and bent closer, neighing laughter, his head bobbing up and down. There were bright, inflamed abscesses on his toothless gums.

His hand clutched a large kitchen knife, and he poked the tip of it into the soft flesh beneath Firecloud's chin.

Firecloud refused to blink. He stared upward, and with sudden disgust realized that the letters were not *written* on the White Trash's cheeks but rather *carved* in puckery scar tissue.

"Thuh-ee meee naameth?" the White Trash bleated unintelligibly, pointing to his face. His tongue flicked through one of the clefts in his upper lip and caught a blob of snot as it slid from his nose. He swallowed it with a crude, gratified sigh and neighed more laughter. *"Thu-thuh-eee meeee naaameth?"*

The knifepoint pricked a little deeper into Firecloud's throat, and a crimson drop of blood welled up. It grew large as a pearl then broke and rilled warmly down to the hollow of his neck.

"Whut mah boy here wants t'know is if yuh can read his name," the other White Trash standing over him said. She was short, bulky, toadlike. Thick wattles of flesh bounced under her neck as she spoke. "That's *Lee*, now. Not *Eel* like it looks. He writ it hisself with the knife while he was standin' in front'a the mirror. Went by his reflection an' got it *backwuhds*!" She tittered, squatted, and whispered with her lips brushing his ear, "Too bad he cain't think as good as he can *cut*!"

Firecloud looked at her without moving his head.

Her hair was bleached nearly white on one side of a middle part, dyed carrot-orange on the other. Wirelike strands, some of which were tied together with red satin bows, fell over a blunt, sloping brow. Her caked, patchy facial makeup failed to hide the erupting terrain of boils, scales, and open sores underneath. Oily trickles and flows crisscrossed her cheeks like irrigation ducts feeding some noxious crop. Ranges of pimples covered her nose and forehead, and there were winegrape-colored scabs and peels of skin everywhere on her face.

Firecloud felt another queasy wriggle of disgust in his

stomach. The trapezius muscles of his upper back clenched in an involuntary spasm, putting strain on the truss that had been devised to hold him prisoner. The crosspiece beneath him pressed into his spine and shoulders. His injured arm sang with pain. The span of rope over his neck tautened chokingly.

His heart knocked, and he became slick with sweat.

Breathe. Slow and easy, he told himself, reasserting control. His nostrils expanded. *Slow. Easy. In and out.*

The woman had straightened briefly and said something to her son that Firecloud missed. The boy mumbled with displeasure and pulled the blade away from his prisoner's neck.

Once more Firecloud wondered why they were keeping him alive.

She looked down at him, scratching under her stained yellow muumuu. A half-dozen platinum bracelets jangled on each wrist. Her pear-shaped diamond earrings glittered like ice crystals. She wore a gold necklace with a large diamond-and-pearl pendant and perhaps a dozen diamond rings on her scabby fingers. Sacked jewelry that must once have been priced at tens of thousands of dollars.

Done scratching, she glanced at the loose flakes of skin that had come off on her fingernails, wiped them on the front of her tentlike garment.

"That ek-zee-ma can drive a gal *nuts*!" she exclaimed, cracks spiderwebbing the thick smudges of makeup on her cheeks as she grinned with hideous good humor.

Then, the benign grin never leaving her face, she shot her hand behind Firecloud's head, grabbed a fistful of hair, and yanked, arching it back.

She bowed low again. And again he was under the smothering heave of her bosom, her mouth moist and hot on his ear.

"Now lissen t'me, sweet thang," she whispered. "Ah ain't gonna let 'em kill yuh, though yuh surely deserves it fore whut yuh done ta Grundy an' his paw. Grundy's hurt bad, bleedin' inside, where it cain't be patched. We got him laid out in th' next room *dyin'*!" She frowned. "Ol' Arlo wants to skin yore hide, no doubt about that, but ah bargained with him. Told 'im that this whole mess only got started on account of him wantin' to rut with the Chinee. Told 'im that ah got as much right to a fresh piece'a ass as he does. You follow?"

Firecloud said nothing. Now he knew why he was being kept alive, and that knowledge made his flesh crawl. He tried not to let the bristling dread show in his expression.

Suddenly, with a violent jerk, she raised him by the hair to a half-sitting position and shoved his face between the voluminous globes of her breasts. Anger chased briefly across her dull, batrachian features, then she shook her head, made a *tsk*-ing sound, and the molasses-and-cyanide smile reappeared.

"Shame on me," she cooed into his ear. "Gettin' riled at yuh for not answerin'. How're yuh *supposed* to answer with mah *mouthplug* shoved back 'gainst yore tonsils?" Her grip relaxed, and she eased him back down. "Now, we'll try again. If yuh followed what ah was gettin' at, blink once."

He blinked. Provoking her would be a mistake. And while she talked he would have a chance to test the ropes and determine how much play he had—if any. He also needed to know what the bar was made of.

He flexed one wrist imperceptibly. Then the other. The tie on the right felt a little looser. Firecloud doubted it was loose enough for him to work the hand free—not without time, certainly not in full view of the woman—but he kept bunching and unbunching his finely developed muscles anyway, trying to give himself more slack.

"Now I gotta talk fast, so listen up t' the deal me and Arlo made," she whispered. "He wants ta knock yuh 'round some, an' maybe Lee gonna do some scribblin' on yuh with his knife. But if yuh behave they ain't gonna break nothin', or cut nothin' off. An afterwuhd ah can have ya t'myself. Got it?"

Firecloud blinked. He had managed to turn his hand in a quarter-circle, placing his thumb, pointer, and middle fingers in contact with the immobilizing pole. The pads of his fingers felt for texture. It was round, straight, made of smooth, coated wood. *A broomstick?* No. Too long and thick. His fingers stretched, reaching bare centimeters from where the pole ended in a coarse peg, the projection obviously fitted for a hole of a smaller circumference than the main length of the rod. *A closet dowel. Or something like that.* Maybe, just maybe, with the right leverage . . .

"So, if yuh be careful not ta hassle too much an' get 'em pissed, yuh'll be okay," the mutant was whispering. Her blistered, sandpapery tongue darted into his ear, and he fought an impulse to recoil. She made a husky, lusting sound. "Later, ah'll make everythin' better. You gonna see. Ah'll make yuh feel so goo—"

"Goddamn it, Itchin' Peg, gimme that sumbitch!" a voice barked from elsewhere in the room. Firecloud had heard it before. It belonged to the White Trash with the gun. The big potbellied one that had knocked him out. "You can get yore rocks off when ah'm through with him!"

"But—"

"Now, woman!"

"Okay, Arlo, *okaaaaay*!" she hollered petulantly. Her lips smacked Firecloud's cheek. "Watch yore man-parts, sweetmeat!"

Itching Peggy rose with a kind of bouncing movement, went around behind Firecloud, leaned down and grabbed the pole. She pulled up on it like a weight lifter, huffing, legs bent.

The floorboards under him creaking and shifting, Firecloud was wrenched to his feet.

And hurled into battle for his life.

Chapter Ten ══════════════════

Vertigo nearly dropped Firecloud the instant Itching Peg let go of the pole.

The room canted like a storm-tossed ship's deck. He staggered, depleted from blood loss, exhaustion, and the blows he'd taken while unconscious; his breathing impaired by the gag and whatever was wedged in his mouth; the pole upsetting his balance. He swayed nauseously, bumped against something. Stumbled around some more, a wall crowding his vision, and retreating.

Then Lee jumped in front of him, one hand reaching out to brace Firecloud by the shoulder, the kitchen knife in his other hand throwing pinpoints of light as he waved it back and forth.

"Steady 'im, boy!" Arlo shouted. "Ah want th' word *injun* sliced inta his face, and ah want it done neat so's ah can read it!"

"How thpell?" Lee blubbered through an overflowing mouthful of something that looked like raw fish.

"I–N–G–O–N, moron! Now get him ta stand still, an' do it!"

His nails clawed into Firecloud's arm, and the shiny blade swung faster. As he moved in, Firecloud backshuffled awkwardly, tearing away from his grip. Firecloud took another step backward, and his hip banged into a captain's chair that was pushed slightly out from a dining table. The wooden chair rocked but stayed upright.

Arlo closed in again, switching the knife from one hand

to the other so that Firecloud could not anticipate which he
would strike with. Firecloud hooked his foot under the leg
of the chair, half-dragged, half-kicked it toward and in front
of himself. It skidded and crashed onto its side between him
and the knife-wielding mutant. Lee hopped back, startled.

Firecloud inhaled, exhaled, inhaled, exhaled, collecting
his wits. The vertigo was passing, and he could feel the
strength and limberness flowing back into his legs. Top-
pling the chair had bought precious moments. Now his
counterattack would have to be fast and decisive.

His eyes made a sweep of the room.

He was in a kitchen. The table he'd kicked the chair away
from was on his right, near the wall and almost directly
below a window. The shade was drawn, and the lot outside
was almost certainly the same brambled patch of ground
he'd seen flanking Ardelia's bungalow.

Firecloud banished questions of where she was and what
they had done to her. If ever he wanted answers, he had to
concentrate on staying alive.

The sink and cabinets were on his immediate left, and
just past them some wooden storage barrels were clustered
against a rectangle of wall on which the paint was brighter
than elsewhere in the room, defining the spot where a
refrigerator must once have stood. The woman called
Itching Peg and the bulking pack leader, Arlo, were to the
right of the barrels, watching Firecloud and his opponent
with wild-eyed expectancy, yipping and hooting like ring-
side spectators. Arlo was brandishing his pistol, a Colt .44.

About a yard behind them was an opening that gave onto
a foyer. Either of the jambs framing the entryway would do
for what Firecloud planned on trying. To get over there he
would have to maneuver past the two mutants. Secured to
the pole as he was, and in the cramped space of the kitchen,
that would be tough. But it was his only hope.

He fixed back on Lee, having mapped his surroundings in
the tick of a second.

The mutant had flung the chair out of his path and was

advancing, sparks of bloodthirsty excitement in his eyes.
Pursing his malformed lips, he made a buzzy kazoolike
sound which might have been comical under far different
circumstances.

He moved in a jerky kind of marionette dance, and as
their gazes locked, he grinned and cupped his free hand
over his crotch and hiked it upward with a perverse
bump-and-grind.

"Oh no, Lee gone *blood simple*!" Itching Peg shrieked.
In her dismay she was pulling at her own hair. "Goddamn
it, sweatmeat, ah tol' ya not ta raise a fuss! Ah *tol' ya*!" She
turned to Arlo, pleaded, "Yuh *gotta* put a stop ta this, Arl.
We made a deal, ya gotta—"

"Shaddup, woman!" he roared, still cranking his gun
hand overhead like a rooter at a boxing match. He was
looking avidly at the combatants with his good eye, his
frenzied gesticulations causing the spongelike mass on the
opposite side of his face to flap and jiggle. "Forget
scratchin' the squawman, Lee! Slice his gutstrings! *Fuck
him up good!*"

With a fierce cry, the mutant stabbed at Firecloud, the
blade held low and flat in his right hand, the cutting edge
outward. His left hand coming up from the fork of his legs
to protect his face.

Leaving his side open for an attack.

As the blade flashed its deadly wink, Firecloud cocked
his leg and delivered a roundhouse kick to his opponent's
kidney, the leg traveling parallel to the floor, his hip and
supporting foot rotating slightly, the ball of his foot connecting with shocking impact as the kick reached the end of
its arc. The mutant doubled over, groaning and wretching,
the knife clattering to the floor. Firecloud moved in for his
follow-up, calculating the precise angle of the kick.

Pain screamed through his arms as his muscles flexed
against the wooden crosspiece. He shut his mind to it,
positioned himself with one foot to the rear of the other,
instinctively making minute adjustments in his stance to

compensate for the pole's off balancing effect. His front leg cocked, thrust speedily up and out in a continuous and linear unit of motion.

The flat of his foot struck the mutant's neck, severing it cleanly from his spine with a wet snap while at the same time pushing him backward across the room, toward the other two White Trash.

The twitching, droopnecked corpse bowled into them, and they flew in opposite directions, looks of utter surprise on their faces. Tangled in her own feet, Itching Peg crashed down hard into the gang of storage barrels. Several of the barrels tipped onto their sides and went rolling over her legs, vomiting grain and potatoes and dried beans and corn. Arlo caromed across the kitchen like a drunk, the side of his head hitting the wall with stunning force, a finger accidentally squeezing two shots out of his Colt.

The first slug ricocheted off the walls like a pinball between electronic bumpers before plowing into the sink cabinet. The second punched into the ceiling. The next spat from the bore of the gun as Arlo's arm was in its seesawing descent and took a searing, whistling trajectory for Itching Peg, who was on her knees, trying to lift her mountainous weight from the floor. It chunked into her meaty breast, and a moment later she looked down and saw a parasol of blood burst open above her heart.

She flopped back in the dry sea of grain and dehydrated vegetables, a crimson lather brewing from her mouth, the front of her shapless garment a mire of gore, the smatters of blood and makeup on her snubby, contorted face making her look like a mad and murderous circus clown that had been stood in front of a firing squad.

"Mmmmph," she grunted, her eyes sliding up in her head.

The last thing she saw before she died was Firecloud rushing past her for the opening to the hall, his arms still pinioned to the wooden bar. His course to the entryway clear, he'd launched into the second and most critical part of his life-or-death gambit.

Firecloud stopped short in the entryway, turned, and backed against the right jamb while keeping Arlo in sight.

Dazed and confused, the mutant was staring at the bloody mound of flesh that had been Itching Peg, blinking furiously, shaking his head as though to fend off mosquitoes, his gun nosed down against his thigh.

In the entry Firecloud closed his fingers around the end of the pole he could reach and planted his feet widely apart. Then, with a tremendous shrug that bulged the muscles of his upper back and shoulders into a corded mass, he slammed himself backward against the jamb, once, twice, three times and more, while prying the pole forward, the wooden bar violently leveraged between the upright beam and his body.

Successive waves of pain jolted up his spine. His jaws involuntarily clamped down on the rag-wrapped object in his mouth, and he tasted blood.

Through a roseate haze he saw Arlo charging toward him, the stupefaction gone from his features, his mouth widened in a bellow of rage.

His gun coming up.

Firecloud slammed back on the pole and pulled, slammed and pulled. He felt it giving, heard it begin to splinter, heard the pounding of his heart match and outrace the pounding of Arlo's footsteps, slammed, pulled, slammed, pulled, his vertebrae grinding. Slammed, pulled . . .

"WE WUZ FAMILY! WE WUZ FAMLEEEEEEY!" Arlo yowled, his gun belting out its own savage roar, the bullet whizzing above Firecloud's head and drilling three inches into the doorjamb as the pole to which he was bound finally, finally broke in two.

Firecloud tightened his grasp on the segment of dowel in his hand and caught the other before it could drop to the floor. Steadying himself, he drove full-tilt into Arlo, keeping low, draggling loose coils of rope, his improvised combat batons crossed to form an X-shaped barricade in front of him. As they closed, the mutant let off another shot and missed, and pulled back the trigger again and the hammer clicked emptily. He had started out with less than a full clip, and now it was spent.

Moving forward, he raised the gun for a bludgeoning swing at Firecloud's right temple, but as it came at him, Firecloud whipped the stick in his left hand up and sideways, striking a crisp, shattering blow to Arlo's forearm. Simultaneously he jabbed the broken, jaggedly pointed tip of the stick in his right hand at the mutant's groin, but Arlo shifted an instant before it would have emasculated him and it speared the inside of his massive thigh instead. He screamed, reeled, the length of wood protruding from his leg, the gun hurtling from his grip.

Firecloud advanced with his remaining club. Though the White Trash was hurt, he had an advantage in size and sheer bulk. Firecloud knew he would have to keep up a relentless assault. He bulled in and made an upward faking motion with the stick, and as Arlo raised his hands from his leg to defend his rolling middle, Firecloud reversed the direction of his swing and slashed the club brutally down and into his kneecap.

It was like hitting a marble pillar. The gigantic mutant grunted in pain but did not fall. The skewered leg forgotten in his heightened, unthinking rage, he lurched forward like a wounded grizzly, his colossal arms spread wide, biceps expanding and rippling under layers of flesh. Snarling, he thrust his arms under Firecloud's and wrapped them around him. Then, his hands pressed into the small of Firecloud's back, he hefted up, and Firecloud's feet left the ground.

His arms tightened crushingly, and Firecloud's nostrils flared. With his mouth taped and the mutant putting enormous pressure on his chest, it was getting harder and harder to breathe. The veins on his temples rose in blue relief. Oxygen squeezed from his lungs and blasted out through his nose. His eyeballs throbbed. His ribs groaned, and he was sure they would soon buckle. He couldn't breathe. If he didn't get loose in seconds, he was a dead man. He raised the stick and flurried Arlo's head and face with blows. He hit the spongy growth on his forehead, and it burst open with an audible *squish*, spewing dollops of malodorous, nearly black fluid. Firecloud swung the stick across his nose and saw his septum crumble bloodily. He barraged the mutant's ears and cheekbones. Hit him in the mouth, smashing his teeth.

Arlo moaned and his grasp relaxed a little. Snorting in air, Firecloud turned the stick so he was holding it near the ends with both hands, then brought it across Arlo's throat and pushed. The stick passed in just below the jawline, where the head meets the neck. Arlo made a strangled sound, and his face began reddening. Firecloud pushed up and in. His sweat mingled with the sour perspiration on Arlo's bulging gut.

Arlo relaxed his grip some more. He coughed violently. His eyes were huge and teary. The redness in his face had deepened by several shades and was now almost purple. Blood gushed from his battered mouth and the remains of his nose. The cystic tumor on his brow leaked rancid black clots. Firecloud continued pushing against the column of his neck. Up and in. Arlo's face had gone bright purple, and one of his eyes was filling with blood and drifting oddly. He uttered a choked, slobbery groan, and his grasp on Firecloud unlocked, and Firecloud fell crashing to the floor on his back.

"Still gon' kill ya," Arlo mumbled, hacking out a bloody cough. His hands massaged his throat. He swayed, rubber-legged, but, astonishingly, remained on his feet.

And after a moment took a shaky step toward Firecloud.

His head spinning, Firecloud rose onto his elbows and dragged himself weakly backward.

Arlo took another step, and another, his strides becoming steadier, covering the floor space between him and Firecloud faster than Firecloud could make his protesting body retreat.

Then Firecloud was in his loom.

The mutant glared down at him, his fingers hooked into claws. His mouth opened in a broken and agonized grimace.

"All this trouble causa the Chinee bitch," he muttered, and started to take another step when suddenly the roof of his skull exploded in a mist of blood and bone.

What was left of the giant keeled forward, and slammed onto the floor like a stack of bricks.

Firecloud rolled sideways barely in the nick of time to avoid being flattened underneath him. A single lifeless finger, still hooked, brushed his booted ankle. Pale and grubby, it looked to Firecloud like some hideously over-sized worm.

"Poor guy lost his head over me," a woman's voice said from beyond the entryway.

John Firecloud craned his head and stared wide-eyed over the hulking corpse at the three strangers that had appeared in the foyer.

None were White Trash.

The woman was tall and lissome, wearing black S.W.A.T. assault coveralls, a leg-mounted gun holster, leather wrist cuffs, and several rawhide necklaces of varying length and thickness. Her midnight-black hair was cropped close to her scalp everywhere but in back, where a tightly wound braid fell midway down to her waist. Bright-red Sprayon makeup banded her large, slanted Oriental eyes like a burglar's mask. A dragon tattoo curled around the bell of her ear, devouring its own tail.

Blue smoke snaked from the bore of the Glock pistol with which she had blown away Arlo's head.

The two men bracketing her were dwarves. It looked as if they were also twins. They were both carrying Winchester Model 97 riot guns in nylon web sling-harnesses and wore electric-blue bicyclist's pants, sneakers, and yellow long-sleeved jerseys that were identical except for the writing on their chests: printed in black on the shirt of the man on the left was the letter M followed by the numeral 1, while the jersey worn by the other man said M2.

"Name's Saralyn. Saralyn Yung," the woman said. "My *paisons* here are Marcus One and Marcus Two. They're brothers. I'll let you guess which one's which."

The broad, stunted men grinned silently.

"I suppose you're the guy Dee's been telling me about," Saralyn went on, grinning herself now. "Johnny Firecloud. Greatest thing since sliced bread, as I hear."

Firecloud ripped the tape off his lips. It smarted. He pincered his fingers around the blood-and-saliva-soaked rag in his mouth and pulled it out. A shoehorn—Itching Peg's "mouthplug"—slipped from inside the wadded rag and clinked tinnily to the floor.

The wound in his arm was bleeding again.

He guzzled air, then said, "Ardelia . . . is she—"

"Dee's had a rough time of it, but she'll be okay. The Trash were keeping her alive as bait for me. She was tied up in the living room next to the body of one of them, looks like a kid. And a pretty damn ugly one at that."

She holstered her weapon, stepped over the prostrate form of Arlo, and crouched beside Firecloud, whistling softly as she glanced around at the carnage inside the room.

Then Saralyn looked down at Firecloud and smiled.

"I'll have you patched up in a jiffy, and get the house-cleaning done before lunch," she said, winking.

Chapter Eleven ════════════════════

Viewed from the air, the 350-year-old Castillo de San Marcos, on the west bank of the Matanzas River in the city of St. Augustine, Florida, resembled nothing more than a star that had flickered out and crashed to the ground—and was, in fact, a classic example of the "stellar" fortress architecture favored by Spanish military designers of the seventeenth century.

Over its long history, this mammoth stronghold had never been captured by an enemy in battle, its fourteen-foot-thick coquina limestone walls and imposing hundred-foot-thick solid-fill bastions having successfully repelled pirates and hostile Native Americans, as well as having withstood prolonged British sieges in 1702 and 1740.

But what force could not achieve, diplomatic wrangling ultimately did. As the result of a series of trades and treaties, from 1763 into the next century, control of the Castillo ping-ponged between England (which during the First American Revolution used it as a staging area for attacks on the southern colonies), the fledgling United States, and Spain. On July 10th, 1821, the Spaniards abandoned the fort for the second time, and the flag of the U.S.A. was raised over its walls . . . also for the second time.

The Stars and Stripes flew high above the Castillo for just short of two centuries—snake eyes seeming to be the magic number with regard to its occupation—until 2009, when they were supplanted by the stars and swastika banner of the

National Front, and the Castillo de San Marcos came to serve as both the Front's main garrison headquarters in Florida and a feared gulag for its political enemies.

Now Commander Joseph Forster Groll stood brooding by the window in his private dining quarters within the ancient citadel, his back to the luxuriously appointed dinner table at which Lieutenant Slade had already seated himself.

The table was set for three.

Groll had been at the window when Slade entered minutes ago. He had not bothered to turn and greet him. His small black eyes stared meditatively out at the parade ground thirty feet below. His mouth was a tight, nearly invisible seam.

He kept his hands together behind him, folded around a sopping wet handkerchief. They wrung it constantly and automatically.

Outside, searchlights worried the rude walls and flag-stones of the rectangular central court from mounts atop the ramparts. The beams grazed each other and occasionally intersected as the sentries made their routine sweeps. On the gundeck once occupied by 18- and 24-pound cannons, sophisticated antiaircraft batteries nuzzled the dark night sky.

The dining room was silent. As was the deserted court. As were the man-eating bull sharks gliding through the saltwater moat which skirted the Castillo on its three landward sides.

Groll was using the time before his other guest arrived to decide whether he should have a Geek pit constructed in the parade ground. He was inclined to think it would be an efficient means of isolating a disruptive prisoner from the rest of the inmate population, while making an object lesson of the troublemaker. Yes, a Geek pit. A full-scale version of the one which was part of his desktop Monster Show. That Geek pit was basically just the empty reservoir of an inkwell. Groll took minimal pride in its invention because he felt it had required minimal use of his talent. The inkwell had been there in his desk to start with. He'd merely adapted it to a new purpose.

The Geek itself was the truly ingenious work of art.

The Geek had started out as an American infantryman in a set of World War Two combat figures. The toy soldier was made of green plastic, and Groll's first modification had been to color its face with white Duco hobby paint. Before applying it he had added a few drops of turpentine to the bottle so the paint would go on thin and smeary, like cheap greasepaint on the face of an actual sideshow Geek. He used women's eye pencil to give the eyes a pitted, blackened look. He glued snips of his own hair onto the head of the figure to conceal the combat helmet and make it appear as if his Geek were wearing a shabby mop wig.

After Groll placed the Geek in the enclosure, he'd had Fran arrange for some bits of raw steak to be sent up from the kitchen. He'd left the scraps on the outer windowsill and waited until they bred maggots and then ordered Fran to dump the squirming pieces of meat into the Geek pit. The revolted expression on her face as she performed her task was priceless. Irreplaceable. The spoiled meat had fallen onto and around the Geek, and Groll had looked in and become totally abstracted. He had mused about levels of human debasement. He had craved the pleasure of reducing someone to a disgusting, filthy creature that would bite the heads off live chickens and eat rats and snakes and perhaps even his own feces with relish.

And, as usual, the commander's mind had drafted an imaginary background for his complete figure. *In an earlier time the Geek had a name, and it was Jack Francis Greer. Jack was clever but emotionally unstable, and his myriad character flaws led him to vice, and his vices led him to become something of a grifter. He was employed for a while as a carny spieler, and though his talk brought in the rubes, they felt cheated by what they found behind the tent flap. Jack barked up hermaphrodites but gave them common transsexuals. His so-called Missing Link was only the preserved fetus of a chimpanzee, his Wild Man of Borneo a simpleton in an animal skin. Audiences denounced him as a fraud and clamored to have their money refunded. Jack became embittered and started drinking heavily. As he deteriorated, so did his shows. Eventually the carny's management gave him an ultimatum: He could either pack his trunk or replace the Geek who had recently died of a failed liver. By then Jack was an alcoholic and would take whatever job he could to support his addiction. Jack crawled into the Geek pen. And there he remained, a sad case whose downfall might have been averted if he had understood how necessary it is for one to always deliver on one's promises.*

Joseph Forster Groll knew the importance of always making good on his word. If he had not, then he, too, might have spent his existence degenerating in a figurative Geek pit, bearing contempt and ridicule. Staring out the window, he could remember the moment in his youth, the precise moment of clarity and consequence, when that knowledge had bolted into his head.

He was twelve years old, and Mother had taken him to the Ohio State Fair. It was a Saturday, and his face was still split and lumpy from the symphony of violence Kenneth Whitman's fists had played on it the day before. Kenneth and over a dozen more of Groll's classmates had cornered him against the schoolyard fence. They were like a dog pack holding their quarry at bay, and they had called him that hated name, *Clam Mouth.* Called him *Clam Mouth* as they hit him, *Clam Mouth* as they jeered and hectored and did things with their lips and tongues to mock his condition. And Groll had looked into Whitman's smug, blustering face and sworn aloud to make him pay, and Whitman laughed and hit him again. They all laughed, and Groll had kept drilling his eyes into Whitman's face and thought, *I will kill what you love the most.*

The next day he and Mother had gone to see the midway attractions and stopped at the tent with the sign that said

there was a Giant South American Jungle Rat on exhibit
inside. And while the picture of the Jungle Rat fascinated
Groll, it was the cretin in the ticket booth that scared him as
he'd never been scared, the cretin with his floppy ears,
bulging epicanthal eyes, and small spade-shaped hands. It
was the cretin who, though he had only winked and leered
and uttered imbecilic grunts as they payed their admission,
by his very appearance promised true horror beyond the tent
flap.

Mother took Groll by the hand and led him in. He'd gone
in shaking, he'd gone in with knees of jelly and acidy saliva
rivering down his chin. She'd led him in, and the Giant
South American Jungle Rat had proved to be just a
common, overfed gopher. And when he left that tent Groll
was no longer frightened of the cretin in the ticket booth.
The cretin had lost his terrifying power, and Groll, having
learned all there was to know about the necessity of keeping
promises, had gained his.

Soon afterward he kept the promise he'd made to
Kenneth Whitman.

"The scientist is here, Commander," Slade said behind
him.

Groll turned from the window, his reverie interrupted. He
would have to decide about the Geek pit another time. He
glanced at the bank of closed-circuit video monitors in an
alcove across the room. The screen offering a view of the
hall outside the door showed Gordon Lansman and the
phalanx of guards assigned to escort Lansman down from
the tower where he was being imprisoned.

Groll dabbed his mouth and chin, discarded the handkerchief, and took his seat at the head of the table. When the
knock came at the door he was ready.

"Enter," he said.

Two of the guards remained out in the corridor. Another
man preceded the scientist into the dining room. A fourth
and fifth followed him in and came to starch attention,
bracketing the entrance.

Groll found the entire display excessive and annoying. Did they really expect Lansman to try and escape? How far could he get? Where was he supposed to go?

"Good evening, professor," he said, nodding curtly. Slade sat like an ice sculpture at his right-hand side.

Groll gestured toward the chair opposite him. "Please be seated," he said, noticing as the scientist went to his chair that he walked with a slight limp. He looked up at the guards. "You may wait outside until summoned. I'm sure my guest won't be any trouble."

The soldiers clicked their heels obediently and left.

"Lieutenant Slade, would you mind very much if I asked you to pour the wine?" Groll said. His eyes were on the scientist.

"My pleasure."

Slade reached for a demijohn, filled the delicate stemmed glasses, and sat back.

Groll continued to look closely at the man facing him across the table. Gordon Lansman was lean and in his midfifties, with thinning gray hair, a prominent nose, and a blue shadow of heavy beard on his deeply lined, clean-shaven cheeks. He had the anemic complexion of someone who has gone too long without proper nourishment and spent too many sleepless nights with only grim thoughts for company. The prison khakis he wore seemed to float on his bony frame.

Groll rotated his wineglass by the stem, sipped, and smiled his humorless smile. "You know, Lansman, I've been wondering about your field of expertise. The sciences have divided into so many umbrellas of specilization, we poor laymen cannot help but be confused." He twirled, sipped, smiled coldly, twirled. "Would I properly call you a biotechnician? A biophysicist? A microbiologist? Or perhaps a genetic researcher?"

Lansman had not yet lifted his drink. In contrast to his sickly pallor, his eyes were clear and probing. " 'Doctor Lansman' would be just fine," he said.

A droplet of saliva slipped from Groll's mouth into his glass with an audible *plunk*. The wine rippled in tiny concentric circles.

Groll flushed, set down the glass, and reached into his pressed black dress tunic for a fresh handkerchief.

"Lansman, it is my hope that we can conclude our business before dinner is served and then enjoy our meal in a relaxed and informal atmosphere," he said graciously, but with a hard note in his voice that emphasized such an atmosphere could exist only if he were so disposed. "Let me be frank. Slade tells me you have been rather uncooperative with regard to participating in certain experiments I've commissioned. This confuses me."

"I don't see why, Commander." Lansman's face was expressionless.

Groll sighed impatiently. "You and your colleague Dr. Roth were integral to the development of a weapon that can potentially take tens of thousands of lives. Then, you did not seem to have a problem complying with the requests of the National Front. Yet your attitude has changed. As I said, I am baffled."

Lansman shrugged. "Your psychotic friend Wiley Pike had a unique way of asking that helped me overcome any silly compunctions."

He held out his arm, pushing back a baggy sleeve to reveal a wide mottled scar which ran from wrist to elbow.

"Old Wiley did that with a soldering gun," he said. "Used an acetylene torch to do even more exacting jobs on my chest, and under my arms, and on the sole of my right foot. Basic table etiquette prevents me from showing you those places, so you'll have to take my word for it." He lowered his sleeve and settled back. "Wiley loves to burn things, you know. But he, at least, was interested in having me work within my . . . *umbrella of specialization*, as you phrased it. He put me in a lab with germ cultures and fissionable elements. Saved the human material for himself."

"Mr. Pike is not a member of the National Front militia but a civilian in its sometime employ," Lieutenant Slade interjected, plucking a wedge of cheese from an ornate salver on the table. "Our concern is only that he accomplishes his designated tasks. We have no interest whatsoever in discussing his methods and personal idiosyncracies."

"The lieutenant is absolutely correct," Groll added quickly. "Never mind Wiley Pike. Here at the Castillo we are engaged in genetic research which may be vital to the continuance of our species. Research which, in its current stage, unfortunately requires human subjects." He paused, dabbed his chin with the hanky. "Survival demands we be strong and do what is necessary without ethical constraint. It is our belief that mankind will have to physically transform itself to cope with an inhospitable post-nuclear environment."

"And that's the reason you had me shipped here from Jacksonville? So I can be part of this . . . this project?"

"Only half the reason," Slade said, leaning forward. "A point that should be stressed is that, as an engineer of the mutated *Pasteurella pestis* bacilli loaded into the bionuclear explosives, you are likely to draw the attention of certain misguided parties in Free Atlanta. Parties who mistakenly think the National Front would consider using the bombs as anything but deterrents to *their* belligerence. Parties who might actually try to take you from our midst in the belief that you are capable of producing, or perhaps have already manufactured, an antidote to the form of bubonic plague caused by the microbe."

"My reputation's evidently a lot better than I deserve, Lieutenant."

"Perhaps." Slade smiled frostily. "At any rate, you needn't worry about our enemies getting their hands on you. *Ever*. The Castillo is impregnable, and we intend for you to enjoy its safety for a very, very long time."

"Consider the citadel to be a huge stone womb, here to keep you well and protected," Groll said. "Though you will doubtless have a comfortable stay in any event, I can arrange for it be especially pleasant if you cease being stubborn. And make further contributions to science by doing as we ask."

Lansman was quiet for a full minute before replying. He looked at Groll and then Slade and then back at Groll. Finally, he said, "Let's cut the Grade-Z bullshit right now. The operations you want me to perform are purely, atrociously, sadistic. As any rational man could tell you, there is no recognizable knowledge to be gained from vivisecting people, or sewing together their limbs, or surgically removing eyeballs and pinning them to the wall like butterflies. Or from any of the other acts of barbarism in which you've sought my participation. I'm not Frankenstein. I'm not Mengele. And, gentlemen, do what you will to me, I'm not game."

Groll was aware that his anger was stepping up the output of his salivary glands. This fool needed to be shown that he would brook no disobedience and be reminded that punishment, the more horrible the better, was the cement and the crux, the *unstated promise*, of the jailer-prisoner relationship.

And Joseph Forster Groll always kept his promise.

"Well," he said, clearing his throat and dabbing his mouth furiously. "Well, now. I hadn't expected such arrogant resistance. Such antagonism." He cleared his throat again and turned to Slade. "Lieutenant, have you informed Lansman that Dr. Roth is also currently our guest?"

Slade shook his head. "I thought you might want to do that yourself, my commander."

Lansman's face suddenly became startled. "Dave? David Roth is *here*?"

"Yes, indeed," Groll said. "He, too, started out with an insolent streak. Raised quite a fuss. But his attitude has much improved." He looked back at Slade. "Perhaps Dr.

Roth should join us. He might help persuade Lansman to have a change of heart."

"A fantastic idea," the lieutenant said. "I'll send for him immediately."

He rose, went to the door, and spoke briefly to one of the guards stationed outside. The devious smile on his face as he sat back down at the table filled Lansman with a sense of terrible foreboding.

The door opened and a white-gloved, nervous-looking private came through, pushing a service cart on silent coasters. The cart, which held only a large, covered silver platter, was rolled up to the table beside Lansman.

"Oh, my! What unfortunate timing. Dinner has arrived before our additional party." Groll wagged his head and clucked his tongue. "Are you certain your orders to have him brought here were understood, Slade?"

"Absolutely." Slade was frowning but his eyes brimmed with evil enjoyment. "I can double-check, if you wish."

"In just a moment," Groll said. "Let's have a peek at our dinner first. I'm anxious for the good doctor to see how creative our cooking staff can be." He looked at the scientist. "Shall we whet your appetite, Lansman?"

Lansman said nothing. He was gazing at the tense, ghost-white face of the young soldier that had wheeled in the cart, and feeling the sweat of his own palms, and listening to the drumming of his own heart.

Groll licked his lips. "Private, *show him*!" he said.

The soldier averted his eyes from the platter as he raised its lid with a shaky hand.

Gordon Lansman looked. Looked only for a millisecond, just long enough to confirm his awful withering fear, long enough to see the severed head of David Roth balanced on its neck stump in a semicongealed gravy of blood. And then, with a stricken cry, he shoved himself away from the table, almost knocking over his chair, biting down on the edge of his hand to hold back his gorge.

"What a surprise! Dr. Roth is with us after all!" Groll

said brightly, raising his drink for a toast. "To heartwarming reunions."

"The rarest of treats," Slade expanded, holding out his own wine.

They clinked glasses.

Chapter Twelve ═══════════════

As Lansman was served his decidedly unappetizing meal at the Castillo, John Firecloud sat among much friendlier company on the front steps of Ardelia Martin's bungalow several hundred miles to the south and west, deliberately studying three photographs—actually xeroxed dupes of photos—on his lap. Stapled to the back of each copy was a sheet of paper which identified and provided salient facts about its subject.

The picture on the right was a grainy, underexposed pre–Rev II police mug of Wiley Pike in a gray jailhouse uniform shirt. The shot on the left showed Drs. Lansman and Roth, along with an attractive woman of about forty who the accompanying fact sheet revealed was Mrs. Barbara Lansman. All three wore lab whites and smiles as they stood posing with their arms around each other's shoulders among long counters crowded with flasks, test tubes, computer terminals, and other scientific apparatus that looked as technologically advanced as they were esoteric.

The middle photostat, upon which Firecloud's eyes now rested, was a medium-altitude, bird's-eye view of Castillo de San Marcos.

"That picture's from a National Park Service tourist brochure that's near as ancient as I am," Ardelia said, noticing where he was looking. She sat to his right on the wooden riser. Saralyn Yung was one shallow step down and on Dee's right, holding and massaging the older woman's hand.

Ardelia winced a little as Saralyn applied pressure to a tender, swollen knuckle.

"Jeez, I'm sorry," Saralyn said, massaging more lightly.

"That's four 'I'm sorrys' in less'n five minutes. Honey, it's never been in your character to be so apologetic. I didn't know you'd started thinking that it's your fault the arthritis took up residence in my hands—which would make no sense, since I've been livin' with it longer than with you."

"I'm edgy, is all. Coming home to find your best friend tied up in the living room, and the person you're supposed to meet over lunch fighting for his life in the kitchen can have that effect, Dee."

"I'm sure. But I also want to be sure it's just finding us in trouble, and not takin' blame for what happened, that has you in a tizzy."

Saralyn looked up at her.

"Maybe I have got a case of the *if-onlys*," she said after a moment, frowning slightly. "It's having your wrists bound that caused your arthritis to flair up. Never mind that, you could have been *killed*." She paused. "I was the one the mutants were after. They'd probably been watching the house on and off for days and just missed me when I went to meet the twins. I should have . . . I don't know. Been more careful. Something."

"You just said yourself that they weren't around when you left," Ardelia said. "Else they'd have made their move right then and not taken a chance you'd be gone a long time."

"Yeah, but—"

"But nothing." Though Dee's tone was mildly admonishing, there was a kind smile on her face. "If you could read the future in a crystal ball, then I'd say you were at fault for not carryin' one around and looking into it every chance you got. Otherwise, I would rather you stopped feeling guilty. And actin' like my fingers are gonna snap like dry twigs if you rub too hard."

"Dee loves giving me the business," Saralyn told Firecloud. But the frown lines were already wearing off her face, and she was massaging with greater verve than before.

"Love her, *period*," Dee said. Satisfied that her words had had their intended effect, she also turned to the man beside her. "Speaking of business, though, we'd better get right to it. The clock's running down on Free Atlanta."

Yes, Firecloud thought, *it is running down and down, and I am chasing events that always seem to be a step beyond my grasp.*

He glanced up at the star-tossed dome of the night. The stars, if indifferent, were at least constant and familiar. Once, he had been told, they had spilled from a basket that was overturned by a mischievous god. In the south he could see Antares in the body of the Scorpion, treading its high path above the horizon Ursa Major, the constellation his ancestors called the Great Bear. White Americans saw its tail as the Big Dipper. Had it been the Orientals that had seen it as a great celestial wagon, making rounds about the North Pole? Or the medieval Europeans? Firecloud couldn't recall.

He looked at Ardelia. "You said the photo of the Castillo is very old. I assume the Front has made changes since its occupation."

"Uh-huh. Put in the guns, for one thing. Big guns, some with four barrels. And what's called track systems—"

"*Tracking systems*, Dee," Saralyn interjected.

"Right. The fancy artillery and equipment's all atop here." She indicated the ramparts. "Here." Her finger went to the bastions. "And here. I think this is called a ravelin." The place she was pointing to now was an outer, arrowhead-shaped fortification which rose out of the moat and appeared to be accessed from the area surrounding the Castillo by means of a wooden bridge. A second bridge connected it to the fort's eastern scarp.

"That slopmouthed bastard Groll's replaced the ordinary walking bridges in the picture with drawbridges," Saralyn said.

"Your cussin' makes my ears smart, Lyn," Ardelia said, "but I'm glad you mentioned what you did. Reminds *me* to mention that there's sharks in the moat. They're kept half-starved, I'm told."

"The fort's brass will sometimes have a local woman brought in from St. Augustine. To please them in sick ways you'd rather not know about. She refuses, she ends up fishfood," Saralyn added bitterly. "Or, if she's a mother, her kid does."

For a long while no one spoke.

At the verge of the lawn the Marcuses were going through what Saralyn had told Firecloud was their nightly workout—and their preferred way of blowing off tension. It was a fascinating display of acrobatic prowess, composed of a seemingly gravityless series of cartwheels, somersaults, flips, leaps, and tumbles. As was common for human anomalies in these times, the brothers had been canvas slaves, sold by their parents to a touring carnival when they were young children, then trained to perform and—until their recent escape—forced to travel with the roadshow under the quick eyes and guns of mercenary biker goon squads.

"They are remarkable," Firecloud said, motioning toward the dwarves with his chin.

"They've got the 'wow factor,' all right," Saralyn said. "You should see them operate in a fight. It's a real eyeful."

Firecloud nodded appreciatively, then looked back down at his lap and studied the picture of the three white-frocked scientists standing chummily together in their lab.

"According to the dossier, Lansman's wife is deceased. Was she executed by the Front?" he asked Dee.

She shrugged. "Only know that she was taken prisoner with him, and passed away sometime after that."

"And Lansman himself . . . can you tell me where in the Castillo he's being held?"

"Man who smuggles out my information says the sentry tower on the bastion that faces northeast, the one they call

San Carlos." She pointed to the photocopy again. "The Spaniards that built the place gave each of them bastions names, and they stuck." She paused reflectively, then added, "I suppose Lansman could be moved at any time."

"Could be, but probably won't," Firecloud said. "Keeping him there makes the most sense. It's the largest of the towers, and guessing from its appearance, also the strongest. Because it overlooks the water it would be hard to approach. And break out of."

"Hard or impossible?" Saralyn asked.

Firecloud looked at her, his brow creasing. He was taking stock, thinking about everything that had happened to him over the past day, everything he'd learned.

After Saralyn arrived at the bungalow and finished off the giant White Trash, she had cleaned and dressed Firecloud's arm wound, binding on a poultice of *wilanv* leaves he had given her from his medicine pouch. The herbal remedy was primarily an antiseptic, but it also worked to relieve some of his pain. Exhausted from his ordeal, Firecloud had then dropped into a sound sleep on the living room couch, as had Ardelia in her bedroom.

He'd awakened still hurting from his injuries but feeling much restored nonetheless, and had been astounded to discover that he'd slept stonily while Saralyn and the Marcuses had not only taken on the disagreeable task of removing the slain mutants, but put the bungalow back in order, eliminating almost all traces of the violence that had occurred. They'd swept away the broken glass, and scrubbed the blood from the walls and floor of the kitchen, and righted the furniture and storage barrels. They had even hunted down a new door and panes for the shattered living room window from among the untenanted homes nearby.

When Dee arose, she and Saralyn had whipped together a delicious vegetable gumbo from odds and ends the White Trash hadn't devoured—Dee's fish fillets were gone—and they'd eaten out on the porch as the sun made its flamboyant descent.

Ardelia had waited until after their meal to tell Firecloud about Gordon Lansman, the bio-nukes, and the countdown to the Tri-territorial Summit—and disaster.

No one knew where in Free Atlanta the bombs had been planted or even if the weapons being employed were actually those developed by Lansman, his wife, and his colleague David Roth. It seemed probable they were, though. As Dee had related, a squad of special-ops, headed by the man named Wiley Pike, had abducted the scientists—all three of whom had been vital to the Free State Union's brain reserve—from FSU territory eight months back and brought them to a laboratory installation in Jacksonville. Exactly what Pike had done to induce them to work on the bionuclear explosives was undetermined. But Wiley Pike was a known arsonist, armed robber, and sadistic murderer; torture would have bee right up his sordid alley.

Ardelia told how an attempt by the Free State Union to liberate Lansman and Roth had been trumped by an intelligence breach that alerted the Front to the impending rescue operation, and how the kidnapped researchers were moved out of the lab where they'd been forced to work before the FSU commandos could launch their strike. Only one thing saved the mission from becoming a complete debacle: The facility's personnel had vacated hastily and left behind telling clues about the nature of the research that had been conducted within its walls. It was from those clues that the Free State Union found out about the bio-nukes and the gene-engineered strain of bubonic plague they contained.

The problem of what had happened to Pike and the scientists and the missing bombs, and further questions of whether progress on the bio-nukes had reached its final stage, went unresolved for months after the raid—until just three days ago, at which point a man named Edward Mason entered the picture.

Mason had landed in a Free Atlanta hospital bed after being involved in a highway collision. When he discovered that his injuries were serious enough to keep him in that bed for many weeks, Mason became extremely agitated and demanded to speak with the Union Police. The bemused staff complied with his wishes. Mason was thereafter found to be a low-level Front mole who, probably out of expedience, had been assigned to convey a suitcase full of bombs to another operative in Atlanta. He'd been given no specific information as to what type of explosives they were, and likewise had been kept in the dark about the identity of the man with whom he'd rendezvoused. Mason was only sure that the Front was planning an act of terrorism to coincide with the Tri-territorial Summit and that the bombs he'd passed on were powerful enough to warrant his earliest departure. It was during his rush to leave that he got into the car accident which laid him up in traction.

The most critical—and frightening—revelation came when Mason was able to recognize his mysterious Atlanta contact as Wiley Pike from photos of Pike in the Union Police files. Communications subsequently flew between Free State Union defense and law-enforcement agencies, and Pike's connection to the Lansman and Roth kidnapping led authorities to believe they had picked up the trail of the bio-nukes.

A trail that would come to a sudden, cataclysmic end unless the bombs were found and defused before the scheduled commencement of the summit . . . just four days away.

Firecloud took in a deep breath. Across the yard the Marcuses had been proceeding with their starlight exercises, and now Firecloud watched as Marcus One high-vaulted from his brother's shoulders and jacked heels over head through the air, then came down in a headstand, backflipped from that position, and amazingly wound up right where he'd started, his legs straddling Marcus Two's head.

Things weren't coming together as well for Firecloud. He'd turned over what he knew, holding each piece of information up to scrutiny and sorting it into place, but there

were still some troubling gaps in his understanding. Blanks
he needed to fill in before the discussion went any further.

"Why us?" he asked Dee bluntly.

The look on her face said she wasn't sure what he meant.

"We're talking here about mass annihilation, the potential destruction of the capital of the Free State Union. All of
which may be averted by finding the bombs and having
Lansman explain how to neutralize them. The FSU knows
where Lansman is. It seems inconceivable that they would
not send military units after him. That they would entrust
such a crucial mission to us."

"A motley crew, no doubt about it," Saralyn said. She
was still kneading Dee's sore joints.

Dee sighed. "Problem is, John, you ain't wise to politicians and their cockamamie thinkin'. First off, you gotta
remember that neither Pike nor the bio-nukes have been
found. There're folks in Free Atlanta with a lot more
influence than brains, the kind that won't admit there's a fire
burning under them 'less the seat of their pants is catchin'."

"Roaches and bureaucrats. You can nuke the world, but
there's no getting rid of them," Saralyn said. "They—the
bureaucrats, I mean—will wait for hard evidence before
they make a move. It doesn't seem to faze them that their
evidence might turn out to be a blasted city and a couple of
million dead bodies."

"That's right," Dee said. "And then there are some that
believe the bombs exist but don't figure on bein' able to
sniff them out before the summit. They think the way to
deal with the problem's to get the territorial leaders to call
off the party and stay home."

"And then what?" Firecloud said. "Evacuate Free Atlanta, all those people, in less than a week?"

"The bunch of geniuses I was just talking about ain't too
concerned with the little guy. By their reckoning, as long as
the honchos are safe, all's well." Ardelia paused. "I don't
want you to think everybody in charge has got squat for
brains. Most appreciate the danger, are takin' steps to deal

with it, and have reasons for not raidin' the Castillo that make some sense."

"Kind of, sort of, maybe make some sense, that is," Saralyn said.

"Hush, Lyn, and let me finish," Dee said. "It boils down to manpower. The lack of it, I should say. The FSU's less'n a decade old. It just doesn't have enough crack military people to search for the bombs, *and* keep order in Atlanta in case there's some kind of emergency, *and* have a go at the National Front on its home turf. You also got to remember that the Castillo is the Front's command center in Occupied Florida. An FSU hit against it might provoke 'em into all-out war. And if that happens, it's a cinch that the Front, with all its weapons an' well-trained soldiers, will be on top when the dust clears."

"So the FSU wants to try and free Lansman from the Castillo while being able to deny any direct responsibility for the attempt," Firecloud said. "And that's where we come in. Grass roots freedom fighters they can wash their hands of if things get sticky."

"Blame it on us natives getting restless." Saralyn smiled thinly. "Which brings us full circle to the question I asked before: Can we do the job?"

Her eyes pressed with all the weight of coming decision and responsibility. In his mind, Firecloud could hear Charlie Tiger speaking of the day he'd assumed leadership of his tribe: *Why me and not someone else? I can't tell you . . . but there was a kind of knitting around me. I felt it along with the rest. I accepted responsibility for the group, and it was heavy.*

Firecloud had never sought to lead anyone. Moreover, he resented the Free State Union government for wanting to clothe him in the wool of its sacrificial lamb. But where societies formed, so did governments, which in their evolution seemed inevitably to swing between the twin poles of republic and dictatorship. The FSU was the only pre–Rev II society where any value was paid to human rights, where the individual was given a voice through representation, where officials could be elected and un-elected. It was, in short, the only heir to the old United States, and however flawed that extinct nation's political machinery had been, mankind had never come up with anything better.

Firecloud might, for that reason alone, have found it worth preserving, but uppermost in his mind was a less altruistic motive. The FSU's success served the interests of his people. The National Front would exterminate the Florida Seminoles within a few years unless they gained outside support. If he aligned with the FSU now, and was careful not to trust them too far, it could be to his tribe's great benefit—as Charlie Tiger, whose practical nature had always been as strong as his spiritual side, must have perceived. Wouldn't that have been why he'd chosen to mention Ardelia's Underground Railroad before his death?

Freeing Lansman, Firecloud thought, would be his first act as his people's champion, their *war shaman*. His chance to begin steering their course toward survival.

He looked at Saralyn Yung, watched her massage Ardelia's arthritic joints as deftly and easily as she'd blown away the mutant Arlo's head, and for a moment wondered what it was that drove her and how she'd come to link up with Dee's budding resistance movement.

"How high are the Castillo walls?" he asked her, finally.

Saralyn's eyes, still steady on him, brightened.

"Been a while since I've been to St. Augustine, but I'd guess about thirty feet," she said. "Right, Dee?"

Ardelia was consulting the fact sheet attached to the Castillo's picture. "Exactly thirty-three. Add another ten or twelve for the watchtower that's holding Lansman, and you got to figure there's about fifty feet between him and the ground."

Firecloud considered that. "It could be climbed," he said after a moment, nodding more to himself than to the others. "I could climb it."

Saralyn looked at him in surprise. "We're talking about a sheer wall, Johnny. No windows. Nothing to use as handholds. And don't forget the moat and the sentries."

"I'm not forgetting," he said, his tone a little clipped. As a Seminole he'd learned to behave with layered reserve and a certain formality. Her calling him "Johnny" was irritating. "The defenses can be overcome. I would use something like a raft to cross the moat. And my experience with Front soldiers is that they are poor observers. They are lazy and overconfident, and their eyes are untrained. At night I could easily slip past them." He paused a moment, thinking. "The wall wouldn't be bare. There would be ledges, ornamental projections, cracks from erosion. I could easily scale it with a grappling hook. Probably even without one."

"The tower window's gonna have steel bars," Dee said. "You'd need some way of cuttin' through them."

"*Blowing* through them, you mean," Saralyn said. "A saddle charge of C-4 would do the trick fast and neat."

Firecloud looked at her, intrigued. "You've access to plastic explosive?"

"Be surprised at the stuff she gets her hands on," Dee said.

"Plastique's no problem," Saralyn said. "I might even be able to scratch up something that'll get you across that moat with style." She paused, tucking in her bottom lip. "Let's say you're able to get up there unnoticed, blow the window, get the prof out. I'm worried about how the two of you are gonna make it *down*."

"I see what Lyn means," Dee said, her expression suddenly dismal. "Front soldiers might be slow as herd cows, but they ain't deaf. That C-4 watchamacallit's gonna raise one heck of a racket. It won't take them but minutes to figure out what's happenin'. And when they do, there you're gonna be, danglin' from a rope with a fifty-year-old man who's probably got one foot in the grave from bein' beaten and starved. They'll pick you off easier'n you could swat a one-winged fly."

Firecloud digested this. He felt as if he'd been forced to pull to a sudden stop after speeding along in a car at 80 m.p.h. They were right. Getting Lansman out was not the same as getting him away.

Momentarily at a loss, Firecloud sat gazing off into space. A meteor blazed briefly overhead, nicking the Big Dipper before it vanished in a train of sparks. It had been the English who described the Dipper as a wagon, he remembered. They had called it Charles's Wain. To the Orientals it had been something else. Something for everyone. A psychological projective test spanning untold light years and generations, an abstract symbol of humanity's dreams and fears. What would tomorrow's stargazers see it as? He sat and looked up at the sky and pondered. He had to keep his mind loose, work around the corners of his problem rather than bash himself against it. He could sense a possible solution floating near the surface of his thoughts, but it needed to be sneaked up on from its blind side, the way one would try and catch a crayfish that will dive to the pond bottom if one grabs for it too hastily.

The Dipper kept drawing his eyes back to it like a magnet. He didn't know why. Then he recalled his dream, or hallucination, or whatever it was he'd experienced returning to consciousness earlier, when the White Trash had held him prisoner. In that odd fantasy, he'd groped for a ladder. A ladder dropped from a helicopter. He'd heard its blades thudding. It had been piloted in to save him. A helicopter. He supposed the Dipper might look like one to the children growing up today, children who'd been taught by their elders to scrabble for cover at the sound of an approaching Strikehawk, who—

A thought streaked into his mind then, as sparklingly bright as the meteor that had flashed across the sky moments ago. Were he a more expressive man he might have clapped his hand over his forehead.

The Strikehawk!

He looked at Saralyn, then at Dee. "I have a helicopter. A Strikehawk."

They stared back at him, mystified.

"What are you talking about?" Saralyn asked, a look of manifest curiosity on her face.

He quickly told them about his following the Front ground patrol to Cape Sable two weeks ago, about the arrival of the helicopter from Vaca Key and his bloody confrontation with its crew and the men it was picking up.

As he spoke, their expressions shifted from bafflement to fascination.

"I knew something would have to be done with the bodies and the copter," he concluded. "Left on the beach, they'd eventually have been found by a search party from the airbase. Had Front officers come to even the faintest suspicion that my people were involved in the attack, they would have torn apart the Everglades searching for our camp, massacred everyone in it. Obviously I could not chance having that happen. After the storm I returned to the beach with a group of strong men from the reservation. The tide hadn't risen as high as it often does during the autumn gales, and most of the bodies were still there."

"And the Strikehawk," Saralyn said, her eyes very large. "That, too?"

"We disposed of the corpses, dragged the chopper into the forest, and camouflaged it."

"Wow," Saralyn said, whistling incredulously. "Dee told me you were something else, and I saw for myself how well you handled yourself against those muties . . . but that is some impressive yarn."

If he was flattered by her words, his face did not show it. "Let's stick to getting Lansman away from the Castillo. I'm fairly sure the copter was undamaged. Say we could find someone capable of piloting it. He could hover in once I've penetrated the tower, airlift us out of there. We'd be gone—" He snapped his fingers. "—Like that. Before any of the troops knew what was happening."

"I don't want to be the naysayer here, but it's a tall order you're placin'," Ardelia said. "Finding somebody who can fly a chopper's one thing. But them Sikorsky birds are complicated, got a whole mess of specialized equipment—"

"I think I might know just the guy for the job," Saralyn said excitedly.

Dee and Firecloud did a double take that would have played well on a vaudeville stage. As both of them turned to look at her, Saralyn held her hand up and waved at the Marcuses.

Bouncing and pinwheeling in their colorful acrobatic garb, the brothers were gaudy blurs against the muslin-blue sky.

"Hey, guys, cut the hijinks a second and c'mere!" she shouted. "It's important!"

The dwarves sprang out of a crisscross somersault maneuver, returned Saralyn's wave, and came toward the porch. Though their legs were stout and bowed, they walked with a nimbleness which would have surprised someone who had never seen them perform, their backs very straight, toes pointed outward like dancers. Firecloud tried to imagine the monumental effort of will it must have taken for them to overcome their physical handicaps.

"We get 'em hooting in the stands tonight?" Marcus One said as he approached the bungalow. He barely seemed winded.

"Always," Saralyn said.

He affected a little bow. Beside him, Marcus Two smiled with satisfaction, revealing a mouthful of teeth that looked as large and white as piano keys.

"So what's up, babe?"

"You two remember a fella named Zeno, a knife-thrower with the Lyle-Ackerman gilly?"

They bobbed their heads in unison.

"Sure. Blond, blue-eyed farmboy from Indiana," Marcus Two said.

"Tall as a giraffe but good people nonetheless." Marcus One.

"Didn't he have some kind of military background?"

"U.S. Army," Marcus One said, nodding. "He was a hotshot pilot before the Revolution. Whirlybirds, I think."

Saralyn's eyes lit up. "He still making the circuit?"

"Last we heard," Marcus One said.

"Except he ain't with that ragtag Lyle-Ackerman outfit anymore."

"Who then?"

"The Praetorius Circus and Curiosity Show." Marcus Two.

"Last we heard." Marcus One.

"He slaving, or on the tap?"

"Praetorius don't pay anybody. You work for him, you're a slave. Born freaks, made freaks, normals, don't matter." Marcus One smiled.

"What's the skinny on Zeno, Lyn?" Marcus Two asked.

"We need him to fly the scientist out of the Castillo. Assuming we can track him down."

"Fly?" Marcus One.

"Out of the Castillo?" Marcus Two.

"We're talkin' three-ring big top!" Marcus One added, impressed.

"Can we find him?"

"Shouldn't be a problem," Marcus Two said.

"None at all. Matter of fact, he's probably on his way there," Marcus One announced.

Saralyn looked at him.

"What my bro means," Marcus Two said, "is that the Praetorius show's been doing a railstop tour along the coast, headin' north up to St. Augy. Mostly overnighters. I hear Clam Mouth Groll himself's got 'em booked for a special gig next week. Right about now they ought to be somewhere between Vero Beach and Orlando."

"We'll have to find out exactly where they're laying stakes tomorrow and the next day," Saralyn said.

"Again, no problem."

"None."

"Me and M-Two'll split outta here at dawn, do some snooping. Be back with what you gotta know before noon."

Saralyn smiled, then turned to Dee and Firecloud, who had been following the conversation attentively. "I can't be sure Zeno's got the know-how to handle the Strikehawk," she said, "but it's a better than even bet he does."

"The carnival won't just let him go," Firecloud said.

"Besides the hired torpedoes, there's sure to be Front troopers to see that the carnies stay in line," Marcus One said.

"Yeah," Marcus Two said. "Groll and Praetorius are tighter than two Fat Ladies in a broom closet. The commander always has a few guards travel with the show, as a favor to his compadre."

Saralyn flapped her hand dismissively. "So what? Only wet-eared punks get assigned to that detail. Freaks are thought of as herd animals. Nobody expects them to act up. Nobody expects *anything* but a milk run." She looked at Firecloud. "We're gonna have to spring Zeno. Ambush the carny train."

Firecloud took a deep breath. He laid the pictures and attached fact sheets in his hand one atop the other, tapped their edges even on his lap, and returned them to the manila envelope in which they'd been presented to him. He placed the envelope between Dee and himself on the porch and leaned forward, his elbows resting on his knees, hands steepled under his chin.

"You're saying," he said, "that we must rescue one man in order to rescue another."

"All in seventy-two hours or less," Dee added dryly.

Saralyn looked at the Marcuses, then Dee, and then at Firecloud.

"Guess we get to see if you're more powerful than a

locomotive and able to leap tall buildings in a single bound," she said to him.

He stared at her, his brow crinkled, having not the foggiest notion what she was talking about.

She shrugged and grinned.

He almost smiled back.

Chapter Thirteen ===========

The carny train and everyone around it glowed bright green.

"How's our man Zeno doing?"

"I lost sight of him. Too much confusion. He must be loading something onto the train."

Firecloud lowered the night vision goggles, resting his strained eyes, blinking away spots as normal darkness returned to swallow the railyard.

"No getting used to it. Those things'll make you green-eyed and silly," Saralyn whispered beside him. "You want me to take over the conning a while?"

He shook his head. "Not yet. I need to get another look at those bikers. See how well they're armed."

"It's your headache."

They were lying flat in the scrub brush on a gentle slope overlooking the rear of the station house. It was 4:00 A.M. on July 16th, a day and small change after they'd hammered out the details of their double rescue on Dee's front porch. The carnival had been slower to wind its way up the coast than the twins initially estimated. Having held over in several locations due to brisk ticket sales, it was much farther south than they'd guessed it would be, and was only now about to pull out of Coral Ridge Beach, a small town about ten miles below Boca Raton.

The show's delay was a stroke of luck for Saralyn, Firecloud, and the Marcuses, more than halving the trip they had to make in order to intercept it. With Marcus One behind the wheel of his Bronco—Firecloud noticed that

he'd rigged wooden blocks to the pedals so his foot could
reach them—the small band caught Alligator Alley a short
jump north of Everglades City, then shot straight across the
state to I–95, where they again doglegged north. All told,
the drive to Coral Ridge clocked in at less than three hours.
After dropping Firecloud and Saralyn off within a mile of
the railroad tracks, the twins went on to their ambush
positions.

The plan they'd devised was simple in theory: Firecloud
and Saralyn were to mix with the crowd of canvas slaves
boarding the train, then, once the trip was under way,
subdue the Front guards riding inside and at a predesignated
location up the line pull the emergency brake. As the train
came to a halt, the Marcuses would cut down the bikers
with gunfire from hiding places flanking the right-of-way,
and Zeno would be taken to freedom.

Simple in theory. And in practice filled with risk.

Firecloud raised the infrared goggles to his eyes and
looked back down. The yard was illuminated only by a trio
of arc lamps wired to a portable generator, the lights
showing as glare spots in his vision.

The train was as curious in appearance as the canvas
slaves thronged about it, having been cobbled together from
an old Amtrak diesel locomotive, two archaic Florida East
Coast–Havana coaches, and six or seven rust-eaten boxcars
and flatcars. Written across the side of the locomotive in
scrolled Old West–style lettering was: THE PRAETORIUS
CIRCUS AND CURIOSITY SHOW. The slaves had already loaded
the trucks and animal cages onto the flatties and were busily
hauling aboard the baggage crates, collapsed sideshow
booths, and miscellaneous tent gear.

At the moment Firecloud's interest was not in the carnies,
but rather their keepers.

He'd previously counted three men on bikes, with another riderless cycle leaning on its kickstand behind a Front
jeep near the station house entrance. Firecloud assumed the
fourth biker was inside, taking care of last-minute business

with Groll's contingent, napping, whatever. Odds were he was the head goon and would emerge only when the train was ready to embark.

The others sat astride their cycles, one at each end of the train, the remaining biker positioned near its middle. They held their weapons loosely in hand. They seemed to be relaxed, expecting no trouble.

The guard posted by the locomotive had on an oilskin duster which flapped about heavy knee gaiters. Underneath the long oilskin he was shirtless. His hair fell greasily around his shoulders, and he wore a thick nose-ring and smaller hoops through his nipples. Around his right wrist was a spiked leather band, on his right hand a studded leather glove with the fingers cut off. An armor gauntlet encased his left hand. His bike was a massive shovelhead Evo with a lance bungeed vertically to its rear fender and a pair of worn leather saddlebags strapped to the seat. Across his lap was a Daisy bolt-action repeater rifle. He was blowing and popping chewing gum bubbles.

Firecloud's gaze shifted to the next man down. He sat on a Harley hog and had a full-face Death Head tattoo which gave the uncanny appearance that the flesh had been stripped from his skull. Furthering the grotesque was an actual human skull mounted between the handlebars of his bike and a dozen or more scalps which trailed from the grips. He wore a cowl, a leather G-string, a bandolier, a silver conchas belt, and riding boots. His naked torso, arms, and legs composed a swirling, bulging mosaic of tattoos. He carried a Colt Delta .223 caliber semiauto with an armored scope.

The biker near the caboose was also seated upon a monster H-D. He was vastly obese, pork-faced, and bald, with a patch over one eye and a tumbleweed beard. He wore fringed leather chaps and a horn-shaped codpiece over dungarees. His T-shirt had the motto I KILL WHAT I FUCK AND I EAT WHAT I KILL! emblazoned across the chest and the Harley-Davidson insignia in back. He held a Thompson

SMG and was picking his teeth with a large bowie knife. Perhaps a dozen additional blades of varying sizes hung in scabbards from the chain around his expansive middle.

"The guards are crazies, and they've got automatic weapons," Firecloud told Saralyn in a hushed voice. "If anything goes wrong, it will be difficult for just the two of us to deal with them."

"Which means what?"

He dropped the glasses from his face and looked at her. "Only that I hope we can depend on your friends."

"The Marcuses would be climbing aboard instead of us if it weren't for having dodgers out on them," she said sharply. "You know that."

And he did. Yesterday, when the group had been debating which of its members should be the ones to slip onto the train, it was Dee who voiced the opinion that the brothers were the most logical candidates. Firecloud had been about to say the same thing. The dwarfism which made them fish out of water among normals rendered them unexceptional in the presence of canvas slaves. They, he'd thought, would be least likely to engender suspicions among the guards as to whether they belonged with the show.

The Marcuses had concurred. But then Saralyn had raised the matter of the dodgers, wanted fliers issued by carnival managers offering cash rewards for fugitive slaves.

"I ain't seen any yet with our kissers on 'em," Marcus One had said.

She'd shaken her head. "Doesn't mean they don't exist. And if they do, you'd be recognized. They circulate those bills between the carnies. One hand washing the other. The guards might not be too up on current events in most cases, but they can smell a buck, and they pay attention to the dodgers."

Her point had been well taken. It was decided that she and Firecloud would board.

Now Firecloud saw that his offhand comment about the Marcuses had tightened her jaw and put flint in her glance.

He tried to think of something to say to relieve the tension.

Behind the rise where they watched and waited, dawn seethed at the horizon.

An owl hooted from atop one of the telephone poles strung into infinity along the railbed. Animal noises from the cages on the flatties mingled with the metallic clang of couplings being made and the general human hubbub filtering upward.

When one of them finally spoke it was Saralyn. "Look, Johnny, I understand where you're coming from," she said, sounding less angry. "I've been taking care of myself since I was a kid, and when it's right down to the wire never depend on anyone. But if you're concerned whether the Marcuses can be trusted to do their part, then just take a look my way. The fact that I'm still breathing tells you they can. You won't ever see me having a lot of friends. But I never undervalue those I've got. Don't take it well when anybody else does, either."

Something stirred in Firecloud. What she'd said about having taken care of herself as a child. Was she, like him, an orphan?

But later for that. Presently no words came to him. In his life he had trusted only Charlie Tiger and Bill Coonan, both of whom he considered family. Friendship was something he'd always been wary of; he found its proximity unsettling.

He lifted the glasses, and the world went vivid green as his attention returned to the rail spur.

It was a beehive of activity.

The head biker was exiting the station house accompanied by three Front troopers and a fifth man in civilian coveralls. The grunts were quite young and seemed to defer to the biker, falling behind him. He wore a goatee and a tricorn buccaneer's hat with a large ostrich plume, and carried a bullwhip which he perfunctorily cracked against the trackbed cinders as he pressed through the clog of slaves. The M-16 slung across his back was fitted with an M203 grenade launcher, and an ammo belt laden with

40-millimeter rounds circled the waist of his leather stove-pipes.

He barked an order, snapping the whip above his head, and the carnies began grouping together between the train and the station house.

Firecloud watched the man in coveralls climb into the cab of the locomotive.

"The conductor's just boarded the train," Firecloud said and passed the goggles to Saralyn. "They'll open the doors for the passengers any minute. We'd better get down there now."

Ardelia had provided them each with a black, lightweight Supplex nylon anorak and black windpants with elasticized waists and cuffs. Saralyn folded the NVGs and stashed them in the kangaroo pocket of her jacket. The loose-fitting pants slandered her figure but effectively hid the silenced Glock pistol strapped below her knee.

"It shouldn't be difficult getting past the guards," Firecloud said. "They're on the lookout for people trying to flee the carnival, not join it willingly."

She nodded. "They quiz us, we're lion tamers. I'll try and do the talking if one of us has to. I've handled cats before and can bluff my way through." She caught his wondering glance and smiled. "Yes, I used to be a canvas slave. And no, there aren't any dodgers out for me. The ringmaster didn't live long enough to get 'em printed. Remind me to tell you about it sometime."

Rising to a crouch, he silently promised himself that he would.

"Follow my lead," he said.

They crept rapidly down the grass-carpeted slope, quiet as smoke, their black-clad bodies bent low and hidden among the shadows, springing from one position of concealment to drop behind another. Some ten yards above the station house Firecloud took cover behind a shrub and paused, his hand raised as a cue for Saralyn to do likewise.

He looked around, eyes questing, listening, alert for any sign that their presence had been detected.

From where they were they could see the back of the station house and little else. The cider glow of a kerosene lamp issued from the single window in its rear wall. The shadows beyond the window did not move. Nobody inside.

His hand made a forward motion, thumb cocked. It was okay to proceed. They scurried the rest of the way down.

They reached the station house wall in seconds. Flattening against it, heads ducked below the windowframe, they inched along toward the corner of the ramshackle structure. At the end of the wall he again gave her the handsignal to stop, and squatted, and craned his head around the corner.

The yard was a riot of fabulous, variant human forms, the born freaks walking and waddling and limping and dragging themselves alongside fellow carnies whose otherness was more a state of mind then flesh, all of them drifting into a ragged line that in places ran three and four abreast. The small Front cohort, meanwhile, had jostled through to the train. Two of the soldiers hoisted themselves onto a passenger coach. They stood flanking its open door as the third grunt and the biker with the Death Head tattoo prodded the slaves at the head of the line aboard. The other bikers, including their leader, sat on their iron horses and watched the carnies with expressions of idle contempt.

Firecloud pulled his head back, straightened, then reached behind him and tugged lightly on Saralyn's sleeve. She came up close enough for him to feel her breath on his neck.

"The guards are looking toward the train," he whispered. "We walk in side by side."

She nodded. There was just a pinpoint of tension in her eyes.

"Let's go," he whispered.

They rounded the corner of the building and entered the yard unseen. They made straight for the line, careful not to hurry, weaving past Bearded Women, Lion-Faced Girls, and a Human Skeleton; squeezing by Fat Ladies, a Snake Charmer with a huge python coiled around his neck, and a man that had the scorched, blistered lips of a Fire Eater; brushing up against a Human Pincushion and a Tattooed Man; passing Flipper Boys, Giants, Midget Quintuplets in belled court jester's costumes, and a host of other canvas slaves who provoked in Firecloud jumbled feelings of wonder, horror, and sympathy.

Seconds later they'd shuffled into line behind a man that was carrying a hurdy-gurdy under his arm and had a rhesus monkey in a red bellhop coat with goat epaulets perched on his shoulder. Not even the slaves took notice of the two infiltrators; the makeup of the carnival was fluid, Praetorius often transferring personnel between his many franchises. There was nothing unusual about having new faces appear, particularly before a major performance like that scheduled to take place at the Castillo.

Saralyn and Firecloud moved forward with the diminishing line, filing past Death Head as they approached the train. The biker's gaze swept over Firecloud with no interest. They were only a few paces from the door when his dull, baleful eyes fell on Saralyn.

"Hey you! China doll!" he snarled.

Firecloud slowed, his stomach knotting. He turned a little to watch obliquely. Death Head was looking her up and down.

Firecloud was armed only with the throwing stars in his waistpouch. If the plan went sour now, he would use one to open the biker's throat, then grab his Colt semiauto and try and take out the rest of the bikers and soldiers. Given the present circumstances, it would probably be the final act of his life. But there was no option.

Death Head licked the tip of his finger and tweaked the nipple of his tattooed breast. An illustration of a werewolf wrinkled its snout. He chuckled, put his finger to his tongue again, then reached out and lightly ran its tip down Saralyn's jawline.

Her face and body were perfectly still.

"Don't recall seeing you before, pretty China doll," he said, and gave her a salacious grin. He withdrew his hand, licked two fingers this time, then extended them and began tracing circles on the side of her neck. His spit glistened on her skin. "How long you been on the circuit?"

He licked his fingers. Lowered them to the zipper of her jacket. Tugged the catch down a little.

"Long enough to know you're an asshole. And that your face'd look right at home in that moldy G-string you wear," she said. "Now get your paw off me."

His vile good humor drained away. "What? *What did you say?*"

"Read my lips: If that zipper opens any farther, you'll lose your hand."

Firecloud nerved himself, snaked a hand toward his pouch. In front of him the organ-grinder's monkey, sensing the building hostility, released a high-strung squeal. It slapped and bounced agitatedly on its master's back.

Death Head's hooded, chalk-white skullface flushed with incongruous spots of bright red. "You gonna find out what I got packed in my G-string, Chinkbitch. You gonna—"

His threat was curtailed by the loud snap of a whip.

The frightened monkey screeched.

Death Head looked suddenly over his right shoulder, toward the end of the line.

Pirate Hat was glaring at him from across the yard.

"Quit gummin' the works, man," he shouted. "We're gettin' paid to watch the slaves, not hassle 'em!"

"But she said—"

"I don't give a fuck if she called your dead mother the scabby whore that she was! You got personal business with her, take it up later. We got to roll!"

Death Head opened his mouth, closed it, opened it again. His furious, frustrated gaze slammed into her. "See you when the train stops, Chinkbitch."

She stared back at him for a moment without answering, then continued toward the passenger car.

A relieved breath hissed through Firecloud's gritted teeth.

Saralyn saw the muscles in his neck and arms unbind.

"Why, Johnny," she whispered, "I think you were actually concerned about me back there."

He gave no indication that he'd heard her.

They got on board the train.

Chapter Fourteen ═══════════

When it went down, it went down fast and hard, and—
thanks to the monkey—not at all according to plan.

The interior of each coach had two rows of double seats
on either side of a central aisle. The first passenger car was
already full as Firecloud and Saralyn entered, so they made
their way to the connecting door and went through into the
second. There they took adjoining seats on the right,
midway down the length of the car, behind a husband and
wife team of mentalists who soon began arguing loudly and
without pause about the necessity of making changes in
their act.

Minutes after they were seated, the train tooted its horn
and pulled from the siding onto the main track, bogies
creaking rustily as it gained speed and traction.

"Did you notice Zeno? He's in the first coach. Fourth or
fifth row, beside the Snake Charmer," Firecloud whispered,
his lips barely moving. He was reclining in his seat, his eyes
slitted, head swaying against the backrest with the movement of the train. If the guard at the head of the car glanced
in his direction, he would appear somnolent. "I think he
might have recognized you as we went by him, but I'm not
certain."

"Been around two years since we've seen each other.
I've got a different haircut, don't wear my makeup the
same. And this is the last place he'd expect me to be." She
had taken the inside seat, and the half of her face nearest
the window was rosy with the light of infant dawn.

Firecloud was conscious of the high, feminine cast of her cheekbones. "The bikers're riding in a diamond formation. One ahead of the locomotive on the right embankment, one following the train on the left, the other two yo-yos flanking the middle of the train."

The mentalist in front of Firecloud called his wife a foul name and sprang angrily out of his seat. He stalked up the aisle, grumbling. Two rows up, the high-strung rhesus monkey poked its head above the organ-grinder's shoulder, its black watery eyes anxiously clinging to the irate performer. The single Front soldier stationed by the door at the head of the car was also watching the man, his face drawn and sleepy.

"Care to tell me where you're going?" he asked mildly as the mentalist approached.

"Been married to me for ten years and she can't get more'n the same two codes straight! How many times does she think the rubes'll fall for the *same stunts*?"

"Alls I asked is where you're going," the guard said.

"To the can, that's where! Always to the can when he gets mad!" the wife shouted from her seat. "Whyn't you tell him to do the world a favor and flush himself?"

"Dummy! Ten years with her and she ain't learned—"

"Spare me, both of you." The guard motioned him on, frowning, and paced listlessly toward the rear.

"We just passed milepost 60," Saralyn said to Firecloud.

He made some simple mental calculations. The Marcuses had told him there were mileposts at twelve-mile intervals all along the route. The previous marker had been back at the station, and the train had been moving for less than fifteen minutes. So it was traveling at better than fifty miles an hour. The brothers were waiting at milepost 96, which meant he and Saralyn needed to take out the guards and stop the train in under three-quarters of an hour. Not much time.

Saralyn's thoughts had coincided with his. "I'd better go talk to Zeno," she said, and then rose and slid into the aisle.

The guard stepped directly into her path. "Stall's occupied, 'case you haven't heard," he said. "Or maybe you got pressing business someplace else."

"There's a rest room in the other coach, too," she said. "And a friend of mine in there's got Dramamine. For my motion sickness."

"Man, I love this run. It's like being a counselor at Goddamned day camp," he said, giving her a look of profound annoyance. "Go ahead."

He shifted aside.

Firecloud watched as Saralyn went through the door between cars, and after the door slammed shut watched through its window as she moved past one of the two guards in the forward coach, then down the aisle to where Zeno sat. She touched the blond man's shoulder and he looked up, his face neutral at first, then flooding with surprise. He smiled delightedly, took her hand into both of his, started rising as if to embrace her or offer her his seat. But she gestured for him to stay put, crouched so their faces were level and very close, and spoke to him. She was also smiling, seemed genuinely pleased to see him. Though Firecloud noticed the underlying graveness in her expression, he didn't think the disinterested, lackadaisical guards would pick up on it. Zeno listened to her, attentive. Said something. Listened again, nodding. They talked a moment longer. Then she straightened, and maintaining her pretense for the benefit of the guards, entered the bathroom stall.

Five minutes later she was back in her seat beside Firecloud.

"Zeno's raring to go," she whispered to him. "He was pretty incredulous, though. Kept looking at me like he was dreaming."

The train rolled on. Through the window Firecloud glimpsed a slumped and faded building that had once been a motor inn. In place of the swinging vacancy sing was a rough plank on which was written RANDY'S HOUSE OF GOOD HEAD and underneath that the word LIVEWIRE—the slang name for the exotic, mind-bending superamphetamine/mescaline/heroin cocktail that had saturated Florida's east coast, putting its addicted users into permanent fast-forward and turning the city of Miami into a doorless lunatic asylum. The drugs, supplied by Cuban allies of the National Front, complemented the Front's intimidation tactics in suppressing any kind of unified uprising, ensuring that hundreds or even thousands of potential rebels remained stoned out of their heads, and thus nullified.

The tracks curved, and the drug emporium vanished from sight. Ahead, beyond a scattering of dogwoods that bloomed unmuted pink in the brightening morning, Firecloud saw milepost 72.

Saralyn gave him a significant look. They had less than half an hour to take the train.

Beneath them, metal wheels pounded their steady, monotonous rhythm, lulling most of the passengers into a doze. But Firecloud noticed several of those still awake flicking intermittent, covert glances in his direction.

Saralyn saw him look at them looking at him. "They're nervous," she whispered. "Zeno's spread word that there's going to be a break. He doesn't want anybody panicking and getting in the way. I think he did the right thing."

"You should have asked me," he said, lifting an eyebrow. "When too many ears hear a secret it stops being one. If the guards get wind—"

"He wouldn't have gone along with us otherwise." She paused. "Put yourself in his shoes. These are his people. Being on the train now puts them at risk, whether they like it or not. They deserve to know what's happening."

He was silent, the concern and displeasure still showing on his face.

"The carnies'll keep mum," Saralyn reassured him. "They—"

She dropped off in midsentence, her gaze darting suddenly over her shoulder as the car's rear door clattered open.

"Check it out, Johnny," she whispered urgently.

He was already doing that.

The soldier had gone out onto the platform between the coach and the flatcar behind it. He'd engaged the latch that held the door open, probably less because he wanted to be able to keep an eye on the slaves than because he didn't want his fellow guards to think he was shirking his duty if they happened to see him outside. Yawning, he slung his gun over his back, then reached into the breastpocket of his tunic, producing a package of cigarettes and a book of safety matches. He yawned again and shook a smoke from the pack. Stifling a third yawn, he jammed the cigarette into his mouth, held a match to its tip, and stood puffing and staring out across the tracks.

"That's our green light," Saralyn whispered.

"I'll take care of the two in the forward car," Firecloud said, nodding. "Keep an eye on me through the window. Wait until after I've—"

"No. It has to be the other way around."

He looked at her.

"Those guards didn't bother me the first time, and I doubt they'll ask questions if I go back in," she said. "Face it, Johnny, I'm the one with the nice legs."

He instantaneously realized three things: that he had taken hold of her elbow, that she had become very important to him, and that he didn't want to let go. But what she'd said made ironclad sense. She looked at his hand on her arm and then looked knowingly into his eyes.

"I'll be all right," she said.

He met her gaze a moment longer. His grip relaxed.

She reached under the elastic cuff of her windpants, drew the Glock pistol, quickly slipped it up her leg and into a sidepocket. The pistol was undiscernible. Her hand remained in the pocket with it.

She moved into the aisle, grasped the armrest of Firecloud's seat to brace herself against the rocking of the train, and then went forward.

He glanced back over his shoulder. The guard was still

puffing on his cigarette and gazing remotely outward, uncaring, his profile to the interior of the car.

Firecloud swallowed apprehensively. There was no moisture. His throat was a desert. He looked straight ahead. Saralyn had entered the other coach. He saw through the window that the soldiers were stationed at opposite ends of the car. Facing one another. Saralyn would be between them when she struck. Whichever man she chose to put away second would see what was happening to his partner and have a chance to react. She would have to be fast, faster than him.

She took a step past the first soldier. The carnies were stirring in their seats, tension evident in their faces. Saralyn took another step and another, and then partway through the fourth step swiveled on her heel, and Firecloud leaned forward and did not breath as the pistol in her hand came out and up, its muzzle flaring. The impact of the bullet spun the guard around and knocked him into the door, his wide-eyed face mashing against the glass, and then his head drooled red blood and gray-white brains as the second bullet to be spat from the Glock rammed into the back of his skull and exited the front to strike the window, causing a star fracture to appear in it. His body slid down the door, followed by chunks of his forehead. Firecloud stared through the smeary, broken window. He saw Saralyn whirl on the other guard, saw him bring up his rifle even as she leveled her Glock at him, holding it in both hands with her feet apart. The carnies in the car huddled together in their seats, all except Zeno, who sprang from his, the gleam of the knife that was suddenly in his hand distracting the guard. For a stalled moment the guard seemed to be trying to decide which of them to fire at, but whatever his choice was or would have been, it was too late for him. In that brief, dangling eternity Firecloud saw Saralyn's wrist buck from recoil as she shot her gun, saw Zeno throw the knife with such quicksilver speed that it seemed to wink out of existence and then wink back in again buried in the guard's throat. The guard dropped his gun and staggered backward and doubled over and fell, clawing at the knife with one hand and clutching his spurting, bullet-stitched chest with the other.

It had played out like a silent movie before an audience of mannequins, the roar and clank of the train muffling all sound from the forward car, the canvas slaves in Firecloud's coach rigid and unspeaking as they watched events run their course. Only the organ-grinder's monkey was animated, shivering and whimpering nervously.

Firecloud left his seat with a bound that carried him into the aisle, then turned, and then was moving toward the back of the car. Taking large strides, almost loping, his keen sense of balance instantly compensating for the lurch of the train. His hand went into his waistpouch and came out with a *shiruken*. He did not like to kill cold-bloodedly, but he would do it now as he'd been forced to before.

The guard was smoking and oblivious. Firecloud cocked his wrist for a toss that would propel the razored throwing star into the back of the man's head and cut the spinal cord where it was connected with the skull.

That was when the tightly wound monkey caved in from stress.

And screamed.

The screechy cry climbed up and up the scale, slicing above the rumble of the train before the organ-grinder finally clamped his hand over the creature's mouth. The monkey, not to be interrupted, chomped down on the organ-grinder's palm, causing him to scream.

An instant later their voices joined together in an aria of ragged shrieks.

By which time the guard had already been startled from his reverie.

He spun toward the inside of the car, the remainder of his cigarette dropping from his mouth, the stock of his rifle coming up against his shoulder, his finger squeezing back on the trigger.

As the gun coughed its salvo, Firecloud dove sideways out of the aisle, falling across the laps of a pair of Siamese Twins.

"Yeeeoouch, you're hurtin' my legs!" one of them hollered, his face crinkling like a baked apple.

"Hurry and get going!" his brother shouted, gesticulating furiously. "He's escaping to the top of the car!"

Firecloud boosted himself back into the aisle. Outside, the soldier's foot stepped up off a metal rung and vanished above the doorway. Firecloud chased after him at once. Wind resistance blasted him as he reached the platform. He fought against it, grasped one of the lower rungs beside the door, and climbed hastily.

He crouched on the roof, hands on the cold steel, his senses adjusting to the sudden openness. Here, exposed, it seemed to him that the train was rocking harder and chugging along at a greater speed than it really was. Sky and countryside welded smoothly and blurred out. Several yards ahead and on either embankment Firecloud saw the bikers keeping pace with the train. Farther up beside the locomotive the lead bike raised a rooster tail of dust. The growl of motorcycles and rhythmical clank of train wheels were far-away sounds in the rushing windstream.

A half second passed. A whole second. His center of gravity settled back into place. He peered ahead, saw the guard a little more than midway toward the front of the car. His head start might have taken him farther, but unlike Firecloud he hadn't yet gotten his bearings. He ran with his arms flailing and his feet stumbling precariously along the roof.

Firecloud plunged forward, hoping to catch the soldier before the bikers noticed them atop the train.

Each step was surer than the last. The gap between Firecloud and his quarry shrank quickly, and he caught up just as the guard reached the edge of the car and was about to leap onto the forward coach. He shot a hand out, clutching. But his arm was stiff from the injury he'd gotten in battle with the White Trash, and he barely missed grabbing hold of the guard's tunic. The soldier chanced a look back over his shoulder, and Firecloud glimpsed his terrified face and the taut, bulging ligaments of his neck. Firecloud's hand snatched at his collar, but again the guard broke away, putting on an unexpected burst of speed. He sprang onto the next car and landed on his belly.

Firecloud made the jump right behind him, his feet coming down solidly. He straddled the floundering soldier, grabbed the back of his collar, jerked him erect. The guard had shouldered his rifle, and now he brought it up and around, gripping it by the barrel, spinning toward Firecloud as he tried to smash its stock against Firecloud's head. Firecloud dodged the swinging gun butt without releasing the guard's tunic, and with his free hand extracted a *shiruken* from his pouch to replace the one he'd dropped in the train. He pulled the guard to him, opened his throat with a vicious slash of the throwing star, then heaved him away.

The guard skid-skated backward, his eyes wet and white, his head rolling loosely on his shoulders. The torn flesh of his neck formed gaping lips which slobbered blood over the gleamingly embedded *shiruken*. A sliced artery lolled from the wound, blurting crimson jets that the wind swirled around his face and then scattered into a fine spray.

His mouth open in a soundless scream, he fell over the side of the train like a sack of wet rags.

Firecloud threw himself flat to avoid being spotted by the bikers. He lay for a moment catching his breath. His injured arm was complaining, but the bandage under his sleeve felt dry, and he didn't think the wound had reopened.

The sky had turned the shimmery bleached-out blue of full morning. It occurred to him with sharp, sudden urgency that the train must be closing in on milepost 96.

He had to get inside.

He scrambled back to the edge of the car on hands and knees, then rose on his haunches, intending to swing down to the platform.

Just then a bullet punched into the roof inches from his feet.

He bellied down again. Two more slugs snapped into the train near him.

He looked in the direction of the gunfire. On the crest of the embankment, the biker in the oilskin duster pumped another round from his Daisy rifle, managing to shoot with only his right hand while wrestling down the cycle's raked front end with his gauntleted left. The bullet whizzed past Firecloud's head; had he not been stretched flat, there would have been nothing left of him above the shoulders. This man was a crack shot even riding a motorcycle, but he wouldn't be able to hit Firecloud as long as he stayed low.

Oilskin was apparently quick to realize that.

Slinging the gun across his back, he jockeyed his custom hog to a wheelstand, juiced its throttle, and took it down the bank in a wailing high-speed run. The fiery breath of its tailpipe scorched the ground. Its rear tire spun up sod and pebbles.

The cycle bounced to the bottom of the grade and zoomed straight across the southbound tracks toward what appeared to be a certain collision with the train. But at the last instant the biker cut a hard right and pulled parallel to the coach Firecloud was riding atop. A mad dog grin on his face, he rose to a standing position on the shovelhead's foot pegs and jumped off, grasping for the rungs on the side of the railroad car.

Incredibly, he caught hold. The motorbike tore from between his legs like an unreined metal bronco. It flipped end over end and then down on its side and scraped over the gravelly railbed at better than 80 m.p.h., sparks flying from its spoked chrome hubcaps.

Firecloud got onto his haunches as Oilskin spidered up the rungs, the wind rippling his duster out behind him. A steel-gloved hand topped the roof of the train. Firecloud stamped down on the biker's arm above the gauntlet. He kept grinning his mad dog grin. His hand briefly retreated, came lunging again. Firecloud backpedaled. But a strong gust pulled him off balance, and he moved a beat too late.

The biker snared his right ankle, *yanked*.

For a moment Firecloud swayed at the edge of the roof. Then his feet slid out from under him, and he went over into space.

His arms and legs bumping against the side of the train, the wind whining in his ears, the ground rushing up fast to meet him, Firecloud reached for a handhold in desperate, lightninglike reflex. His fingers strained to their limit, skidded off a rung, blindly grabbed nothing but air, grabbed again—

—And caught onto Oilskin's sleeve.

The biker thrashed and jerked crazily, trying to shake him off, like an animal shaking off fleas. But Firecloud's fingers had dug in hard. He climbed up Oilskin's back, one hand locked on his elbow, gathering the cloth of the duster in his opposite fist. He felt seams rip, then thought he felt the billowing overgarment sag and begin to tear away in his hand . . . though it may have been the biker himself that was slipping, losing his grip on the rung.

Firecloud slid down a little. He gasped, his heart knocking. The train negotiated a hump in the trackbed and bucked. He held on, pulled himself up, but knew it couldn't go on much longer. Something would give. His grip, the biker's grip, or the duster. Whichever, he'd fall. And if hitting the ground didn't kill him, the other three bikers surely would.

They hung with Firecloud's chest against Oilskin's back, their legs dangling. The wind slapped at them, tried to peel them from the side of the train. Firecloud still had his right hand on the biker's right elbow and the other hand clenched around a wad of his duster above the left hip. He let go of the duster, shot his freed left hand up over the biker's shoulder, and grabbed a rung . . . the same rung Oilskin was clutching.

Oilskin swung his head around and glanced at him. The

grin was gone from the biker's mouth. It had curved into a
snarl, and there were white petals of foam at its corners. His
eyes were raging white disks. The veins in his temples
bulged like mountain ranges on a topographical map.

"*Off me!*" he shouted. "*Get off me, fucker!*"

His gauntleted fist swung down on the hand with which
Firecloud had snatched the rung. Pain flared through
Firecloud's knuckles. The metal rung clanged like a bell.
The fist hammered and hammered. Firecloud ground his
teeth, holding on. His fingers bled and grew numb under the
crunching blows. His right hand released the biker's arm,
reached up and across Oilskin's body, grabbed the long,
greasy hair at the back of his head, and whacked the biker's
face down against his own spiked wristband. The biker
groaned aloud. Firecloud pulled his head back, slammed it
down again with a mashing, twisting motion.

Bloody gouges appeared on the biker's face. He cursed
and, through torn lips, gasped like a drowning man. Blood
and mucus dripped over his nose-ring. A wide gash
had opened above his eye, and a hunk of skin flapped from
his cheek. The muscles of his neck thickened as he
struggled against Firecloud, but Firecloud was stronger and
had leverage working for him. His arm cranked Oilskin's
head relentlessly.

A spike on the wristband sank into the biker's eyeball and
popped it like a grape. He made a weak, froglike sound, his
iris oozing down his collapsed face in a wash of blood and
vitreous jelly.

Then, at last, his hand went slack, and he slumped down
between Firecloud's arms and fell to the rails.

Firecloud hauled himself back to the top of the car. In
seconds his upper body was on the roof, then his leg. Then
the other leg hooked over, and he was up. He squatted. The
train shook and pounded along the tracks, and underneath
its thunder he could hear the sound of gunfire. He looked
down, saw the three remaining scooter tramps peppering the
coaches with bursts from their automatics. Return fire was

coming from the windows—that would be Saralyn and her friend Zeno.

He looked up the line.

And saw milepost 96 not a quarter mile ahead, reflecting glary dashes of sunlight, the stretch of track that ran to the marker vanishing like a lit fuse beneath the wheels of the train.

No time to waste. Histamines flooding his bloodstream, he raced to the rear end of the car, dropped down onto the platform, and pulled open the door to the coach in which he and Saralyn had ridden.

Most of the carnies were ducked low in their seats, some of them under the seats.

As he'd expected, Saralyn was at the window. In her battle frenzy her face had taken on an expression that was almost like lust, her cheeks flushed, jaw muscles working, eyes slotted. The M-16 she'd grabbed from one of the dead Front guards jolted and racketed against her shoulder.

A peripheral glance into the forward coach showed him Zeno chopping bullets out the window with another appropriated M-16. The turbaned Snake Charmer that had been seated beside Zeno had also joined the gunfight. His python was a living collar around his neck. In his hand was Saralyn's Glock.

Firecloud dashed toward the metal box on the wall that held the compressed-air emergency brake. A matter of yards now until they reached the milepost. He opened the door, reached in for the braking lever . . . and a blitz of armor-piercing slugs chewed through the wall of the train inches to the left of the box. Jagged metal nuggets flew inward. His hand fluttering from the brake control, he ducked to the right and backward an instant before the storm of shrapnel would have minced him to ribbons.

He was aware of Saralyn's voice rising above the screams of the panic-stricken carnies.

"The milepost!" She was shouting. *"Johnny, pull the brake. I can see the milepost!"*

He literally vaulted across the aisle and shoved his arm
into the box again and wrenched the lever.

The train grated to a squealing, shuddering halt. Carnies
spilled into the aisles, screaming and waving their arms.
Saralyn was thrown from the window, her gun rabbiting out
of her hand. Firecloud stumbled backward against a chair,
clenched its armrest to anchor himself against the violent
jarring. The organ-grinder's monkey bounced past his head
in a furry, howling ball.

Outside, the confused bikers momentarily held their fire,
sat revving the dynamo engines of their bikes while trying
to understand why the train had stopped.

Then the Marcuses' Winchester riot guns bellowed their
strident thunder into the uneasy silence. Firecloud sprinted
out between the coaches for a better look at what was
happening. Saralyn scooped up her rifle and followed close
on his heels.

The Marcuses had taken positions on either embankment,
about ten yards to the rear of where the bikers had been
tooling. Surprised and outflanked, two of the goons met
their ends almost immediately. One of the riot guns
boomed, and on the left embankment Death Head's cycle
kicked up onto its front tire and threw the biker over its tall
handlebars. He sailed toward the crest of the slope, buckshot tearing into his half-naked, tattooed body and knocking
him out of the air like a skeet. He landed in a sprawl across
the railroad ties, intestines dolloping from an opened
middle.

The fat biker with the tumbleweed beard was on the right
bank. He dropped next. One moment he was astride his
Harley, gaping down at the tangled spill of guts that had
been his confederate. The next instant Marcus Two appeared from cover across the tracks and blew the biker off
the saddle. His hog slewed over the bank, its massive
eight-hundred-pound frame pancaking heavily onto Death
Head's corpse.

The biker in the pirate hat now had only himself to lead—and he wasn't going down easy.

He'd been riding point on the left side of the tracks, keeping a consistent dozen yards ahead of the locomotive. Now he wheeled his bike around, throttled it, and dragged straight for Marcus Two. He waved his M-16/M203 over his head like a saber, his finger on the trigger of the rifled aluminum grenade launcher attachment.

Both Firecloud and Saralyn recognized the characteristic bloop of the tube ejecting a 40-millimeter cartridge which spun toward the dwarf at 3,700 RPM.

"Christ!" she hissed, her body pressed against Firecloud's side on the coach platform. Her hand locked on his arm. "He shot a fucking grenade at Mar—"

An explosive roar gobbled her words as the fragmentation round, armed by its centrifugally activated fuse, slammed a smoking crater into the embankment.

But the dwarf that had been its intended target was already gone. He'd evacuated a split second before impact, leaping down over the seven-foot slope to the tracks, avoiding both the blast and the ensuing hail of shrapnel. He came down on his feet, bounced as if on a pogo stick, then sprang into an evasive pattern of flips and somersaults as Pirate Hat pulled his bike to a screaming halt and again tried to draw a bead on him.

Over the next twelfth of a minute Firecloud had cause to remember a comment Saralyn had made about the twins on the night he'd watched their exercise session: *"You should see them operate in a fight. It's a real eyeful."*

It was, indeed, something to see.

In the first second, Marcus One came sliding down the right embankment, his riot gun strapped across his back, shouting coded signals like a football quarterback. In the following two seconds, his twin responded with a well-rehearsed combination of athletic flips, drawing Pirate Hat's machine gun fire while Marcus One cut across the tracks and moved into position for a counterattack. At the top of the fourth second, Marcus Two pulled a handstand on the rails almost directly below the biker, who was by then stuffing another shell into the grenade launcher tube. At the bottom of that same second, Marcus Two did a full flip, and landing with his feet on his brother's—their soles coming together like the opposite halves of a playing card—was cannoned into the air with a synchronized thrust of both their legs.

In the fifth second, having soared above the crest of the embankment, Marcus Two swung his gun around and pumped a load of buckshot almost point-blank into Pirate Hat's dumbfounded face.

Then the Marcuses were triumphantly hugging and high-fiving each other. They pranced about in circles, their feet raising puffs of gravel and sandy earth. After a minute Marcus One turned toward Saralyn and Firecloud on the train and waved, his fingers forming the V-for-victory sign.

Saralyn raised her hand in an identical gesture.

Firecloud heard her release a prolonged, unmistakably relieved sigh.

"They did it," she said to him, sounding proud and relieved at the same time. "I told you they'd do it."

"Yes," he said. "Yes, you did, Saralyn."

They looked at each other and smiled.

"Well, that's one rescue down and one to go," she said after a moment. "Our team's gotten off to a honey of a start, huh?"

"Yes," he said. "We—"

His smile suddenly disappeared.

"I say something wrong?" she said.

"The conductor," he said. "We forgot about him. He may have radioed for help. And if he restarts the train—"

"C'mon," she said.

They ran back inside, wriggling through a mass of carnies whose mood had shifted from terror to cheering elation—and found the conductor unconscious on the floor at the forward end of the coach.

Zeno and the Snake Charmer were standing over his body.

Saralyn gave the blond a questioning look.

He grinned and nodded toward the swarthy, whipcord-thin Snake Charmer. "Mohammed here ran into the loco-motive cab and knocked him out," he said, raising his voice so it could be heard above the jubilant commotion around them. "Mo's got these darts. He dips them in all kinds of homemade concoctions."

"He will sleep for many hours," the Snake Charmer said, looking pleased with himself. His Indonesian accent turned the word *will* into *vill*. "I stick him with extract of chinaberry tree. Very, very potent."

He petted the big snake that was coiled around his neck.

The Siamese Twins Firecloud had fallen across earlier sidled up behind him and began slapping him on the back.

"You cut our shackles, man," one of them said. "Thanks."

"No hard feelings about the bruises on my legs," the other said. "Not after what you did."

"Nice to be appreciated," Saralyn grumbled.

Zeno introduced himself to Firecloud, offering his hand. The gesture was not automatic for Seminoles as it was for whites, and it took Firecloud an instant to reciprocate. If the blond man noticed, he didn't seem offended.

"Saralyn tells me you need a helo jock," the knife thrower said, leaning closer to Firecloud so that only he would hear.

"Someone that can pilot a Strikehawk." Firecloud's voice was also hushed.

Zeno scrubbed his cheek thoughtfully. "Won't say I've actually handled one of those birds . . . but I flew Apaches and Cobras back before Rev II, and don't think there'll be too much of a problem. 'Course I'll have to check her out, to be sure."

"The conditions you'd be flying under . . . what we are planning . . . will be jeopardous."

"Hell," Zeno said, laughing suddenly. "I didn't think you

went to all this trouble to free me just so I could take you sight-seeing!"

Firecloud nodded, then looked at Saralyn. "We'd better tell the carnies to get moving. In case the conductor called ahead for help."

"The ones that *want* to leave, that is. I'll bet some of them are so well trained they'll sit around and wait for the Front to come get 'em."

"Their choice," he said.

"Speaking of which," Mohammed broke in, "I would very much like to—"

Several feet to the right of where they stood, the door to the bathroom swung open with a loud crash. The mentalist stepped out of the stall, tucking his shirttail into his pants.

"They oughtta put shocks under that toilet bowl, way you feel the bumps on it," he complained, glancing around. "Anybody know what's holding us up?"

Firecloud just looked at Saralyn and tiredly shook his head.

Chapter Fifteen ═══════════════

Tuesday, July 17th.

Though Ed Mason's room at Piedmont Hospital in Free Atlanta was dark and silent when the nurse entered at 3:00 A.M., Mason himself was starey-eyed awake.

He'd been resting poorly since his admission six days ago, and during the last forty-eight hours in particular hadn't been able to sleep a wink. Like a salmon swimming upstream, his mind kept returning to his troubles, no matter how battered and weary it became, and in spite of his every effort to steer it toward calmer waters. Not that there were many opportunities for diversion while stuck in a traction frame. He'd even tried daydreaming about women. Sleek, naked women with scented oils rubbed into their breasts; ready, waiting women moaning like panthers in heat spread-eagled on beds the size of Asia, their nipples hard and palpitant, muscular harvest moon buttocks invitingly propped on tassled, satiny pillows; women whose moist, expert lips would—

He sighed inwardly. Fantasies like that just would lead him to physical rather than mental stress, considering that Molly Hand and four of her five daughters were presently slung to his traction frame in ten-ton casts, and that little Miss Pinky couldn't get around much on her own.

Dashing himself against his troubles seemed to be the lesser of two evils.

As the nurse opened the door, her body was briefly silhouetted in a bar of light from the hall. Eddie heard the *chock-chock!* of a lever being pulled on one of the snack machines somewhere past the nurses' station. That would be his so-called guard doing what he did best. The nurse didn't have a bad figure. The regular nurse on this shift—or anyway the one who'd been coming around all week— looked like the backside of a tractor trailer. He hoped she'd been replaced. For good. Not that for good meant much in his case. Not when his world would probably be coming to an end within two days.

The door quietly closed behind her, and the bar of light shrank out of existence. She faded in the dark. Her crepe-soled shoes moved like air across the floor. He wondered what she was up to. This late, they didn't usually do more than slip their heads in and out, maybe have a peek at the monitors to make sure his readings were okay— leastways they hadn't since the first couple of nights, when everybody'd been real concerned about his health. Union cops, the military boys, the special government agents in their blue suits. All of them with their stack of photos, sketches, and endless questions.

Ed had really found himself the toast of the town after he'd looked at the mug shots and recognized the face of the whackadoo to whom he'd given the bombs. Wiley Pike. Arsonist, kidnapper, nasty guy. Pike and the bombs, Ed had learned, had been old friends at the time of the delivery. He'd had something to do with their production, and gotten separated from them somehow or other, and someway slipped into Free Atlanta without them. Being a wanted man in the FSU, he'd figured that if he got caught sneaking over the border, it was better to be nabbed without his explosive babies—to keep them out of the FSU's hands so that someone else could finish the job he was coming to do. Pike and his zookeeper Slade had decided to smuggle them in separately by courier, which was where Ed had been brought into the picture.

And when his troubles had begun.

The nurse was at the foot of the bed, looking down at

him. She was carrying a tray. He remained still, keeping his eyes nearly closed, not wanting her to know he was awake. Maybe the doctors had decided to step up his medication. Maybe she was going to jab him with a needle or make him pop some pills or stick a thermometer in his face. Now if she wanted to stick a tittie in his face, that'd be another story, heh-heh. But he didn't want to be hassled. Not tonight. Didn't even want more painkillers. Regardless of how many he took, he felt constantly as if mechanical ants were gnawing at his bones with steel mandibles. And no amount of painkillers or medication would save him from the blast. He just wanted to be left alone in his misery.

The initial attention he'd gotten from Johnny Law had been different; he'd kind of liked feeling important for once in his life. Like he mattered for something. But that hadn't lasted. He'd been able to identify Pike for his interrogators, which had made them happier than pigs in shit, but they'd quickly soured on him after they discovered he couldn't help them beyond that. He didn't know what alias Pike was using or where he was staying or where he was planting the bombs. He couldn't tell them. Was it his fault he was just a courier? His fault Slade had kept him in the dark? Anyway, he'd started out at the hospital with an army of guards posted at his door round-the-clock. He was a valued informant, and the FSU wanted to make sure he stayed safe and sound. Then, three, four days ago, after the bastards had squeezed everything they could out of him, his stock had dropped. *Plummeted*. The army of guards had been reduced to a handful. And for the past couple of nights there'd only been some rumpled slob assigned to watch him. That guy spent most of his time checking out the nurses at their station and the rest of his time at the snack machines.

Now Ed felt used, lied to, and discarded. Now he could think about nothing but his unceasing pain and the fact that he was still in Free Atlanta. Still here, just two days before the scheduled Tri-territorial Summit, forty-eight hours be-

fore the city was supposed to be blown to kingdom come.
Still here, though he'd begged and pleaded to be moved out
of town and refused to talk until the law boys had promised
him they'd do so. Still here, without adequate protection
from the Front, and specifically from Lieutenant Slade,
who'd surely consider him a squealer and . . .

And why was the nurse creeping around his room at this
odd, ungodly hour anyway? She had come around his bed
and set the tray on the rolling night table, and why the fuck
was he pretending he was asleep when all he wanted was to
be left alone!

"Hey, you, you're disturbin' me," he said crankily.
"Ain't do for no medicine, and I'm trying to catch some
shut-eye."

"I'm sorry if I woke you," she said. "I'll try to be more
quiet."

He saw her smile sweetly at him in the dim light coming
through the window blind. Her face rated up there with her
curvacious bod. Smooth high forehead under her nurse's
cap, good cheekbones, button nose, pouty, sensitive kind of
mouth. Pouty mouths were a definite turn-on. But so what?
Why be nice to her? She wasn't about to strip out of that
cute white skirt and swing from the traction rig in only a bra
and panties. She wasn't going to let him cop a feel of her
perky little ass . . . or do anything but be a pain in his.

"Quiet doing what?" he asked. "I'm breathing. My
heart's tickin'. What's so important it couldn't wait?"

She laughed a little and reached for something on her tray
and sat in the plastic chair at his bedside. "I'm going to give
you a shave."

He blinked, wondering if he'd heard her correctly.

"Huh? A *what*?" he asked.

"A shave," she said. "A clean, close shave."

"At three in the morning? You're kidding." He looked at
her. "I mean, you are kidding me . . . right?"

She shook her head. Smiling. "No joke. It's our policy."

He looked at her hands and saw that the object she'd

gotten off the tray was a roll of bandage tape. She snapped off its outer ring and set it down on the tray and picked the edge of the tape off the spool.

Then she measured out a length of tape and held it taut above his face.

Suddenly his annoyance and confusion hardened into a cold brick of fear. "Whose pol—?"

She slapped the tape down onto his mouth before he could complete his question.

"National Front policy," she said, leaning close, her hand on his mouth. He thrashed, whinnied, as the ends of his broken bones ground together. "Lieutenant Varnum Slade's policy," she said, reaching back to her tray again, slipping a straight razor from underneath a folded towelette. Her sensitive smile had become a gallow's grin.

"*My* policy, you filthy snitching worm!" she said.

And slashed the blade deep into his throat, dragging it across from earlobe to earlobe.

When she left the room minutes later, closing the door quietly behind her, the guard was just returning from the vending machines. He'd been there for almost half an hour trying to decide what to munch on, finally settling upon some sugar-glazed peanuts, a chocolate bar, two bags of potato chips, and a soft drink. He'd already eaten most of the chips.

Passing him, the woman in the nurse's uniform smiled.

He smiled back, wiping a crumb off his mouth. Then, lowering himself into his chair outside Ed Mason's door, he watched her walk to the bank of elevators down the hall.

His eyes tracked her shapely legs until the elevator doors shut them from view.

At eight o'clock on the morning of July 17th, two plainclothes Union Defense Force agents were having breakfast in an unmarked sedan parked behind a No Parking sign across the street from the Omni Hotel at the FNN Center. The windows of the old 1998 Dodge were rolled

down because its air conditioner was on the fritz. Replace-
ment auto parts were by and large manufactured in the
Japanese-controlled eastern United States and their cost was
exorbitant. UDF funds were tight, and the money allocated
to the car pool went toward keeping the vehicles in basic
running condition. The comfort of the agents assigned to
those vehicles was not given a high priority.

Though it was early in the day, the Dodge's overhead
digital thermometer registered a stifling 86 degrees outside
the windshield. Such hot spells had once been rare due to
the city's high elevation; but the Greenhouse Effect had
changed that forever.

Thanks to a moderating cross breeze, the agents in the
Dodge were only half-cooked. The junior of the pair,
Investigator Second-Class Vince Neal, sat in the front
passenger seat eating custard doughnuts and drinking cola
from a can. The older, heavier man behind the wheel,
Investigator First-Class Tom Lombardi, was nibbling without relish at a wedge of whole wheat toast smeared with a
soybean-derived butter substitute and sipping lukewarm
herbal tea. At his last required physical he'd been told that
his blood pressure was dangerously high and that there was
enough cholesterol in his arteries to clog a city water main
and that he needed to lose at least thirty pounds. The doctor
had put him on a strict diet, which his wife had been
enforcing with thuggish zeal. You survived the nuking of
New York, she'd reminded him, as if he had needed
reminding. I will not let the cause of your death be
something as stupid as drinking too many vanilla milk
shakes, Shirley had said. You are going to promise me you
will stick to this diet, or else. Being wisely afraid of her *or
elses*, he had promised. And being a man of his word, he
was sticking. He'd tried very hard to convince himself that
Neal's reckless eating habits in no way enticed him to cheat.
Right now he was eyeing Neal's doughnut and thinking
he would trade his teenaged son into slavery for a single bite
of it.

"Can't believe you actually like those things," he said, glumly swallowing a bite of his toast. The artificial butter tasted like . . . well, artificial butter.

"What things?" Neal asked, smacking his lips.

"That custard doughnut. Sugary stuff in general. I mean, I used to have a sweet tooth when I was a kid, but now . . . I dunno, guess it's something you have to outgrow."

"Uh-huh." Neal reached into the bag beside him on the seat, pulled out a second doughnut, and sank his teeth into it. "I seem to remember," he said, swallowing, "you having a fondness for Boston cream pie. With extra topping. Not long ago." He took another bite. "In fact, I saw you eat several slices maybe two weeks back."

Lombardi looked at him. "You are making a mistake, Vince. Thinking about Robby Conners, probably. Or somebody else you've been teamed with. Because I am a health-conscious man."

"Uh-huh." Neal finished his doughnut, wiped his hands, and dropped the crumpled napkin into the bag. "Tom, I gotta talk to you about something."

Lombardi saw that his partner's expression had become serious. Whatever his question was about, it would have nothing to do with food.

"Shoot."

"You really believe the bombs we're looking for might be nukes?"

Tom Lombardi did not have to think about his answer. He'd been asking himself that same question, and considering its ramifications, for almost a week. It hung unspoken between those involved in the secret hunt for the bombs, as if to mouth it were to risk incurring some terrible curse.

They were all so afraid to admit they were afraid.

He was glad Neal had finally chosen to raise the subject. He wished he'd been the one with guts enough to do it.

"You ask me, this town's getting a little too hot," he said. "If the bombs ain't found by tomorrow afternoon, I'm going to call in sick, pack Shirley, the boys, and whatever else I can fit into our car and take a spin into the next state." He cleared his throat. "You want to hear something else? Just between you, me, and the shitty vinyl seats sticking to our asses?"

Neal gave him a look of strict confidence.

"Before I leave on my little excursion, FNN is going to get an anonymous tip about the bombs. Because that kind of news has got to be broadcast to the general citizenry. So that it isn't just us cops and the high-and-mighties, but every poor schnook in Free Atlanta that gets a chance to decide if he's suddenly in the mood to go somewhere and beat the heat."

Neal sat back in silence, looking out his window at the Omni's main entrance. After several moments he checked his wristwatch.

"Eight-ten, Tom," he said. "The morning desk clerk ought to be on shift by now. Sooner we talk to him, sooner I can make up my mind whether to start planning my own vacation."

Lombardi nodded. He dumped the remainder of his tea out the window, dropped the empty cup and his mostly uneaten toast into a refuse container below the dash, and reached for the door handle.

"Come on."

The floor of the Omni's lobby was gleaming marble. There were many overstuffed chairs, and elegant stands with oriental vases on them, and large abstract paintings on the walls. On each side of the lobby were doors leading off into convenience shops and dining places.

The UDF agents went straight to the front desk. They'd made two previous, unproductive trips there—the first at four yesterday afternoon to speak with the evening clerk, the second at six this morning to interview the clerk on the midnight-to-8-A.M. shift.

Neither of them had recognized Wiley Pike from his photograph. Prints of the same photo were being shown to hotel and motel staffs throughout the Atlanta area by hundreds of UDF agents and an assortment of other under-cover military and law enforcement personnel who, like Neal and Lombardi, were involved in the urgent manhunt for the Front terrorist. So far the massive search had yielded nothing but frustration.

The morning clerk was a brisk little man with a pencil mustache, short, slicked-back hair, and fingernails that looked as if they were manicured and buffed once after every meal. His fretful, darting eyes reminded Lombardi of a poodle he'd owned as a child. The dog had liked to be petted—unless you happened to touch one of the ninety-nine spots on its body where it didn't like to be petted. The location of those spots would shift daily, and if you were unfortunate enough to hit one, the dog would take a chunk out of your hand.

He hadn't cared much for that poodle after a while.

The clerk was gazing at Tom's ID with something like distaste.

"It isn't very good," Tom said. He waited for the clerk's quizzical glance to arrive before going on. It arrived. "The picture on my identification, that is. The angle it was taken from weakens my chin and detracts from my boyish charm."

"Mine's even worse," Neal said. "Makes me look like I eat too many sweets or something."

"How may I help you gentlemen?"

Lombardi laid the photo of Wiley Pike on the counter. "We need to know if you've seen this man at the hotel."

The clerk literally looked down his nose at it. His sour expression intensified. "He appears to be a hard character," he said.

"Folks we're after often are," Lombardi said.

"Sir, the Omni attracts and caters to a refined clientele," the clerk said, brushing an invisible fleck of lint off his suit jacket. "Business people. Politicians. As you may have heard, the Tri-territorial Summit is to be held here the day after tomorrow."

Golly gee, Lombardi thought.

"So what you're implying," he said, "is that you would refuse to take a reservation from the man in this photograph based on his appearance? You'd send him away regardless of whether he could afford to stay here?"

"Well, as I'm sure you are aware, that would be prohibited by FSU discrimination laws. But—"

"Look," Lombardi said, "I'm not arguing that you run a nice place. It is a beautiful place, and I would be proud if my son decides to hold his wedding reception here when the time comes. But that's beside the point. It is very important we find the man in the snapshot. I'd appreciate very much if you could take a minute to think about whether his face is at all familiar."

The clerk lifted the photo rather prissily, gave it a quick second glance, and held it out for Lombardi to take. "I have never seen him before in my life. To the best of my knowledge."

"Exactly what's that mean, to the best of your knowledge?"

He huffed out an exasperated breath. "Our hotel has nearly five hundred rooms and suites, plus meeting rooms that can accommodate as many as fifteen hundred people. I am a very busy man. It is possible he could pass through without my notice." He huffed again. His high-gloss fingernails tapped the desk. "Perhaps you could try the night clerk."

"Already have. And Mr. Reynolds on the overnight shift."

"Well then," the clerk said, and made an idle gesture. "What more can I tell you?"

"That I'm a lot cuter than I photograph, for one thing," Lombardi said.

The two agents turned from the desk. Neal stopped abruptly partway to the entrance doors.

"What is it?" Lombardi asked. He could practically see his partner's wheels turning.

"I was just thinking," Neal said, "that maybe we should do some asking around in the hotel shops. I'm not saying Pike'd be buying cards to send his sick grandma in the nursing home. But he might be eating out. Buying clothes. You know?"

"Worth a shot," Lombardi said. "It's still early. Let's see which places are open."

As happens in investigative work rarely enough to be considered a lucky fluke, they struck paydirt on their first try.

The kid that managed the shoe repair shop was just unlocking the doors when they approached. He was short, dark, and handsome and spoke with a faint Creole accent. He nodded with recognition the moment Lombardi handed him Pike's photo.

"You bet I remember him. He's upstairs in room 1403. Or at least was a couple of days ago. Real cheapskate."

Lombardi looked at Neal. Neal's eyes were as wide as poached eggs. He supposed his must be also.

"You're positive?" he said, looking back at the kid.

"You bet. And not just because of his freaky ear." He grinned wryly. "He had a pair of beat-up old loafers, couldn't've cost him more than ten bucks brand-new. Like the kind my dad would've bought at Pay Less Shoes before the war. But he acted like they were some real fancy flats." He chuckled, remembering. "They had all man-made uppers. When manufacturers say man-made they usually mean plastic, y'know. Most people wear shoes like that out after a month and trash 'em. Even with the shortages these days, people still trash—"

"What day was it?" Neal said.

"That he came in with the shoes?"

Neal nodded impatiently.

"Would've been last Friday," the kid said. "I know without having to check the receipts because it was a last-minute rush order, and I was going out on a date that night and wanted to get home. But I figured, what the hell, I'd do the work and get a decent tip. Every little bit helps."

"Rush order . . . ?" Lombardi motioned for him to expand.

"I finished work on them a half hour after he brought them in. It was just before closing. I resoled them and locked up and took them up to his room myself. Even though the shoes were man-made, I thought he'd tip a few dollars. To rent a suite here, you have to have *beaucoup* bucks. Anyway, I ended up with zip. And a dirty look. Don't ask me why."

Lombardi turned to Neal. He felt as if every nerve in his body was suddenly jumping. "Vin, I think we better call HQ and then get our butts upstairs to that—"

He broke off midsentence.

His partner was already on his way out the door.

At 8:30 A.M., as agents Lombardi and Neal sprinted toward the elevators in the Omni's main lobby, Wiley Pike was in his room fourteen stories above them taking a bath. He'd been soaking since six that morning—having climbed in just after hiding and activating the final bio-nuke.

On the shelf formed by the flattened rim of the tub were several 1.5-ounce bottles of complimentary toiletries Wiley had discovered in the bathroom upon his arrival last week: hair shampoo, hair conditioner, body lotion, and cologne. The bottles were empty despite the fact that this was the first occasion on which he'd cleaned up during his stay at the Omni and that, as was SOP, the bottles had been freshly set out by the maid after the previous guest vacated.

In order to drain the bottles Wiley had needed to shampoo, condition, smear himself with lotion, and slap on cologne seven times in the past two hours. It hadn't been pleasant. He didn't enjoy washing much. The body lotion had been especially problematic because he'd never used such a product before and wasn't sure whether it was supposed to go on while he was in the tub or after he'd toweled. He'd decided on the former, and now oily globs of it were scumming the water.

The cologne was another story. He was familiar with cologne. He knew it was supposed to go on after you shaved. Before the war he'd favored a brand called Elvis, named after the performer whose singing he'd enjoyed. He knew about cologne but had been using it up in the bath along with the other stuff. Using it all up *fast*.

There was of course a reason. A principle.

He was going to show Them that he was as good as They were. Before the Holy Fire consumed Them, They would know.

On the tub rim beside the empty bottles was a small bar of soap. Like the other toiletries, it had been provided courtesy of the hotel. Unlike them, it was only partially spent. He had already lathered over a dozen times, mountains of suds had heaved and fallen on his chest, foam had bearded his cheeks and brewed like yeast from the cavities of his underarms a dozen times and more, and the bar of soap seemed hardly to have dwindled. It was a test. He realized that. A test of Patience. A test of Worthiness.

At first he'd wondered why the bottles and soap bar were so small. That had been part of the test, of course—having to figure out why. And he had. The bottles and soap were small because the Rich Shits that normally stayed at plush joints like the Omni wanted to make a big show of how clean they were. They wanted the maid to come in after They had left and see the empty bottles of shampoo and conditioner and body lotion and oooh and aaah at their oh-so-marvelous personal hygiene and think things like "They've finished it *all*, how *often* they must bathe." They wanted the maid to think that. But give Them *regular* size bottles of shampoo and conditioner and body lotion, give Them sixteen ounces instead of one and a half and make Them *pay* for it like everyone else, and then you'd see that They were just a bunch of dirtbags.

Wiley chuckled and lathered his stomach furiously. He knew the score. Yes indeedeee, he did. The Lord had shown him the Truth and the Way.

Revelation 6:15: ". . . *and the great men, and the rich men, and the chief captains, and the mighty men, and every bondman, and every free man hid themselves in the dens and in the rocks of the mountains.*"

"And said to the mountains and rocks, Fall on us, and hide us from the face of Him that siteth on the throne!" Wiley shouted aloud, recalling the next verse. His voice bounced off the bathroom tiles. "For the great day of His wrath is come, and who shall be able to stand?"

He laughed again. Somewhere in the back of his mind the voice of his father tried to make itself heard, but it was nothing now, nothing more than a faint crackle of mental interference, nothing more than the buzz of a fly trapped in a bottle. Wiley had eclipsed him. Father had burned him, oh yes, Father had held the branding iron to his body often, and his flesh had seared and bubbled and melted like rubber, Father had held the iron to his ear until it charred like a blob of fat in a pan, but Wiley Pike would soon outdo him in a big way, the biggest: He would burn an entire city, he—

A knock sounded at the door to his room. He drew up straight, the soap bar slipping out of his hand like a fish, and grasped the side of the tub. Whoever was out there rapped again. Then he heard a man's voice: "Hello?" And again: "Hello?"

He thought a moment. Interruptions were common in this place. He was always being disturbed. The dry cleaner, room service, that brown-skinned kid who'd fixed his shoes. But the thing was . . . the thing was he'd placed no orders. No clothes were out.

Who was it?

He sprang from the tub and catwalked, naked and sopping, to the open bathroom door. He hadn't paused to rinse off or grab a towel, and wispy caps of foam rolled down his arms, legs, and chest. He padded out into the bedroom and stood before the entrance door.

Another rap. He backed from the door, slowly, as if it were a bull rhino about to charge.

"Yes?" he said. "Who is it?"

"This is Investigator Thomas Lombardi of the UDF. My partner and I would like to ask you some questions."

"I was taking a bath," he said. He heard the sharp intake of his own breath. "Why don't you come back in fifteen minutes, I'll be glad to—"

"Mr. Pike, will you open the door immediately."

Mister Pike.

So They knew.

"Okay," he said. "Just give me a second to get dressed."

He turned, went to the dresser, got his S & W .44 Magnum from the drawer. The cylinder was loaded. He always kept it full.

"Mr. Pike?"

His thoughts sped. Was anything left undone? The bio-nukes were in place. He had hidden the third here in his room. Right under Their noses. He'd slit open the under-lining of the hassock and slipped the canister inside and remote-activated both the timer and motion sensors. No great loss if They found it now. And They would. Find it and the others. In the inside pocket of his sport coat were his notes, his city map with the Carter Center circled in red, his schematics of the FNN center. They would find the bombs. Good. Jostle the suckers and *wham*! True, the explosion would occur prematurely. But what did it matter? There was no escape for him, his stay on earth over, he would be unto God forever and ever. That was fine. And if They knew about the bombs, then the summit would be canceled anyway. That was all right, too. The sinners that would die in the Fire and subsequent Plague were legion.

"Mr. Pike, open the door, or we will break it in."

"I'm coming," he shouted, and cocked his Magnum, and went to the door, still without any clothes on, and turned open the latch, and instead of pulling back on the handle, fired four shots *BOOMBOOMBOOMBOOM!* through the door in quick succession.

"Woe to the sinners that inhabit the earth! Fuck you all!" he screamed as the splintered door was banged open from outside. The cop he'd drilled was a heavy, older guy, should have quit his line of work while he was ahead, the stupid, devilspawn sonuvabitch; he was on his knees bleeding out there in the hallway, an expression of what might have been protest on his face. Still on his knees, the fat cop came waddling forward, and Wiley put another slug into his face because he couldn't stand that look on it, and then the face was gone.

"Go ahead and tinker with the bombs! Go ahead and see what happens!" Wiley laughed, fanning his gun across the doorway. He saw the second cop in the hall and triggered a sixth shoot *BOOM!* and the cop ducked and fired back with the gun in his own hand. Wiley felt a bullet mulekick his chest and flew backward through the air and was dead before he hit the floor.

Inspector Second-Class Vince Neal saw Lombardi lying there on the carpet with his blood flowing out like lava, and when he was certain Pike was not going to move, ran over to his partner, and dropped to his knees, and cradled the body in his arms.

The salt of tears was on his lips.

"Oh Christ, Tom, it isn't fair," he muttered, his own voice seeming to reach him from a distance. "Isn't fair, isn't fair, isn't fair, isn't . . ."

Chapter Sixteen ══════════════════

Midday sunlight touched the Cape Sable shore; smooth expanses of sand, ocean, and sky bled together, softly undulant, in the constant glow.

At the fringe of the sea, storm and tide had left a signature bank of broken coral, seashells, and driftwood from which a flock of egrets launched in a burst of amplified whiteness that looked oddly like sudden snow. The birds wheeled inland over the crescent of beach dividing ocean from shaded forest and made sweeping, exploratory passes at the sand.

The Cape Sable beaches are an instinctual nesting range for the seafaring loggerhead turtle, and the egrets flock there to hunt their eggs and newly hatched young as delicacies.

In the steamy mangrove woods beyond the strand, an excited horde of mosquitoes buzzed around a party of four men and a woman, attracted by the scent of the rich, warm blood that was their own preferred nourishment.

"Damn!" Zeno said, slapping at the attacking bugs with both hands. "These little bastards are turning me into a sieve!"

Firecloud looked at him with cool serenity. His lean form was a clear break in the milling, biting cloud that had settled over the pilot, Saralyn, and the Marcuses.

"Flapping your arms will just aggravate them," he said. "It would be better if all of you moved about as little as possible and also tried breathing exclusively through your noses—and next time we're in the swamp, do as Saralyn has, and wear bandannas over your mouths."

"*Next* time?" Marcus One interrupted. "Me an' my bro are like appetizers before lunch to these skeeters. We won't *last* till next time."

"The respiratory damage that can be caused by inhaling the mosquitoes is of greater concern than their bites," Firecloud went on. "Their wing scales irritate the mucous membranes of the lungs." He glanced downward, belatedly acknowledging Marcus One. "I suggest you worry less about the mosquitoes and watch out that you don't brush against any scorpions."

"Scorpions?" Marcus Two gagged, as if there were an obstruction in his throat. "There're *scorpions* around here?"

"Fat, lethal ones, in abundance," Firecloud said. "They often cling to tree stumps and roots. Objects that are close to the ground . . . you understand."

The twins shuffled and examined themselves uneasily.

"Only one thing I want to know, John," Zeno said. He struck at a mosquito on his neck, glanced at the splotch of his own siphoned blood that the tiny carcass left on his palm. "Namely, why's it you Indians don't get feasted on by these vampires?"

Firecloud's expression was blank. "We have a peace treaty."

Saralyn laughed under the bandanna, shaking her head, the corners of her eyes crinkling prettily. "He's getting our goats, fellas. I'm starting to think our leader actually has a sense of humor."

"I don't know what you mean," Firecloud said flatly. "Better stop laughing or the noise will disturb the water moccasins."

To an observer, it would have appeared that the small rebel band was gathered around a teardrop-shaped hummock about sixty feet long, fourteen feet wide, and thirteen feet high—the approximate dimensions of the Strikehawk that was, in fact, at the core of the mock rise, camouflaged beneath a huge tarpaulin festooned with clay and vegetation.

An armadillo was snuffing about for insects near the top of the hump, going about its business as if there were no humans present.

"Sorry to make you move, little one," Firecloud said. He lifted a frond from the camouflaging and swished it near the animal. His gentleness fascinated Saralyn. "I'm sure you'll find another good place to dig."

The armadillo looked at him, the flattened tip of its nose curling up. It grunted—seemingly more in annoyance than alarm—then abandoned its perch, jogging swiftly into the woods.

Firecloud turned to the others. "I'll show you where the edges of the tarp are, and then we'll peel it away."

It came down without a problem, and seconds later the chopper stood revealed in the dripping brush like a strange time machine that had gotten stranded in some prehistoric epoch. Globules of moisture had condensed on its black skin. There were tailor ants and a six-inch-long centipede crawling on it.

"We tied down the blades," Firecloud said to Zeno. "That made concealing it much easier."

Zeno nodded and walked up to the gunship. His hands glided over the giant "cheek" beneath the cockpit window which, along with an identical structure on the opposite side of the fuselage, housed the Strikehawk's avionics. His eyes followed his fingers as they moved up to the canopy, not resting on anything, just probing. The expression on his face was like that of an archaeologist who had unearthed an ancient chamber filled with treasures.

"Awesome," he said under his breath.

"And deadly." Firecloud came abreast of him.

"Yeah, that, too." Zeno gave him a quizzical glance. "I can't imagine how you and your people dragged her all this way upbeach. Even without a full load of weapons, a chopper like this weighs tons. And she's *bristling* with firepower."

"My father used to say: 'The hardest thing I ever learned is that nothing's ever that hard,'" Firecloud said, smiling in reminiscence. "The copter has wheels. There were a lot of us, almost all the young men from camp. We rolled it across the sand on planks and put our minds and backs to the task. And, you know, it wasn't that hard."

Zeno gave him an appreciative nod. "I mostly just remember my own dad telling me to quit playing with knives and model aircraft."

"I see you were the type that always did as you were told."

Zeno laughed.

"Let's go have a look inside," Firecloud said.

Zeno jumped onto the catwalk on the side of the copter, leaned over the canopy and popped it. The snug two-man cockpit had side-by-side seating with full dual controls. He scrunched into the left-hand seat, maneuvering his legs around the cyclic lever. He was already studying the instrument panel as Firecloud climbed in next to him.

There was a reddish stain on Zeno's padded headrest. Firecloud remembered the pilot he'd killed, slumped dead in that seat with an arrow skewering his face. That had only been weeks ago, and yet it seemed a lifetime.

"Very neat and uncluttered," Zeno said, gesturing around him. His eyes were narrowed in concentration. Firecloud felt as if he were seeing the man revealed in full light for the first time. "The layout of the console, I mean. Facilitates readings and gives quick, simple access to the weapons controls."

"Can you check whether the copter's flightworthy without actually bringing her up?" Firecloud asked.

"Pretty much." Zeno nodded his chin at the console. "Somebody was kind enough to leave the key in the lock for us," he said, reaching for it and turning it to the "on" position.

He began expertly flipping switches. "Just got the battery started. Now we should have juice in the cockpit. See that panel up over there? We'd see warning lights blink on if any chiclets were blown on the engine instrument display. Looks good so far."

He reached over to a panel labeled MASTER CAUTION, pressed the test switch. This time all the gauges lit bright green and red.

"The various systems are almost totally self-diagnostic," Zeno said, "and what they're telling me is that they're all shipshape."

He was still working the controls, his fingers gaining facile speed, eyebrows scrunched almost together. "What I'm doing now is flicking on the APU. That'll power up the engines. There. There it goes. You hear the humming?"

Firecloud nodded. He heard it, and another sound as well, a clatter from the passenger cabin. He leaned out of the open cockpit and saw the twins climbing aboard.

"They're making sure the first-class accommodations are to their liking," Saralyn said, looking up at him from outside. She stepped closer. "How're you guys doing?"

"Marcuses shouldn't be messing around back there," Zeno said hurriedly. "Since they're already in, tell them to stay put until the test is over. I don't want them getting baked behind the engines when I fire them."

"Don't think they'd care too much for the idea, either," Saralyn said, and went aft.

"Okay, let's see, I have to hold this switch here down, probably for thirty seconds," Zeno said. Firecloud realized that he was thinking aloud. "That'd be about right. And now this one, to get the engine cooking." Suddenly he was grinning helplessly at Firecloud, indicating a circular gauge. "The needle's climbing, which is exactly what it ought to be doing. When it tells us the exhaust gas temp's at 25 percent, I'll throttle one of the turbines to 'idle,' and after that to 'fly.' Then we go through the same thing with the other engine."

Within minutes Firecloud heard the whine of turbines sucking in air. The Strikehawk shivered.

"That's it," Zeno said. "She's like a racehorse itching to charge at the gate. If the blades were up and the chopper was clear of the trees, I'd raise the collective, and we'd be in the air." He sat back, examining his palms. "God, look at how they're sweating. Almost forgot how much I loved being in this seat."

He wiped his hands on his pants and sat quietly. Firecloud said nothing, sensing he needed time to wind down.

"I'd kinda quit thinking anyone'd stand up to those National Front loonies. Quit on myself, too, I guess," Zeno said after a little while, his eyes turned inward. There was another moment of silence, and then he reached for the controls again. "Better put her back to sleep."

The engines subsided.

"Will you be ready by midnight?" Firecloud asked.

The blond man looked at him and breathed a long sigh. "I'd like to take her for a dry run. Get the feel of her. But that's out of the question, isn't it? I mean, we need to get Lansman to Free Atlanta, and get him there fast."

Firecloud's thoughts turned back to recent events. After their successful interception of the carny train, he and his fledgling band—joined by Zeno and the Snake Charmer Mohammed, the latter having to all intents *insisted* they take him along—had roared back to Everglades City in the twins' Bronco and spent the night at Ardelia's bungalow. In the predawn darkness, Dee had awakened Firecloud and asked him to accompany her to the marina, where he'd been introduced to her Georgia contacts. They arrived in an old cabin cruiser that had launched from the vicinity of the Okefenokee Swamp, wended its way down the Suwannee River, then cleared the bay into the Gulf and plowed southeast hugging the Florida shoreline—a trip of hundreds of miles in pitch darkness, through waters thick with enemy coastal patrols.

If the daring of the three men that had been on the vessel

had impressed Firecloud, the news they'd brought had galvanized him. The terrorist Pike had been killed in a bloody shoot-out at a Free Atlanta hotel. Documents found among his belongings had revealed the location of the bombs and confirmed that they were indeed the long-sought bio-nukes. The papers, coupled with statements Pike had made to one of the UDF agents that ran him to ground, had further revealed that the bombs' timed detonators had been activated, and that they possessed motion-sensitive fallback mechanisms, which meant that any attempt to render them inoperative would bring on the devastation Free Atlanta authorities were scrambling to avoid.

More than ever the FSU's efforts to save its capital hinged upon having Lansman delivered from captivity. Perhaps he could break this hellish Catch-22. As Zeno had said, he had to be gotten to Free Atlanta fast.

Now Saralyn came around from behind, jumped onto the catwalk on Firecloud's side, and leaned into the cockpit.

"Sounds as if we have a healthy bird," she said.

"Sang like a well-fed canary," Zeno said.

Firecloud emerged from his woolgathering. "Are you going to be able to do the flying and deliver the weapons at the same time?"

"In a less radical copter that'd be a real problem," Zeno said, shaking his head. "I'll want to go around to the main cabin and have a gander at the helmets you took off the crew . . . the former crew, that is. But if they're the kind I think they are, I ought to be okay."

Firecloud waited for an explanation.

"Judging from your description they've got built-in IHADSS—Integrated Helmet and Display Sighting Systems. That'll give me comprehensive navigation and weapons systems information displayed on a sort of reticular lens mounted to the helmet. Airspeed, height, magnetic headings, target range, you name it, they show up as alphanumerics that are superimposed wherever I turn my eyes. And if I get everything calibrated right, I'll be able to slave the guns and missiles to my line of sight . . . in other words, aim them at a target just by looking at it."

"Awesome," Saralyn said.

"Same word I used," Zeno said. "Of course the weapons are still engaged, and, in some extreme cases, fired, manually. Which is why in a more conventional sortie you'd have a gunner scanning for targets while the pilot keeps his mind on the flying." He gave them a tepid smile. "I suppose there isn't much about us that's conventional."

"So, while we're being different, why not take me on as a co-pilot?" Saralyn asked.

She saw the skepticism on Zeno's face and raised her palm in a preemptory gesture. "Don't dismiss me out of hand. The Marcuses'll be in the cabin when we take off, and they can handle everything that has to be done back there. With them, I'd be extra weight. But maybe I can be of some help in the cockpit. I'm a quick study. And anyway, what's the matter with you having some solid moral support?"

"I don't know," Zeno said, rubbing his chin. "Having an unskilled person in the cockpit, well—"

"I think Saralyn's idea is excellent," Firecloud broke in abruptly. "I think she should fly beside you."

She smiled. Zeno's eyes swung from her to Firecloud, then back to Saralyn.

"Guess we've got ourselves a date, babe," he said, finally acquiescing.

"Tonight, fly-boy," she said. "Trust me, it'll be one to remember."

"It's tonight? You're absolutely certain?"

Madas, the inmate physician that had come to examine Gordon Lansman in the northeast tower of the Castillo de San Marcos, nodded and took his stethescope out of his black bag. He was a thin man in his sixties, with lifeless gray hair and a tendency to squint. Lansman supposed the doctor needed glasses, though he neither had them on now nor had been wearing them on any of his previous visits.

Madas slid closer to Lansman on the hard, narrow cot that served as Lansman's bed and sofa and held the diaphragm of the stethescope to his chest. "Take a deep breath and hold it for the count of five," he said, and then, lowering his voice to a clandestine whisper, added, "They will be coming for you at midnight. Be prepared."

Lansman inhaled and counted. His ribs were bruised and fractured as the result of numerous beatings inflicted by Slade's torturers, and they hurt badly—but the pain in his left arm was far, far more severe. It had throbbed sharply and unabatingly since the night before last, when they had entered his tower prison, shattered his humerus about an inch above the elbow with a ball peen hammer, and then hung him from the ceiling by the broken arm.

He'd been left to dangle for three excruciating hours before they'd finally taken him down and let Dr. Madas apply the long-arm cast.

Lansman liked and admired Madas, and moreover was grateful to him. He'd tended Lansman's injuries with a skilled, delicate hand after each brutal going-over. He did his earnest best to carry on in the face of Dantesque conditions, attempting by whatever means possible to alleviate the suffering of patients forced to endure hunger, deprivation, and wholesale abuse. And beyond that, he'd bravely established himself as a liaison between the Castillo's inmate population and the increasingly active and well-organized Underground Railroad that sheltered and transported fugitives from National Front persecution into the FSU.

It was through Dr. Madas that Lansman had been informed of the dire situation in Free Atlanta—and about the impending mission to rescue him.

Lansman glanced up at the small, barred window in the heavy steel door of the tower that was his cage. He saw no one peering in. He had searched for bugging devices in the tower, and found none. There would be few places for his captors to have hidden a transmitter since his furniture

consisted of the cot, a washbasin, and nothing else. But a
button mike could easily have been implanted in the courses
between masonry stones. It was also probable that one of
the stones in the wall or ceiling had been replaced with a
hollow facsimile. He had to be cautious.

"What other information do you have?" he whispered.
Had he spoken any more quietly his words would have been
inaudible even to Madas. "Do you know the people that are
going to free me?"

"Turn around and let me have a listen from behind,"
Madas said, and placed the cold, smooth nose of the
stethescope between Lansman's shoulder blades. "*Inhale.
The man who will come for you is a Seminole. Code name
Swampmaster. Exhale.* I know nothing else about him. Nor
do I know the true identity of my contact, or how the escape
is to be accomplished. *Exhale.* The secrecy is for the
protection of all involved, in case any of us are caught and
interrogated. *Inhale.*"

The doctor folded his stethescope and returned it to his
bag. "That's all," he said at a normal volume. "You're
mending well, Professor Lansman." He smiled. "Perhaps
soon we won't be seeing each other so often."

"Thank you, doctor," Lansman said, buttoning his shirt.
"Thanks for everything."

Madas rapped twice on the door, signaling the turnkey on
the landing outside to release him. The doorlatch clattered
open. He held his hand up to Lansman and exited.

His ersatz smile faded as he began descending the
staircase that wound to the San Carlos bastion.

Lieutenant Varnum Slade stood waiting for him on the
third step down.

"You have done as I instructed?" Slade asked.

"Exactly," Madas said. "I told him to get ready. He
hasn't any suspicion that you're on to tonight's planned
breakout."

"Thanks to you." Slade grinned frigidly. "I'm proud of
you, Madas. You've become even more skilled at duplicity

than medicine. I'm glad you'd never be foolish enough to test your abilities as a liar on me."

"Never, Lieutenant." Madas looked at him. Slid his tongue across his lips. "My reward. Do I get my reward?"

"You mean your booze? Is that what you're asking for?"

"You know that's what," Madas said. "You kn—"

"*Refresh* me, Madas. Spell it out."

Madas felt shame, guilt, and self-hatred worm through him. What he had done, the part he'd played in the trap, disgusted him. But he needed. He *needed*.

He wondered if Lansman would understand. He did not expect or think he was deserving of forgiveness . . . but understanding—perhaps that was not too much to wish for. Would Lansman know what it was like for him here? What it was like being a doctor, trying to uphold your Hippocratic vows in a place where human misery was an all-encompassing, fundamental condition of life? Knowing all those you treated as patients were ultimately doomed? Feeling that what you were doing was as futile and senseless and absurd as replacing a roof shingle on a house while it was burning, being reduced to ashes? Could Lansman—could *anyone*—know?

"I want a drink," he told Slade. The void was a beast eating at his gut. He had to appease it. "I want alcohol."

"Spell it out." Slade's tone was full of dark amusement.

"A-l-c-o-h-ol." Madas's eyes were hot. "Now, please, please, I beg you, please . . ."

"Oh, my good, thirsty little pet. My eyes and ears among the bottom dwellers! How you gratify me!" The lieutenant laughed haughtily and turned down the stairs. "Come. Come along," he said, crooking his finger. "I'll see what ambrosia I can provide."

Chapter Seventeen ══════════

Night over the Atlantic, a slight chop to the water, its surface imperfectly reflecting the quarter-moon and its coterie of stars.

The blacked-out, shallow draft Cougar patrol boat streaked over the water like hot oil on Teflon. The lightweight craft was constructed from glass-reinforced plastic and measured ten feet from bow to stern. Its compact but muscular outboard motor raced it along at close to eighty knots, and the wake that rose in its slipstream was like the contrail of a jet fighter.

Its pilot and passenger were one and the same. A mere shadow in the shadowcraft, he stood at the helm in a black anorak and windpants that repelled the spray. Bands of lampblack masked his eyes and cheekbones like war paint. The clean, salty wind whipped back his hair, shot into his sinuses, and slapped his cheeks. His garments snapped crisply around his body. The speed imparted a headiness that he enjoyed.

Alone, he was most relaxed.

Ahead and to the left, he could see the southeastern tip of Anastasia Island. The western side of the bar faced the mainland and the scarred walls of Castillo de San Marcos across Matanzas Bay. He would keep to the open water east of Anastasia, then swing around its northern spur through the St. Augustine harbor mouth.

Tough and sleek as its namesake, the Cougar had carried Firecloud from the Ft. Pierce inlet of the Indian River to his present position approximately two hundred miles north of there in under two hours—ahead of schedule. Which was good. The more time available to him the better. Saralyn had provided the craft. She had come through. Thinking about her, he was unaware of the smile that came onto his face. He was honest enough with himself to acknowledge that he was attracted to her. And that he liked her. But he was convinced the doors to his heart were locked tight. As certain as he'd been the day Charlie Tiger had taken him from the orphanage.

Wiping drizzle from his face, he discovered his smile and willed it away.

He passed Matanzas Inlet and then Crescent Beach, and then Anastasia was directly portside, perhaps a half mile distant. He could see the foamy crests of breakers flinging themselves against the moonsilvered shore. On his starboard side the ocean swell was endless and dark. No other vessels were visible. Traffic on the waters had been sparse tonight, for which he was thankful. He hadn't needed to make any time-consuming detours.

Buoys blinked in the harbor inlet. Beyond, he could make out the long sandspit that was Ponte Vedra.

He veered off to port and minutes later turned into the harbor entrance.

The Castillo was ahead of him now, the AA machine guns on its bastions thrusting at the thin scud of clouds moving inland over the bay.

Firecloud cut the engine and paddled toward shore, navigating past the few darkened ships at anchor in the harbor. The tide was coming in, and the current aided his progress, pushing at the stern like a mittened hand.

There was a pair of Front sentries looking out over the seawall. Neither man saw the Cougar gliding close between the hulls of two larger vessels. Firecloud reached for his bow, waited as a searchlight mounted on the west wall made its regular inspection of their post. They waved an all's well to the light operator.

The beam roved on.

A beat later the guards went down with arrows quilling from their throats.

Firecloud heaved to in the shallows beneath a split, rotted portion of the Castillo's seawall. He waded from the boat, dragged it up the sand that rimmed the outer wall, then pulled it through the crumbly breach.

The moat was only four or five yards across the covered way, and needling above it, the tower of San Carlos where Lansman was imprisoned.

He checked the diver's watch he was wearing: 11:05. Saralyn had an identical, synchronized timepiece on her wrist. He supposed she must also be feeling the shave of minutes.

The Cougar weighed a hundred pounds at most; he had no problem towing it across the slick, dewy turf. Near the lip of the moat he paused, thinking he heard a swish of feet on grass. Yes. He glanced around tensely, brought the bow around his shoulders. The patrolling guard rounded the point of the southeast bastion and started along the wall in Firecloud's direction. About a hundred yards separated them. Lurking in the shadows, Firecloud watched him come closer. Closer. Thirty yards away, the guard halted and stretched. He was whistling. Unaware that anything was amiss.

An arrow and then another fired from the bow—*whit whit!*—and the guard dropped dead on the grass.

Firecloud broke from his crouch and returned to the Cougar. He pulled it the rest of the way to the moat, then slipped it into the forty-foot-wide barrier of water that surrounded the fortress. It hit with a dull slap and some listless ripples. He swung his legs over the edge of the moat, dropped onto the speedcraft, remained standing. It was a buoyant, wobbly platform under his feet.

Suddenly a triangular dorsal fin rose from the water to the right of him. A second appeared beside it. He cast his gaze over his opposite shoulder. More fins. A dozen of them

coming at him like torpedoes, attracted by the disturbance
his entry had caused, their submerged bodies long and gray.
One of them knocked against his boat, turning it 90 degrees.
The short, rounded snout of another man-eater bumped his
keel. The Cougar fishtailed in the water. Firecloud crouched
and steadied his feet. He had planned for this attack. His
bow was raised. He awaited opportunity.

A large head surfaced in a burble of water, dipped down
before he could take aim. The head reemerged six inches to
the left of where it had been and smashed the side of the
Cougar. Its cavernous mouth was snapping. Firecloud
glimpsed row upon row of cusped, bladelike teeth. He
released an arrow. The shark dove. The shaft bobbed
harmlessly in the water.

Then the stern was bumped. Hard. The boat tossed and
rocked. He turned and saw the surface of the water swell. A
shark reared up almost vertically. Its underside was white.
Its eyes gleamed with black hunger. Its pectoral fins were
like scythes. Its gills pulsed, and there was froth around
them, froth on its mouth. Another arrow hurtled through the
air, sank into the omnivore's pale belly. His second arrow
shot into a gill slit. It made a kind of deep tubalike sound
and fell back splashing.

Now the triangular fins cut away from Firecloud's boat.
The shark he'd hit was bleeding dark, oily streamers into
the water, and the scent had whipped the other beasts into a
feeding frenzy. They went cannibal. The water around the
wounded shark churned as they converged upon their dying,
thrashing prey.

Firecloud slung his bow across his back, kneeled, flipped
open the door of a small storage bay. Inside was a grappling
hook and fifty feet of scaling rope, and a duffel containing
the C-4 saddle charges. He had tied knots in the rope at
one-foot intervals to make climbing easier.

He looked upward at the battered, ancient fortress wall.
The duffel was over his shoulder. In his throwing hand he

had the hook and a few coils of rope. The remainder of the rope, in loose coils, was in his other hand.

There was a molded cornice about a dozen feet below the base of the tower. Sixteen feet above him.

He prepared for his toss.

It was 11:27.

Lieutenant Varnum Slade's handpicked five-man detail had assembled in one of the eight high-arched bombproofs lined along the Castillo's east curtain. They wore the smart all-black tunics, breeches, and knee-boots of his elite guard. Runic symbols inscribed the blades of the daggers hanging from their belts.

All had silver skulls on their kepis.

All had lean, hard bodies and golden hair and eyes that were the pale blue of blameless innocence.

Behind them in the huge stone hearth were charred scraps of a woman's clothing and a scrabble of carbonized bone chips.

Above them the vaulted ceiling was capped with a swastika.

Slade walked past the rank of soldiers, inspecting them with pride. Tonight his ambition was a bonfire at the very heart of his being.

"Soon, my obedient guards, my pedigree crop, soon you shall distinguish yourselves above all others," he said. "You shall be *exalted*."

"Your will unto death!" one of them proclaimed, his eyes bright and overmoist.

"We are lightning at your fingertips!" another enthused.

"Yes, lightning," Slade said. "And how surprised the rebels will be when they find you waiting to strike them down."

He glanced at his watch.

It was 11:30.

Almost time to lead his men up to the tower.

The Strikehawk hopscotched across the dark ocean of vegetation once known as Silver Springs National Preserve, the blast of its rotors lashing the forest canopy. A low

ground mist coiled and swirled over the tree trunks like
steam over a cup of hot cocoa.

The neck of a browsing giraffe derricked unexpectedly
above the top of a mimosa, and Zeno hauled on the cyclic.
The chopper nosed upward, avoiding a collision by inches,
wind riffling the shock of strawlike hair on the ruminant's
stub-horned head.

"Was that what I *thought* it was?" Saralyn asked from the
right-hand seat. The breath she'd held whooshed out of her.

Zeno nodded. In his enormous helmet he looked like a
cartoon Martian. "Used to be one of those jungle wildlife
parks here—you know, the kind you drive into or take a tour
boat through. After the war, the imported critters outspread
their original habitat. Now they're all over Silver Springs.
Lions and tigers and bears."

"Oh my," she said giddily. "Don't you think that you
ought to—"

Her words sucked back into her throat as the helicopter
whopped between the column of two soaring pines, clipping
branches on either side.

"You were saying?" Zeno said.

Her hand came off her mouth, and she cleared her throat.
"Just that maybe it'd be safer if you took her up a little
higher."

"Oh," he said. "So it's the NOE that's got you frazzled."

"N-O-*what*?"

"That's nap-of-the-earth flight." He smiled. "Give me a
bird to pilot, and I start speaking in acronyms."

"So what about it?"

"Flying at a higher altitude, you mean?"

She nodded.

He shook his head.

She frowned.

"Staying close to the terrain keeps us masked from radar.
And offers cover from visual detection. Strikehawk's *engi-
neered* for this type of flight."

"Oh."

He made a small adjustment in pitch, his hands nudging the sticks, feet tapping the pedals. A grassy meadow rushed into sight beneath them and then was gone.

"Bet right now your stomach can't decide whether it's up or down."

"Didn't think it showed."

"We're zipping along at an indicated airspeed of a 150 knots—around 170 miles an hour. That's fast by any reckoning, and the lower you travel the more you feel the effect of speed. It takes some getting used to." He laughed. "I can imagine what the Marcuses are saying about me back in the cabin."

Saralyn shifted in her seat harness. She and Zeno both wore fire-resistant Nomex flight suits and survival vests.

She glanced at the VDU on her console, tried without success to make sense of the numbers tickering by on the screen.

"I've been thinking about the Castillo's defenses," she said. "These copters are easy targets for heat-seeking missiles, aren't they?"

"Not with the kind of jamming we've got. Did you notice that little turret behind the main rotor? Shaped kind of like a lighthouse?"

"Uh-huh."

"It's an IRCM—whoops, there I go again—an infrared countermeasure device. What it does is pump out infrared radiation in a coded, on-again off-again sequence that confuses heat-seekers. Makes them lose interest, in a manner of speaking." He paused. "There's some other stuff like that as well."

She looked at the green video display again and thought suddenly about John Firecloud. Right about now he ought to be starting up the citadel wall—or getting ready to, anyway.

"How much longer till we reach the Castillo?" she asked.

"A few minutes. I'm going to swing across the St. Johns River, which you can see through the trees if you look to

your right. That'd put us just east of Flagler and something
like twenty miles from St. Augustine." He paused. "Concerned about John?"

She nodded. The thought of his climbing that wall,
exposed, made her edgy.

"Me, too," Zeno said.

They lapsed into silence.

Her eyes returned to the console in front of her. She
supposed there had to be a readout of the time somewhere
among the digital meters and gauges. How hard could it be
to figure out which of them was the *clock*?

After a moment she gave up and checked her watch.

It was 11:31.

Dee looked at her Timex: 11:32.

God, how the minutes crawled. Would this long, long
night ever end?

She was sitting on her favorite recliner in her living
room, having a cup of tea that Mohammed had brewed.
Over the last few hours he had regaled her with stories of his
escapades in Malaysia, told her all about carny life, and
gone into an extended lecture debunking commonly held
fallacies about the temperaments of various species of
reptile, and given her a discourse on the comparative
effectiveness of holistic versus traditional medicine.

John had left him behind so she would not be alone with
her grief if the rescue went bad, though he hadn't stated his
reason exactly like that. What he'd said was something
about her having to be careful and keep someone around in
case more White Trash showed up. Well, at least he'd
picked an excuse that made sense.

In other circumstances she would have found Mo to be
pretty decent company. Much of what he was telling her
was quite interesting. He was knowledgeable and polite.
And he kept his snake away from her and off the furniture.
True, he was a mite overtalkative . . . but what was so
wrong with that? He was fresh from being a canvas slave.

After having been treated like a subhuman for who knew how long, the poor man was probably just starved for attention.

Problem was, she couldn't keep from thinking about Saralyn and John Firecloud—the woman she regarded almost as a daughter and the man that had been Charlie Tiger's son. Them, and the others who'd gone with them.

Children that even now might be heading toward their deaths.

Dee looked at Mohammed over the rim of her cup and suddenly realized that she'd lost the flow of his conversation.

"I'm sorry," she said, embarrassed. "My mind just wandered a second. What was it you were talking about?" *Food, that was it. Something about food.*

He looked at her soberly. "I was asking you what time it is," he said. "I was thinking about our friends."

Firecloud lobbed the grappling hook up gently, with an even upward throw. His other hand was loose around the rope, releasing it as it played out.

The first three flings were unsuccessful. It was not that his aim was off, but rather that the masonry blocks and the lime mortar holding them together were badly eroded. The hook was snagging and breaking off chunks of cornice the way a dentist's pick will chip away at a rotten tooth.

The hook caught what seemed to be a solid hold on the fourth throw. He pulled hard on the rope to test the bite. It stayed put. He fervently hoped it would continue to stay once his entire weight was pulling down on it—the sharks wouldn't turn aside another portion of fresh meat.

Carefully, purposefully, he made his ascent.

In some distant era the wall had been finished with a hard waterproofing of which only cracked, peeling vestiges remained. The sunbleached material scraped away under his soles and fell to the moat in a dry and crumbly shower. He slid his hands from knot to knot, his feet scuffing over the coarse stone blocks.

His legs quivered from the effort of each deliberate step. His shoulders bunched. His breath came in strained rasps. The thin rope burned into his hands. The wind whispered, rippling his clothes. From the moat came the sound of the sharks crashing against his speedboat.

He kept his eyes on the wall in front of him as he climbed, putting the final goal out of his mind, trying not to think of the fragile stone and the insatiate beasts circling in the water below—concentrating instead on getting one foot ahead of the other, on grabbing the next knot.

At last the cornice was just above him. He reached for it with one hand, then the other, and scrambled onto it.

He paused just long enough to fetch a single deep breath. The tower rose on his left, the ledge which formed a collar around it was perhaps nine feet above him. The barred window a couple of feet above that. He dislodged the grapple from the cornice, reeled up the length of scaling rope, and threw the hook again. This time it fixed on after just one try.

He moved up the tower like a bobcat climbing a tree.

And then he was there, kneeling on the wide ledge below the window. His right hand came up to grasp one of the rusted steel window bars.

An electric light was on inside the tower room.

He pressed his face against the bars and peered through them.

Professor Gordon Lansman was looking back at him, an amazed, exceedingly joyous grin on his face. The man was haggard and pitifully thin and one of his arms was in a cast—but Firecloud had half-expected to find him in much worse shape. He'd even tried to gird himself for the possibility that he'd achieve the tower only to discover a shackled corpse within.

He motioned for the scientist to step back from the window and reached into the sack that held the plastique. Each of the three saddle charges of sliced plastic explosive was one-third a block of C-4, shaped to form an isosceles triangle.

Firecloud took a charge from the duffel, peeled off the waxed paper in which he and Saralyn had wrapped the charge to protect it en route to the Castillo. The plastique was as easily molded as sculpting clay, and he pressed the charge around one of the window bars, covering half the bar's circumference. He repeated this with the rest of the charges until three of the window bars were sheathed in C-4.

The explosives had been primed with nonelectric blasting caps crimped to equal lengths of homemade fuse, the fuse itself manufactured from shoelaces soaked in a solution of potassium nitrate, granulated sugar, and hot water.

When the saddle charges were set, he braided the ends of the fuses together, produced a cigarette lighter from his anorak, and fired them.

He had five seconds. Silently counting down, he scampered to the end of the sill on his knees, hugging the curved outer wall of the tower. *Four, three*. His hand found a raised coat of arms and clawed at it for additional support. *Two, one*.

The blast clapped his ears with a terrific *pow*! A tongue of flame licked the sky, angry red in the center and deep violet around its tattered edges. Chunks of coquina torn from around the window hailed down in clusters. Firecloud clung to the side of the tower for dear life, dust and stinging pebbles sweeping against the back of his head, the ledge trembling beneath him.

As the blast's shock wave died away, Firecloud shuffled back around the ledge. A glowy veil of smoke hung outside the window.

The bars were twisted and cut.

He leaped in over the sill.

Lansman was clinging to a wall beside the door, disheveled and shaky but still with that expression of intense, stunned happiness on his face.

"Thank God you've come," he said stepping toward Firecloud. "I—"

Just then the door crashed open.

Lansman and Firecloud whipped their heads toward the entry in precise unison.

Lieutenant Varnum Slade and his elite guard came flooding through the door in a black wave.

Their guns were drawn.

Slade's gloating laughter was like the sound of a steamroller crunching over a pile of brittle bones.

His eyes stabbed into Firecloud's.

"I'm sorry, *Swampmaster*," he said, cackling. "But your friend the professor can't come out and play."

The Strikehawk crept up on the Castillo's landlocked western curtain, coming in a bare yard above the bayonet-like spiny yuccas lined along its earthwork perimeter wall. The helicopter's exterior lights were off, and it was only when it passed directly over the barricade's small circular redoubt that the firefight began.

Saralyn heard the hiss of her own breath as tracer rounds from the 12.7-millimeter machine guns below lit the sky with noonday, then the *tickticktick* of flak sprinkling the fuselage.

"Shit!" Zeno hissed. "Thought the dumb mothers'd at least try to hail us first! This *is* one of their own craft!"

"Guess they don't like unexpected visitors." She slid the boron armor shield on the right side of her seat forward to protect her torso.

Zeno was looking down at the redoubt, his IHADSS informing the Hellfires on the chopper's stub wings of its position.

"G'night, fuckers," he muttered, punching a button.

In a heartbeat: The Hellfire cooked off into the darkness following the Strikehawk's autonomous homing laser, the chopper climbed with a burst of acceleration, and the illuminated faces of the soldiers in the redoubt vaporized in a dazzling fireball.

Saralyn glanced at her watch. "Five of midnight," she said.

"I'm gonna bank hard and then jump to the tower," Zeno said, nodding. "This might make you a little queasy."

His hands squeezed the control levers.

The copter shot upward at a rate of 3,000 feet per second, withstanding 3.5 positive g's of lift a lot better than Saralyn's stomach.

She emitted a sick groan.

No sooner had the Strikehawk climbed level with the parapet than the AA's came alive. Rounds sleeted into the bullet-resistant windscreen. Tracers spiraled and streaked brilliantly in every direction.

Saralyn could see dozens of men in the seats behind the pivoting guns—then suddenly some of them began darting for nonexistent cover. Faintly she heard the chatter of the Marcuses' door guns returning fire.

Zeno sent another missile gliding from the pylons, and a hedge of flame arose where a gun emplacement had been a second before. The incoming flak, however, seemed hardly reduced.

"We're taking too many hits," Zeno said. "I hope to God Firecloud's got it all together."

The chopper had ascended with its nose pointed at the fortress wall. The tower was off to the left. Saralyn saw it across Zeno's body as the 'hawk turned left, lunged forward, and pulled to a hover outside the tower—its window only a matter of inches from her right shoulder now.

She looked through the canopy into the window.

"Can you make out what's happening in there?" Zeno asked. "Is John—"

Her head snapped around at him, and he saw that she had gone livid.

"He's in trouble," she said.

Firecloud stormed into action, the whirlwind suddenness and fury of his attack taking them all by surprise.

The black-clad Front guard had formed a line in front of the door upon entering, and Firecloud charged into it at a full run, bouncing them off the walls like pool balls on a break. He dashed the man nearest him back against the wall with a headbutt to the chest, then delivered two quick uppercuts to his throat with his right hand. As the man was sinking with a crushed larynx, Firecloud's right hand fired out and yanked the unconscious guard's knife from its scabbard. He swung the knife backward in a horizontal arc and slashed a second guard open across his midsection. The guard flowed to the floor like a punctured accordion.

The other soldiers were shouting in the melee, trying to gain position on him. One charged from his left, and Firecloud thrust the bloody six-inch dagger into his stomach, then hauled it up between his ribs, twisting the blade as he did so. The soldier exhaled moistly and crumpled, dying, the knife buried in his guts.

Firecloud's mind registered the whop of rotors and staccato outbreak of overlapping machine gun blasts outside. He heard the door slam loudly to his right.

All at once a powerful forearm locked around his throat and arched him backward. The arm was like a vise. Firecloud struggled for air. Dots spinning across his vision, he cocked his right elbow by placing the arm across the front of his body, fist over the left shoulder, palm downward. Then he swung his elbow hard back to the right into his attacker's rib cage. The guard staggered backward, his breath whoofing out. His vise-grip loosened. Firecloud struck him twice more in the ribs, and his arm dropped. Firecloud spun, and while the soldier was trying to compensate for his counterattack, hit him with a rib-shattering front kick that sent him reeling toward the window. He followed through instantly with a second, and then a third kick, and the man got tangled up in his own feet and tripped out the window. His scream dopplered upward and then cut out abruptly as he splashed into the shark-infested moat.

Panting, Firecloud glanced out the window, his face limned by the tracer flashes that sequined the sky outside the tower—

—And his eyes met Saralyn's. She sat in the cockpit of the hovering Strikehawk, staring in at him, her face tense.

They were here. They'd come for him.

He whirled 180 degrees, bracing for further combat.

The room was empty.

The slam of the door replayed in his memory like a tape recording.

They'd taken Lansman. The lieutenant and his remaining guards had fled with him.

He considered and immediately rejected the idea of pursuit. He could hear Klaxons wailing elsewhere in the Castillo. The fortress garrisoned hundreds of men, all of whom would be consolidating at active alert. And by now a second wave of soldiers must surely be racing up the tower stairs.

There was nothing to do but get himself out.

He turned back to the window. The chopper had lifted above the upper sill and dropped its rappel line. The webbed snaplink belt swung at the end of the line just past the ruined window bars. He reached out and grabbed the belt and locked it around his waist, then climbed out onto the ledge.

Around him the night was a bizarre hell. Smoke strung across the sky in churning, nebulous garlands. Guns roared and muzzles flashed. He could hear shells pinging off the Strikehawk's fuselage. For as long as it waited for him the chopper was a sitting duck.

He looked up, tugging at the rope. Marcus One craned his head out of the cabin and waved acknowledgingly. Firecloud leaped into space, dropped for a dizzy instant as the line's slack played out, then was jerked suddenly and hauled up toward the open cabin door. The rotor blast was deafening. It flapped his clothes around him and blew his hair back in a wild stream.

It was only by pure chance that he glanced earthward as he rose and saw the convoy speeding away from the Castillo on Route 214, some thirty feet below him. There were three jeep convertibles with their tops retracted tailgating a squat Bradley M2 infantry fighting vehicle.

Gordon Lansman was in the rear of one of the jeeps, sandwiched between a pair of guards. The lieutenant that had surprised Firecloud in the tower occupied the shotgun seat of the vehicle ahead of it.

Firecloud raised his eyes back to the copter, saw Saralyn looking at him, and gestured urgently in the direction of Route 214. Her eyes followed the angle of his pointing finger. She nodded her understanding.

Two seconds later the Marcuses clamped their hands around his shoulders and were pulling him aboard.

The Strikehawk went screaming after the convoy.

A TOW flew from the M2's rocket launcher and needled toward the swooping Strikehawk.

"No way you're gonna hit us, bastard, no way," Saralyn swore under her breath, and jabbed the chaff button on the left-hand section of her weapons console. Instantly a cloud of radar-reflective slivers of aluminum-coated plastic dispersed from a box on the tail boom, blanketing the inbound missile and disrupting its guidance system. The TOW blindly swerved off course and exploded harmlessly in the air yards from its target.

Zeno glanced at Saralyn. "Did I show you how to do that?"

She didn't answer.

Treads eating up the road, the M2 was spitting a different form of death now, its 25-millimeter turret cannon blasting a spiral constellation of armor-piercing APDS ammunition at the copter. A round impacted with the hull, and the bird shook woundedly.

His hand on the Hellfire launch controls, Zeno craned his head toward the M2. The armored vehicle was boxed and centered within video cross hairs on the monocle of his IHADSS. He fired the missile.

The M2 suddenly roared into nova flame. Behind it the jeeps weaved berserkly off-road, tires screeching as their drivers wrestled with their steering wheels.

The Strikehawk dove for the closest jeep as it bumped past the soft shoulder.

"You see Lansman in that one?" Zeno asked.

Saralyn shook her head.

"Me neither," Zeno said. "It's history."

The chopper's 20-millimeter chin cannon howled.

Four sets of horrified eyes looked up from the jeep, and then the jeep's fuel line ruptured, and it went up in an engulfing spume of flame that hurled chunks of metal for dozens of yards.

"Two down, two left," Zeno said.

"Yeah, and take a peek down at three o'clock," Saralyn said.

He looked. The jeep carrying the lieutenant had swerved onto the roadside dirt and was doubling back to the Castillo, its rear tires spraying pebbles and clods of soil.

"That's Varnum Slade, Groll's right-hand man, turning tail," Zeno said, banking toward the road. "Game's up and he knows it."

Saralyn nodded.

The final jeep was dead ahead.

"Let's go get the prof," she said.

Zeno pulled pitch, and the Strikehawk dropped steeply in hot cat-and-mouse pursuit. The jeep accelerated, burning rubber at almost 80 m.p.h., but the chopper caught up to it in seconds, kept pace almost directly overhead. The jeep zigged and the copter zigged with it. Zagged and the chopper zagged. The jeep's driver put the pedal to the floor, and the vehicle leaped forward to 90. The Strikehawk crossed above it in easy figure eights.

And then, unexpectedly, the jeep slowed and came to a halt.

"Am I seeing what I think I'm seeing?" Zeno asked Saralyn. "Because what I think I'm seeing is them surrendering."

She looked out the windscreen at the soldiers that had poured out of the car, their hands on their heads, their weapons tossed into a pile in the center of the road.

She grinned. "Either that, or they're getting ready for morning calisthenics."

"I'm bringing her down," Zeno said.

The Front soldiers stood near their evacuated jeep with their own weapons trained on them, held in the Marcuses' ready hands.

Overhead, the moon was a jaundiced, slitted eye.

"I say we kill 'em," Marcus One said.

"They definitely wouldn't be any great loss," his brother said. "And besides, we ain't exactly equipped for prisoners."

"Maybe we should ask the professor," Saralyn said. She motioned at Lansman, standing with her and Firecloud beside the Strikehawk, which had landed several yards up the road from the jeep. "He's gotten the worst of it from those creepoids."

Lansman glanced at her and sighed. He looked totally drained and seemed to speak with a supreme effort. "Just send them back," he said flatly. "There's been enough blood spilled tonight."

"Glad to hear your opinion, but I think that idea sucks," Marcus One growled. The muzzle of his gun swept up at the soldiers, and a horrified gasp came from all three of them at once.

"Bye-bye guy—" Marcus Two started to say, the gun in his hand also elevating.

"No," Firecloud said with quiet authority.

Everyone looked at him.

The twins' trigger fingers slackened.

He walked over to the Front soldiers, taking long, slow strides, and spoke to one of them suddenly.

"I have a message for you to deliver to your lieutenant."

The soldier stared at him, fish-eyed, sweat gushing off his face. "W-w-whatever you want me to say," he pleaded. "Whatever."

Firecloud smiled ferociously. "Tell him that when Swampmaster comes out to play, he plays for keeps."

Epilog One ═══════════════════════════

The Strikehawk clipping through the Florida night, John Firecloud and Gordon Lansman settled back in adjacent troop webbing seats, the Marcuses across from them, gazing out a portside window into inky darkness.

"How are you feeling?" Firecloud asked the scientist.

Lansman sat thinking for a while, then shrugged.

"Tell you the truth, I don't know," he replied at last. "Physically, I'm all right. But emotionally, I'm still trying to catch up with everything that's happened to me. Not just tonight, but over the last eight months." He shrugged again. "You understand?"

"Very well," Firecloud said.

Brief silence. The copter's rotors blatted.

"Are we heading for Free Atlanta now?" Lansman asked.

Firecloud shook his head. "It wouldn't be wise to make the trip in the Strikehawk. The Front will be looking for it. A friend of mine in Everglades City will put you on a boat before dawn, and you should reach Georgia by midmorning." He thought a moment. "Will you be able to neutralize the bio-nukes?"

Lansman massaged the bridge of his nose and released an odd, aching laugh. "The nukes, yes. Quite simply," he said. "But *bio*-nukes? Ain't no such dog."

Firecloud looked at him.

Lansman laughed again, softly. "All this time, the Front has believed that Dr. Roth, my late wife, and myself developed a strain of *Pasteurella pestis* that is not only resistant to almost limitless heat and radiation, but *thrives* under such conditions. All this time they've been wrong. Oh, we claimed we'd done it, just to throw a wrench into their plans. We pulled a few scientific sleights of hand, fudged test results, whatever it took to dupe them. And it worked. Famously."

Firecloud was surprised. "What about the nuclear explosives?"

"Like I said, *they're* real enough. Any school kid can put together a kitchen nuke if he's able to get hold of the right materials. If we'd tried scamming the Front when it came to constructing the actual bombs, they'd have found us out right away. The technology's too commonplace."

"And the detonating mechanisms—the motion sensors . . . ?"

"Also real. And also simplicity itself to deactivate. You don't have to touch the bombs to do it, or even be that close to them. Matter of fact, all it takes is this—"

He whistled four short, brisk notes.

Firecloud stared at him as if he'd gone crazy.

"Each bomb contains a tiny computer chip that will shut down the detonator upon 'hearing' a specific musical sequence. There were toys that worked on the same principle *thirty years ago*." He smiled. "It was my wife's idea. She thought of it shortly before she died. Sick as she was for so long, she never lost her goofy sense of humor. Did you recognize the tune?"

Firecloud shook his head.

"It's part of the intro to an old dance number from the early 1990's. By somebody I think was known as The Hammer, that Sara liked when she was in college. The song's called 'Can't Touch This.'"

Firecloud smiled, and fell silent as the Strikehawk flew without disturbance toward the Everglades.

Epilog Two

Front Commander Joseph Forster Groll was whittling at a toy Indian with a paring knife when Fran knocked at the door.

"Yes!" he answered quickly. His arm swept the mound of plastic shavings from his desk. A few of the shavings stuck to a wet spot, and he picked them off. Quickly. He was anxious to meet Slade's bounty hunter. Most anxious.

He looked down at the carved, disfigured face of the Indian and felt nothing, absolutely nothing. The pleasure was gone. It had been that way with his customizations since shortly before the Lansman travesty. Since the Indian, Swampmaster, had ruined, had *dismembered*, his favorite carnival.

It was not that his work on the miniatures was lacking. His workmanship was excellent as usual. But lately . . . lately he was unable to concentrate on drawing imaginary backgrounds for his creations. His mind kept returning to the Indian, the *real* Indian, and the affront he'd committed.

It was a crime that must be punished.

He hadn't modified a human being, not with his own two hands at least, in many years. Since he had abducted the sister of his childhood tormentor, Kenneth Whitman, *the person Whitman had loved the most*, and kept her in a basement, and sliced her, and sewed her, and . . . and now the old urge was upon him again.

He would have the Indian. Swampmaster.

Fran's head thrust in the door. "Lieutenant Slade is here with his—"

"I *know* who it is, imbecile!" he screamed. His saliva was thick as mucilage. "I've been *expecting* them, and I want to see them this *instant*!"

"Yes, sir," she said.

The bounty hunter that entered with Slade did indeed look impressive. He was a huge, barrel-chested man with a red walrus mustache and hard, weather-beaten features. The handle of the machete at his waist was discolored from frequent use, but its blade gleamed brightly.

"My commander, permit me to introduce you to the man who will bring you Swampmaster," Slade said. "His name is—"

"I can introduce myself, thanks," the redhead said. "The name's Coonan. Bill Coonan. And for the right price I'll bring you anybody you want—dead, alive, or somewhere in between."

His seared face broke into a grin. "Anybody, includin' my own brother."